CLUCKED

TROY HOLLAN

Black Rose Writing | Texas

ISBN: 978-1-68513-309-2
PUBLISHED BY BLACK ROSE WRITING
www.blackrosewriting.com

Printed in the United States of America
Suggested Retail Price (SRP) $21.95

Clucked is printed in EB Garamond

*As a planet-friendly publisher, Black Rose Writing does its best to eliminate unnecessary waste to reduce paper usage and energy costs, while never compromising the reading experience. As a result, the final word count vs. page count may not meet common expectations.

To my dad, Neill, who was a master of the art of oral story-telling, and to my mom, Beatrice, who always provided a ready audience for both his tales and mine. Thank you both for inspiring my love of history and books filled with tall tales of pirate ships and sunken gold - while showing me that the greatest treasure of all is the love of family and friends.

To Melissa, my wife and best friend who always supports my adventures (real and literary), and our two rescue dogs, Tripp and Lizzy Lou, who have no qualms about waking me up well before dawn to get busy writing.

Thanks to Terrance Grundy, editor and proof-reader extraordinaire, who was my first "real" reader and an early fan of Hank, the rat terrier (arguably *Clucked's* main character).

While this is a work of fiction, and I make many references to real places and historical events, I have chosen to make specific reference to the Gullah people of South Carolina. My intention is to honor their history and spirit and through the collective efforts of my book's characters, to show a very genuine, if fictional, attempt to honor their quest to retain family-owned land.

CLUCKED

CHAPTER 1

As his old sailboat, *Lonesome Dove*, rocked in the water, tugging restlessly against her anchor, Matt ran his fingers along the thick, salt-crusted line that ran from beneath the waves to the bow cleat, checking carefully for any signs of wear. The twelve-strand rope was stretched tight where it ran through a well-worn brass fairlead, polished from countless anchorings over the years, yet still capable of causing chafe on the line. After a quick search of the multiple pockets in his threadbare, baggy shorts, he found a scrap of soft leather and wiggled it up under the line to buffer the friction between nylon and metal. Then he stood, tipped his head back to gaze at the gently tilting mast and took a deep breath, savoring the heady aroma of salt and sea—of life and decay—that mingled pleasantly with sharp notes of diesel and freshly varnished wood.

His heart thrummed in his chest and his pulse quickened as he took in the spread of grayish-blue water and the blushing sky. It was one of those perfect Gulf Coast sunsets, the horizon flushing deep crimson from particles carried here by a dust storm from somewhere way out in West Texas. Rippling in the light breeze, the gentle waves that rolled across the wide reach of Corpus Christi Bay shimmered in the red glow. Feet braced easily against the slow side-to-side roll of the old sailboat, Matt was keenly aware that he stood poised at the brink of his own personal sea change. So, for a time, he remained where he was, feeling the grit of stray bits of sand and sawdust against the soles of his feet, absorbing the sound of the halyard tinkling against the mast in the breeze, and waves slapping lightly against the hull. He was both excited and terrified, longing to be underway and yet loath to unglue his feet from the deck and set the whole machine of change in motion. For the first time in a long time, he felt painfully conscious of how alone he was in the world and how much more so he soon would be. But the alternative—staying put and just running through the motions of living—was worse than solitude. And so he forced himself to get moving, crossing the cockpit in two easy strides and climbing down the sturdy ladder to the cabin below.

The space below was compact and cozy, lit dimly by old-fashioned-looking brass sconces that were powered by an array of modern solar panels up on deck. Matt drowned out the nagging doubts in his mind by noisily opening and closing cabinet doors as he pulled out the ingredients for a dinner of Spam and grits. It wasn't the fanciest of meals, but it was comfort food that reminded him of the home he'd lost, and of Julie. His wife had made him the simple meal whenever the darkness threatened to overtake him— when he'd tunneled somewhere deep inside himself and needed something, or someone, to pull him back out. Spam and grits, and Julie's quiet comfort, had always helped. The salty tang of fried mystery meat was almost as powerful as her quiet voice calling him back to waking as he thrashed in the grip of some nightmare, *but not quite*. Maybe the taste for Spam came from way back in the earliest of his army days, reminding him of the best of the worst times of his life, when most of his best friends were still alive and trying to survive their deployment to Iraq. Miguel, one of his buddies from a neighboring county in South Texas, would often get a can of the meaty product in his care packages. The Spam, and the other goodies from home—sweet bars of *leche quemada*, small tins of pickled jalapeno peppers, and jars of homemade barbecue sauce, were a welcome reprieve after the monotony of weeks of consuming MREs.

"Spam, what are you...really?" he mused fondly, cranking open the can with its little key and shaking the jellied meat concoction onto a cutting board. It landed with a squelch, quivering slightly in accompaniment to the waves softly rocking the boat. The pink, fleshy block sliced easily, revealing its glistening red-and-white marbled interior. Matt cranked up the gas on the little gimbaled stove whose pivot would keep the cooking surface level, even if the boat was heeled over, and began frying the slices in a drizzle of oil. The pork product popped and sizzled, seeming to issue small squeals of complaint as he boiled water for the grits and pulled out the last of his precious store of butter and milk. When these were done, he'd be relying on canned milk and Pam—staples from his tiny pantry. Turning the heat off under the browned Spam, he poured a little milk

and a lot of butter into the grits, stirring the concoction gently.

"*Lovely Spam, wonderful Spam*," he crooned, his mealtime musical homage to Monty Python, while dicing up the fried-meat product and mixing it in with a hillock of buttered grits. He set his full plate down on the table of the dinette and scooted onto the bench, pushing aside his jumble of nautical charts so he could give his full attention to the meal. As he shoveled in a mouthful of the greasy comfort food, he tried hard to ignore the pleading, bug-eyed stare of Hank, his little senior rat terrier-chihuahua mix, who was now wide awake and shamelessly begging for a bite of his human's dinner. "Soon," he promised, with a nod in the canine's direction, turning his attention back to his meal.

Spearing two cubes of Spam with his fork, Matt considered the irony of his guilty culinary pleasure. While he'd enjoyed the occasional treat of Spam as a soldier, WW2 grunts had consumed so much of the convenient protein source as a staple during their service that many refused to eat it when they returned stateside. When his four years were up, Matt had missed the taste of fried-up Spam so much that he'd kept a generous supply on hand so he could indulge his guilty pleasure whenever he wanted. He'd become slightly obsessed with the history of the mystery meat, even paying a visit to the Spam Museum in Austin, Minnesota, as well as competing in Spamarama, the quirky annual festival and cook-off in Austin, Texas, where "his" recipe of Spam and Truffle-Cheese Grits (borrowed in part from Julie's), had once earned top prize.

He now recalled having heard several stories about Spam being considered a coveted delicacy in some remote villages in the highland jungle of New Guinea. According to the tales—or more likely wildly fictionalized urban legends—it was Spam, not chicken, that was favored by local connoisseurs, as having the flavor most closely approximating that of "long pig". One sensational story even claimed that, when Western missionaries brought both the Holy Book and cans of Spam on their journey to spread Christianity, they ended up, quite by accident, reviving what was then a dying tradition: cannibalism. The sudden availability of the portable, congealed meat product was reputed to have reawakened ancient, long-dormant taste buds, resulting in a reversion to practices from the not-so-distant past.

Just thinking about those rumors caused Matt to drop his fork on the table and lock eyes with Hank's pleading gaze. With a sigh, he pushed the plate over to the little dog, who immediately propped his little paws up against the table and gobbled up the remnants of Matt's meal. He and Julie had adopted the rescue dog from a shelter in Austin when the mutt was a youthful senior of ten, so happy to be in a real home that, on arrival, he went on a wild run through their old farmhouse, finally jumping on and burrowing into a warm pile of freshly folded laundry. Now sixteen years old and the last living member of their original pack of five, Hank was half-deaf and sported thick cataracts that filmed his big brown eyes. Despite his age, the dog was Matt's faithful shadow, and his human knew he could never leave him behind, even on a journey that might be uncomfortable—or even a little dangerous. Matt had prepared as best he could, though, purchasing a well-fitted, top-of-the-line doggy life vest and rigging up the boat with safety lines and netting to keep his little buddy secure when they were underway.

Plate licked clean, Hank skittered across the tabletop and dropped into Matt's waiting arms. Cradling the warm little body, Matt watched the red sun drop below the horizon, and the deep crimson sunset give way to a light shade of watercolor purple. The brisk wind had tapered to a softly sighing breeze, and the settling waves slapped gently against the hull. With his free hand, he pushed the slider to the galley window all the way open, relishing the cool evening air against his skin and the sensation of the comforting food filling his belly. He was grateful for the hearty fare, as this might be his last chance to cook a real hot meal for a few days. Tomorrow they'd be sailing out of the tranquil shelter of Shamrock Cove, then on to Port Aransas, out past the long stone jetty and beyond—to the dark sprawl of ocean in which Matt yearned to lose himself. It would be the first of a ten-day journey that would take them across the vast thousand-mile-wide Gulf of Mexico and spit them out somewhere in the Florida Keys. From there, it was just a coin toss as to their next destination.

Matt had a vague plan of sailing around the world in the old vintage 1960s Pearson Vanguard *Lonesome Dove,* wandering aimlessly from port to port until he'd had his fill of journeying. Matt and Julie had christened the vintage sloop in homage both to their favorite western movie and the autobiography *The Dove*—a book they'd shared and loved about the teenage sailor, Robin Lee Graham, who had circumnavigated the globe when he was only sixteen years old. Once upon a time, traversing the globe in their own sailboat had been his and Julie's dream. They'd talked for years of one day, sailing out of Corpus Christi Bay and far beyond to the Caribbean, spending their days swimming and snorkeling in the turquoise waters. Once they'd had their fill of the West Indies, they would head slowly down through the Windward and Leeward islands, stopping in the San Blas Islands of Panama, before transiting the Panama Canal and crossing the Pacific to Tahiti—and wherever the wind carried them next.

It wouldn't be the same without her, yet the dream they had shared and the promise of one day fulfilling it were all that was currently holding him together. And here he was, finally, ready to haul up anchor and head off into the unknown...*alone*. His eyes filled with tears, and he ran a thumb over one wet cheek. *One day at a time*, he reminded himself as he drew in a deep breath, holding at the top and then counting to five before releasing the exhalation. Except his addiction wasn't alcohol or drugs: it was his memories.

With Hank snuggled securely under his arm, and his last cold beer tucked in the deepest pocket of his cargo shorts, Matt grabbed an old sweatshirt and climbed up into the cockpit for a final look around. Lowering himself onto a damp seat cushion, he stretched out his legs. While the little dog curled himself into a comfortable ball in his lap, Matt sipped the beer, savoring the cool slide of the drink over his tongue, enjoying the tangy scent of the ocean air and the soft slap of the waves against the hull. When he and

Julie had first started dating, they'd visited Shamrock Cove often, spending hours anchored in the calm waters, watching slick gray porpoises chase schools of mullet around the boat, cooling off with a quick swim, and catching an occasional red drum or "redfish" for dinner. More often than not, they'd spent a good part of the afternoon up in the V-berth, moving together in a sexy tangle of sweaty limbs. After they'd married and were working around the clock to manage mortgage payments on their old farmhouse, they hadn't been able to visit their little cove as often as they had that first summer. And so *Lonesome Dove* had mostly stayed neglected and a little forlorn in her slip down in Corpus Christi.

Over the past year, since that time when everything had gone to hell, the old sloop had grown a thick beard of moss and barnacles on her hull, and gained a generous spatter of seagull poop that clung stubbornly to her formerly pristine decks. When he'd first arrived at the marina, still heavy with grief and rapidly losing faith in his plan, Matt had lost himself in work. He'd spent weeks suited up in a "shorty" wetsuit, mask and snorkel, scraping away on the hull in the murky coastal water and then up on deck with a hose and rags, scrubbing away the poop and grime. When *Lonesome Dove* emerged from the damage neglect and time had wrought, Matt went to work sanding and re-varnishing the weathered teak and polishing the old brass work. Cleaning up the mess, restoring *Lonesome Dove* to her former modest glory and getting her ready for a voyage to somewhere— anywhere but here—had helped Matt take his mind off the living hell that simply existing had become.

Matt shifted on the cushions as he gazed off in the distance. In his lap, Hank stirred slightly, then let out a contented moan. From far off, the lights of Corpus Christi were a distant sparkle against the darkening sky. As he prepared himself mentally for the journey ahead, running methodically through his safety checklist and rehearsing for departure, his mind, unbidden, began slipping backward, falling into memories and finally tumbling into the darkness that reached up to greet him.

CHAPTER 2

The images came as clear and ungraspable as a spill of water. He closed his eyes and sighed as his thoughts curled backward in time, smiling as he remembered: *Julie, curled up in bed, his faded T-shirt riding high on her long, tanned legs, smiling an invitation as shafts of sunlight played on her curves. Julie, her long dark hair pulled up in a shining mass of curls and flowers, winking as she raised the hem of her lacy white wedding gown to reveal her favorite pair of well-worn high-tops.* Matt flashed through all of her faces: her wide, dimpled smile, her frown of deep concentration, her tears, her delight, her rare flashes of anger, and her fleeting sadness. He reveled in his memories of her body: the slope of her belly, the pout of her breasts, the long sweep of her back, and the flash of her eyes—sometimes green, sometimes blue, depending on the light. His mind cast back to all the places they'd been, the friends they'd shared, and the adventures they'd had. And then, the very worst came—what he'd never seen, but had imagined a million nightmarish times: his beautiful wife, her hands carefully fixed at ten and two on the steering wheel, that dreamy half smile that lit up her face, dropping and opening into a scream as twin headlights slashed through the darkness, heading straight toward her.

He sat up quickly, breath catching in his throat, heart pounding. He struggled to wipe the image from his mind—a gruesome jigsaw of sight and smell and sound whose pieces would come together and connect unbidden whenever he thought about that night.

· · ·

It had been just before the winter break, when Julie stayed late to help wrap things up at her school's annual holiday concert. She'd hugged her kinder students and many of their parents, loaded her "teacher gifts"—mugs and candles and homemade goodies—into her small hybrid SUV, and waved goodbye to the stragglers. After pulling out of the parking lot, she headed east down the county road and merged, just below the speed limit, onto the highway. She'd barely made it a mile down the road when a large semi-truck, owned by a major chicken products company, had crossed the double line and struck her vehicle head on, crushing it like a ball of aluminum foil. The heavily over-loaded truck had been traveling well over the posted speed limit, and from the lack of any skid marks on the pavement, its driver hadn't so much as tapped the brakes. If there was anything that helped Matt cling to life in the disaster's aftermath, it was the medical examiner's assertion that both Julie and the truck driver, who'd fallen asleep at the wheel, had likely perished on impact and avoided prolonged suffering.

When news of this heartbreaking tragedy had reached Matt at work, his whole world had collapsed, crushing every whisper of hope he had from that day forward. When he got the call, he was working high above the ground in a bucket lift, insulated lineman's pole in hand, struggling with a tangle of electric lines. As his phone slipped from his grip and crashed to the ground below, for just a moment he imagined reaching out, touching one of those twenty-thousand-volt lines, and stopping his own heart. Instead, he screamed his rage, pounding his fists against the side of the cage until his knuckles wept with blood, and his coworkers half dragged him, sobbing and collapsing, from the lowered lift. From that day forth, the only thing that kept him moving forward—and literally kept him alive—was a single-minded quest for justice: justice for Julie and for everyone she left behind.

As the months passed by, and police investigators did their part, the ugly and unmistakable truth had been revealed. A whistleblower finally came forward and offered solid evidence of several egregious safety violations on the part of the truck's owner. The company that employed the driver who'd fallen asleep at the wheel—Clawson Chicken—required their employees to drive many more hours per day and week than the Department of Transportation legally allowed. All employees were instructed to regularly falsify their electronic log books with an override code that altered the official records, allowing them to drive farther and faster than allowed by law. As soon as the workers had finished loading the trucks with frozen chicken products and were ready to leave the dock, Clawson managers would immediately start their employee-tracking software and time the drivers to see how long it took them to reach their destination. The company didn't make allowances for bad weather, mechanical issues, or exhaustion— and the trucks were always loaded far beyond the weight limit allowed by the DOT. According to the whistleblower, the drivers made it to their destination within the brief window of time allotted by the company man, or they lost their jobs. The bottom line? All that seemed to matter to Clawson Chicken was their profits. As the largest global supplier of chicken nuggets, they had reached the pinnacle of corporate success, not by creating tasty food or by dint of good old-fashioned hard work, but by cultivating only the most ruthless business tactics.

Clawson's massive operation, based out of Texas and South Carolina, operated dozens of large, mostly automated factory farms and processing plants and supplied the lion's share of the ninety-seven-million tons of chicken nuggets sold in the U.S.—everywhere from the frozen-food section of major grocery chains to school lunchrooms and fast-food restaurants. In one restaurant chain they'd be doused with a little MSG and extra spices and called "Cajun Poppers," while just across the street, they'd be served as the main course in a kid's "Fun Meal." To actually qualify as "chicken" according to the rules set by the FDA, (where Clawson's former head of operations now served as director), they needed to contain only a minimum of 50 percent chicken and "chicken by-products." The rest of the pink-slime slurry comprising the nuggets consisted of everything from hydrogenated wood cellulose fiber and high-fructose corn syrup, to a proprietary seaweed-based filler that gave the nuggets a "chewier" texture. The result of all this corner-cutting was that consumers got the worst end of the bird, and Clawson Chicken reaped obscenely inflated annual profits.

The company could easily have afforded to pay their truck drivers a living wage, and to hire more recruits, rather than forcing human employees to perform like robots. Matt wanted Clawson Chicken and its owner, Clyde Clawson, to pay for what they'd done to his Julie. So, shortly after the revelation of the accident's true cause, Matt hired a local lawyer to help him in his quest for justice. Unfortunately, at every turn, his small-town lawyer was outwitted and outmaneuvered. Clawson Chicken even went so far as to slap Matt with a "defamation" lawsuit in order to hinder the progress of his negligence litigation, causing him to bleed even more money he couldn't afford to lose. After a few months, it became painfully obvious that the multibillion-dollar company's tactics were more than his modest lawyer could manage, and Matt had to let him go, moving on to some bigger and much pricier guns out of Dallas. The big city firm, whose owner called himself "the Jackhammer", specialized in trucking accidents - and in over-the-top but strangely compelling commercials.

Matt felt a twinge of mortification as he recalled how he'd been roped in by one of the Jackhammer's late-night attention-grabbers.

"Have you or someone you know been hurt by a big truck? I'll make 'em pay big time!" the lawyer bellowed from atop the cab of a semi-truck while brandishing a crudely animated jackhammer. The scene cut to a close-up of the hammer in action, smashing the semi into gold coins, which were promptly snatched up by a motley crew of bandaged accident victims.

After hiring "the Jackhammer", the legal fees had really spun out of control. Persuaded by his lawyer that justice was right around the corner, Matt persisted, maxing out every credit card he had before finally visiting his bank to take out a second mortgage on the farm.

The lawyer's offer to take the case on a "contingency basis" had initially sounded reasonable, but what Matt had failed to grasp was that any legal fees incurred while defending himself from Clawson's spiteful defamation lawsuit would be coming out of his own pocket.

In one short-lived victory, a lower court had ordered Clawson Chicken to pay more than ten million dollars in fines and restitution—what still amounted to a slap on the wrist for a multibillion-dollar corporation—along with requiring them to perform a complete overhaul of their entire transportation division. Clawson was directed to hire more drivers as well as agree to a regular inspection of the electronic driver logbook system that was used on all of their semi-trucks. Never again would one of their sleep-deprived drivers use eighty-thousand pounds of speeding metal as a killing machine. Tragically, following an appeal, the state supreme court struck down this earlier ruling. The state's decision came down to a vote from a single judge, who Matt later found out had deep business connections to the owner of Clawson Chicken. All that was left of Matt and Julie's temporary justice was a stinging rebuke by the judge to "those who sought to hinder free enterprise," delivered to the obvious delight of "Colonel" Clyde Clawson and his corrupt company of corporate chicken pluckers. Clawson, who'd evaded the Vietnam draft on account of a fabricated medical condition, reveled, with no sense of irony, in being called "The Colonel," and had made it a personal mission to buy off nearly every judge in the South.

Matt knew that many wealthy southern gentlemen had anointed themselves with the moniker of "Colonel" without having ever seen a day of battle—a practice dating back to the Civil War era, but boldly carried forward into the twenty-first century by Clyde Clawson. Many of these self-titled "Colonels" had remained safely ensconced in their elegant mansions, while directing thousands of poor country boys out to fight and die in their name during the "War of Northern Aggression," as some in the South still called it. The closest Mr. Clawson and his imaginary bone spur had ever come to military service was his annual donning of a vaguely military-looking uniform for the Charleston Christmas Parade. Riding in his shiny vintage Rolls Royce and clutching an uncomfortable-looking Corgi to his brass-buttoned chest, he would throw handfuls of little plastic toy chicks and other Clawson Chicken-themed trinkets to children along the route. The cheap toys, recently banned from his frozen "Clucky the Clown' kid's meals for being a choking hazard, were but one small representation of the true nature of the Colonel's "generosity"

It was apparently an endless source of irritation to Clyde that another militarily titled chicken magnate had beaten him to both the moniker and control of a large share of the fast-food retail market. Because of this, the company forced all new employees to sign a legal document stating that they would not discuss or consume "the other colonel's" products during their employment. After all, he insisted, what did those heretics up in Kentucky know about chicken, anyway? They really needed to stick to their moonshine and ponies.

Matt had spent the past year on autopilot, putting one foot in front of the other, trying to restore some kind of order to the chaotic mess his life had become. One night he'd sat at the kitchen table of their old farmhouse, finally facing the mountainous stack of unpaid bills that he'd left unopened for weeks. Clicking away on an old student calculator Julie had used in her classroom, Matt finally reached the end of the stack and totaled up the damage. The math didn't lie. One thing was clear: he'd have to sell their small acreage and the old farmhouse to pay off the debt he'd incurred. The next morning, Matt called a local real estate agent whose ad he'd seen prominently displayed on a billboard he passed daily en route to work. "Summer Sutherland" was her name, and "Sell Sooner with Summer" was the catchphrase emblazoned next to her oversized, platinum-blonde billboard likeness. He sensed Summer was dreaming of generous commissions as she assured him she'd be on her way to the farm at once.

In under an hour, Summer's glossy new Land Rover had pulled up outside the farm's rusty gate, a couple of

hundred yards from the farmhouse. Matt could see that the
big-city agent was having some trouble figuring out how to
open the gate's latch, so he fired up his old John Deere Ga-
tor and, with Hank in the bed wagging his tail, the pair
went down to lend a hand. Clearly Matt's little farm was
not the country estate that she'd envisioned, and she struggled to keep up her "sunny Summer" persona as her sky-
high heels struggled to find purchase on the rocky front
lawn. Still, she apparently sensed enough of an opportunity
to encourage Matt to list the place with her as a "Summer
Special." She scanned the property with ill-concealed judgment in her eyes, wincing as her gaze reached the tangle of
dying tomato plants and cornstalks in the old garden that
Julie had always kept so tidy.

"In this market, buyers from Austin are starting to consider homes this far out," she said, in a tone that did little to
hide her disdain for the "boonies" as she called any area five
miles beyond the city limits. "I should be able to get you
market value as is, but we could increase that a bit if you
tidied up and painted that front porch," she pronounced,
with as much of a furrow in her brow as her heavy-handed
Botox treatment would permit.

Matt had mulled over the prospect. It would be just
enough to pay off what remained of the legal bills, with
enough left over so that he could buy an old travel trailer he
could live in until he got back on his feet. He'd paid off the
note on *Lonesome Dove* and he vowed he'd do everything
in his power to keep the old boat docked at a marina down
in Corpus Christi. Some of his best memories with Julie
would always linger there.

Matt had spent the next few weeks tidying up the place. He plowed under what was left of the garden with his old tractor, then put a *for sale* sign on the old Farmall and parked it down by the road. He washed and put away a sink full of dirty dishes, cleaned the bathrooms and, for the first time in many months, properly made his bed. After a couple of days, Summer returned with her Land Rover full of props for the house. Soon, their minimalist, uncluttered home was chock-full of a city slicker's idea of country chic: dried flowers, burlap throw pillows, and rustic-looking pictures of farm animals. A cutesy wooden sign bearing the sentiment "Farm Sweet Home" now nestled over a bowl of plastic vegetables in the kitchen, replacing the fresh apples Julie always kept there. His wife would have had a fit. She couldn't abide *fake*, hated what she called "tchotchkes" and loathed anything that served no purpose other than gathering dust.

Soon the local real estate agents had begun scheduling showings and a parade of "lookie-loos," along with a few potential buyers (mostly rich folks looking for a weekend escape), began to file through Matt's home. Hank, who stayed behind while Matt went off to work each day, seemed to be taking the invasion of his home in stride, even gaining a bit of weight as the local real estate agents bought his trust and quiet with generous offerings of dog treats. Matt finally received a decent offer on the place and agreed to sell their old farm to a young couple from Austin who were looking for a place to grow organic vegetables. It had been his and Julie's idea to start a modest market garden with vegetables in spring and summer and a pumpkin patch in the fall. Hoping to one day maybe even grow their own little family, they'd envisioned themselves teaching their future kids about the simple joys of farm life: the taste of a freshly plucked strawberry, a sun-ripened cherry tomato, or even a slice of succulent, sweet watermelon they'd all helped nurture. They'd even hoped to have a farm stand out by the road one day that they could take turns running when they were home from their oceangoing adventures.

Matt could no longer wrap his head around things like meals and chores, much less plan for retirement. Nothing made sense anymore, not even his job. He'd always tried to be a provider for his family, never refusing to work overtime, and frequently missing suppertime and Julie's school functions when a power outage occurred and he was stuck out on some dark county road working with his crew to replace a broken power pole.

He often thought back to the night when Julie had died. *What if he hadn't volunteered to be on call over the winter break and had been free to drive with her to the Christmas concert? What if they'd bought a place in town, one that hadn't dragged her out in the dark along that stretch of highway? What if she'd been driving their sturdy old four-by-four farm truck instead of her cute little SUV? What if, what if, what if . . .* played on a loop through his sleep-addled brain, gobbling up all his free-thinking space to the point that he could no longer focus. One fateful afternoon, his mental exhaustion and the supreme effort required to make it through each day had collided head-on, sending him hurtling toward a new destiny.

It had been an unusually hot summer day, even for central Texas. The sky, bleached and cloudless, offered little relief, and relocating a section of power line alongside a new highway promised a long and joyless afternoon of sweaty labor up in the bucket lift. With a new trainee observing from the ground, Matt began his ascent toward the target. He noticed the sunlight bouncing off the rookie's hard hat, turning its red surface ablaze. As the bucket lift cranked to a stop, he flexed his grip around the wire cutters, and with the back of the lineman's glove on his free hand, wiped away a trickle of sweat from his face before lifting the tool toward the taut wire. Squinting as the harsh rays of the sun glinted off his safety glasses, he opened the jaw of the cutters and prepared to sever the thick, twisted strands of aluminum wire at a point next to a heavy ceramic insulator. Just as he raised his hand to make the cut, a voice from below made him start, and he peered down at the upturned face.

"You're sure it's isolated...right, boss?"

"Of course it is," Matt had snapped, barely concealing his irritation. Then he glanced down at the base of the pole below and saw the mistake. He'd flipped the wrong disconnect lever, turning off power to a nearby line, but not to the one that he was about to touch.

"Oh shit...no! I pulled the wrong disconnect!" he yelled, dropping the wire cutters with a clatter and running a shaking hand over his mouth.

For a moment, Matt had just stood, heart pounding and hands braced against the walls of the bucket lift's cage as he grappled with the enormity of the near-miss. For the rest of the afternoon, adrenaline kept him hyper-focused, and he moved slowly and methodically through each task. Matt tried to keep it together and play it cool, but when the workday was over and they were back at the electric co-op yard, rather than waving the rookie on his way, he called him over. With a lump in his throat that threatened to snatch the words from his mouth, he managed, "Hey man, thanks. Don't ever be afraid to check your partner. You saved my ass back there."

Then Matt had turned, and with a heavy sigh, headed over the dusty gravel yard toward the head boss's trailer. He'd stared at the cracked toes of his work boots as he paused outside the door, then pushed it open and smiled wearily at the older man inside.

"Eldon...do you have a few minutes? I need to get something off my chest."

Matt had nearly broken down as he recounted the almost fatal error. Eldon was a sympathetic listener, and he came around and sat on the edge of the desk as Matt spoke, leaning over more than once to pat the younger man's shoulder. He had been with the electric utility for nearly forty years now and had hired Matt nearly a decade ago. Everyone at the yard knew what had happened to Julie, but it was Eldon—a good friend to both of them—who had seen Matt at his most broken. They both knew that mistakes like the one Matt had almost made were unacceptable for a lineman, especially one as experienced as he. Grief was an explanation but could never be an excuse. There was silence for a moment as Matt finished speaking, then Eldon took a deep breath and smiled kindly.

"Son, you need some time off to get yourself together. It's not a suggestion. You need to get your house in order. You're a good worker...my best worker in fact...but you're falling apart and we both know it. You need at least a couple of weeks off."

Matt sat silent for a moment, tumbling Eldon's words around in his mind. A whisper of an idea filled his ears and he paused, letting it take shape before he spoke. Silence yawned between them, and then Matt breathed life into the bare bones of a dream.

"What if I wanted to take more time?"

Eldon had lost his own wife to a heart attack just a few months before Julie's accident. The couple had taken Eldon out on a sunset cruise on Corpus Christi Bay a couple of weeks after the funeral. The older man knew Matt's pain better than anyone. He rubbed his creased forehead and smiled slowly.

"What did you have in mind?" he asked.

"Well..." Matt hesitated.

"Spit it out, Matt. Let me know what you're thinking and we'll see what we can do." Eldon leaned forward and threaded his fingers together.

Matt took a deep breath and continued.

"Would you still have a spot for a lineman if I was to, say, 'go on walkabout' like the Aussies say, for maybe . . ." He paused, then plunged.

"Like, a year? I've been thinking about that trip Julie and I always talked about taking...of sailing, maybe even through the Panama Canal. Or...farther?"

Matt spoke haltingly, his tone betraying his lack of certainty. His plan was only half-formed, the pieces coming together only as the words left his lips.

Eldon replied with a slow smile. "Aw, hell, Matt. Do what you need to do. You know I'll never find another worker half as good as you. You'll always have a job as long as I'm here, and I'm not planning to go anywhere, anytime soon."

Relief flooded Matt and when he spoke; even his voice felt freer.

"I'll have about thirty grand left over after selling the old place and settling our bills. It should be enough for at least a year if I'm careful. After that, I'll probably have to trade my Hawaiian shirt and flip-flops back in for a hard hat and steel-toe boots."

"You got it, but you gotta promise that you'll send me some pictures of your adventures," Eldon said, giving Matt's hand a firm shake. The older man breathed slowly and deep and nodded his head. "Go for it, son. If I was your age, I'd want to do the same damn thing."

•   •   •

Matt finished the last of his beer and gazed out at the inky night, now with a smattering of bright stars. He was just rising to his feet when he saw a flash of light streak across the sky—a falling star. By force of habit, he made a wish, crossed his fingers, then climbed down into the cabin with a slumbering Hank clutched to his chest. Gently lowering the little dog onto the bed of the V-berth, where Hank immediately tossed the bedding into a comfy nest, Matt took a few minutes straightening up in the galley, then followed the beer with a generous shot of Jim Beam hoping the chaser would ease him to sleep. Chores complete, he settled down with Hank in the V- berth. Hank immediately woke and waddled up to the top of the bed where he curled up against Matt's chest. As the little dog's snorts turned into snores, Matt shifted around, trying to get comfortable on the thin mattress. Despite the dark thoughts that often chased away sleep, tonight the Jim Beam, sea air, and gentle rocking waves caused his eyelids to droop, then drift closed. Tomorrow their adventure would begin, and maybe, just maybe, he could put some sea miles between himself and his ever-present pain.

CHAPTER 3

Matt awoke early the following morning, a brilliant red sunrise greeting him as he came up on *Lonesome Dove*'s deck. The adage "Red sky at morning, sailor take warning," popped into Matt's head as he yawned and stretched, the cool morning breeze ruffling his hair. He'd learned that in places where the trade winds blow, such as here on the Gulf Coast, a red morning sky often foretold a coming storm, since bad weather most often traveled from east to west with the prevailing winds. Matt checked the NOAA weather channel on his marine VHF radio. The forecast for "offshore and out to one hundred miles" called for four-to-six-foot seas—with winds up to thirty knots. This wasn't terrible news, even for a relatively inexperienced oceangoing sailor. Matt was confident that *Lonesome Dove*, a sturdily built, well-seasoned 33' Pearson Vanguard, could handle these waves with ease. He was nervous and excited—and eager to be under way—a condition that quickly propelled him back into the cockpit to start preparations.

As Matt finished listening to the morning weather report and absentmindedly downed a cup of tepid instant coffee, he set about getting the boat underway. First mates came first, though, so he fed Hank a handful of kibble, grabbed a pee pad, then lifted the dog up on deck and watched him run to his little patch of Astroturf. Out in calm seas, and in international waters, doggy dad could just get a bucket and wash Hank's mess off the deck, but not here. Because of strict environmental regulations, Hank's poops would have to live onboard, sealed in a couple of Hefty trash bags, until they reached Florida. Matt had wondered if it was the right thing to do, bringing his old, half-blind companion along, but he and Julie had agreed to give Hank his "forever home" and he planned to keep that promise, even if their current home was headed off on a seafaring journey.

He was happy he'd have his buddy along for the ride, and figured that if Hank always wore his custom yellow life jacket and a safety tether attached securely to the boat, the little dog would be just fine. Besides, Hank might even meet some "lady love" and have a doggy adventure of his own in the islands. Matt reached Hank with the pee pad just in time, the dog quickly assuming the hunched position to complete his business. Hank was turning to watch the cleanup when a majestic gray heron swooped in low over the bow of the boat. The shaggy bird startled Hank, and he barked angrily at the intrusion. Just as quickly, the heron responded by emitting a sloppy, chalky-white payload on top of the little dog's head. Matt quickly grabbed an old towel and threw it over his dejected first mate, scooping him into his arms. From the folds of the towels, Hank's filmy brown eyes telegraphed an obvious message: *Dude, where the hell is my yard?*

Matt had read that sailors consider any mishap aboard a boat involving a bird to be a pretty bad omen. Despite a chill of foreboding at the thought, he chose to chalk this one up to bad timing on the heron's part—and even worse, on Hank's. After washing and towel-drying the stout little body, he slipped the old dog's life vest on and fastened this to the tether that would keep him safely connected to the boat. Then, Matt assembled a wall of cushions and pillows up in the V-berth that would keep his buddy secure and comfortable when the waves really began to rock the boat. Hank's needs checked off, Matt began getting everything shipshape and ready for the voyage ahead.

Pulse quickening with excitement, Matt leaned over the deck and began hauling up *Lonesome Dove*'s anchor, feeling the cold slide of the links running through his fingers. Anchor stowed away, he scooted starboard, and checked once more that the cords holding his inflatable dinghy and its outboard in place against the gunwale were secure. Then he ducked down into the cockpit, and with a fist held to his heart, and a silent prayer said for Julie, cranked up the little Yanmar diesel engine, eased the throttle lever forward and—as soon as he saw *Lonesome Dove* was pointed directly into the wind, her prow dipping eagerly into the spreading waves—lashed the varnished teakwood tiller handle into position. Checking that his safety harness and jackline that connected him to the boat were both secure, he again made his way forward on deck, loosened the last of the small ties securing the mainsail to the boom, then pulled hard on the halyard line, hauling several folds of heavy synthetic material skyward up the sail track until they were stretched firmly against the mast.

He gave the halyard line a final snug with the winch, tied it off, then scurried back to the cockpit to release the mainsheet that held the boom in place. The big white mainsail flapped overhead in the wind—as if it were as excited as he to get going. As soon as he felt the boom begin to sway, he reached up with a free hand to help swing it out over the port side while deftly nudging the tiller handle with his knee to make a slight course correction. Matt heard the familiar crack of the sail as it filled with air and adjusted the mainsheet. Then, holding the end of the jib sheet that was loosely wrapped around the port side winch with his left hand, he carefully untied and paid out a second, smaller line, allowing the wheel of the Harken roller furling to rotate and unfurl the boat's front sail—the jib.

After giving the jib sheet a quick trim with a couple cranks of the winch handle, Matt finally let out a sigh of relief that they were underway. At last, after completing a procedure he knew he'd be repeating countless times in the coming months, he reached down and switched off *Lonesome Dove*'s noisy auxiliary engine, allowing the morning breeze to ease them slowly forward. He'd dreamed of this very moment for years—the start of an around-the-world-voyage—just not like this. If not for Clawson Chicken, Julie could have been there at his side, sharing equally in his joy as she helped get *Lonesome Dove* underway. Matt felt alone and hollow, yet still his heart swelled—enlivened by all the adventures that might lie ahead—as the trade winds carried the sloop forward. He wiped his eyes, cleared his throat and somehow managed a brave voice as he called out to his sailing companion, "All right, Hank, ol' buddy, let's do this thing!"

Knowing that the journey ahead would be a solitary one, Matt had rigged up his sailboat for single-handed sailing, making it manageable and safe for him to handle alone. He'd installed a "roller furling" type of sail—favored by many single-handed sailors—which he could control safely from the boat's cockpit when really heavy seas might make it perilous to run along the deck. The whole process of getting *Lonesome Dove* underway had taken only a couple of minutes, and soon, the crisp white sails billowed out, the force of the trade winds pushing his new home forward at a steady and comfortable pace of six knots. She surged ahead as the wind picked up, and flecks of foam from the waves peppered Matt's sun-warmed skin. Seemingly from out of nowhere, a lone gray porpoise emerged alongside the boat. Much to Hank's delight, it emitted a loud spout of warm air and water that they both felt up in the cockpit, before it turned to frolic in *Lonesome Dove*'s wake, its slick gray body crossing the "vee" several times before finally disappearing from view.

Near Pelican Island, at the northeast end of Corpus Christi Bay, Matt finally allowed his steady grip on the tiller to relax. Out here in the vast spread of water, with his floating home moving along briskly, he suddenly realized that he'd finally "done it"—cast off all the lines that tethered him to the painful monotony of his Julie-less life. For the first time in a long time, he felt a surge of something like hope, and he tilted his face up toward the sun and let out a whoop of pure joy. From the cockpit, Hank joined in with a sharp chorus of barking

Feeling more like a real seafarer, and not just a weekend sailor, Matt periodically rechecked the course he'd mapped out on his old-school paper chart and consulted the wind indicator—a small plastic arrow up on the mast—to gauge the true direction of the wind, the better to trim his sails. Now, glancing up at the indicator, Matt caught the glint of morning sun striking something reflective just below the top of the mast. He smiled fondly. It was his dad's old eyeglasses, a bittersweet reminder of yet another of the losses that had steamrollered their way over the past few years. Matt's dad, George—"Coach" to his friends—had fought and finally succumbed to a decade-long battle with cancer not long before Julie's accident. As the cancer ate away at his fragile body, his sight had rapidly begun to fail. Before his vision was completely gone, Matt and Julie had taken the old man down to Corpus Christi to see the latest upgrades to *Lonesome Dove* and see the coast from the water, one last time. As Julie prepared to hoist Matt up the mast in a bosun's chair to install the wind indicator, his father had pulled a worn pair of eyeglasses from his pocket and pressed them into his son's hand.

"These ain't doing me any good now. If you don't mind, would you duct tape these up on top of the mast for me...looking forward? I know it's silly, but maybe my old glasses can help guide you on your journey, even after I'm gone."

At the memory, Matt smiled sadly and pressed a palm to his chest. "Okay, Dad, he breathed, "I'm heading out now. Please help me find my way."

After what seemed like hours, they finally made it across the wide bay, with the coastal vacation town of Port Aransas finally coming into sight off in the distance. *Lonesome Dove* was soon passing rows of moored shrimp boats, dockside T-shirt shops, and bars before finally easing out Aransas Pass into the vast sprawl that was the Gulf of Mexico. There was the salty smell of countless commingling forms of Gulf marine life, combined with faint but pungent notes of seafood cooking, charcoal briquettes, and suntan oil from shore. *It smells like life*, he thought, as the complex aroma slowly faded from his nostrils and was replaced by the cleaner, more uniform, salty-sweet brine of the open ocean.

Just as they cleared the end of the jetty, gliding past the big red marker buoy with its sonorous clanging bell marking the channel entrance, a large U.S. Navy ship passed them on its way into port. High above on the ship's deck, Matt could see scores of sailors engaged in a frenzy of activity as they prepared for docking, and he was awestruck by the sheer size of the massive vessel. Matt tipped his head back, regarding the majestic ship with both admiration and trepidation. The "road" ahead, albeit a watery one, would be filled with both wonders and dangers, and he would have to watch his little home around these monsters of the sea.

As the long white strand of sandy beach that crowned Mustang Island faded away in the distance, a brisk southwest wind, unusual for this time of year, allowed Matt to trim the sails nice and tight, so *Lonesome Dove* could increase her speed.

To the left of the bow, to the northeast, and 873 nautical miles ahead, was Key West, a journey which would take them about eight days of nonstop sailing. To the right, some 4,700 miles and due east, were Morocco and West Africa, which, under the right conditions, could be reached in just over a month, without ever seeing land if one wanted. For now, to the left. They'd take it slow and easy as they figured out this offshore-sailing thing and earned their sea legs.

For now, the Keys were calling Matt's name, beckoning with water that was bluer and clearer than anything he'd seen on the Texas coast. Once he'd checked out the coral reefs around the handful of tiny, unpopulated islands, he might even head into Key West, see a six-toed Hemingway cat, and drink a rum runner while strolling down Duval Street. Or he could bypass civilization altogether and thread his way north to the Upper Keys, leading *Lonesome Dove* into the crystal turquoise water he and Julie had once dreamed of sailing together. He'd pilot the dinghy ever so slowly into the shallow, lazy waters near shore, seeking out seagrass beds where the shy, sluggish manatees sometimes lolled, careful not to disturb them as they grazed. Once he'd swum with a manatee, he might be ready to take on the powerful, swift-moving Gulf Stream, heading east to the Bahamas for the winter. When spring came, he'd chart a new course—chasing more sunsets westward across the Caribbean—and beyond.

The southwest wind kicked up a bit, ruffling Hank's fur as they picked up speed. *Lonesome Dove*'s dancing bow seemed to be drawn forward as if pulled by an invisible hand or a cable. The blue water deepened to indigo ink, and Matt saw that a pod of dolphins had joined them, arcing and diving in the waves, escorting them into the wide expanse of the Gulf.

Matt spent the next few hours readying the boat for nighttime solo sailing. He secured his heavy, padded sailing harness, which had a ten-foot-long nylon tether with a heavy-duty clip that he could attach to various points on the boat. If anything happened—a collision with a wayward log or a rogue wave—the harness would keep him connected to the vessel, preventing him from falling overboard and becoming lost at sea.

After his furry buddy had his dinner and a quick trip to the pee pad, Matt made sure that Hank's life jacket and lifeline were all snug and shortened the tether so he couldn't fall out of the V-berth where he was securely and comfortably, stowed.

Matt knew that most boats always kept a two-way VHF radio turned on and tuned to channel 16, especially while out at sea. Whether they were little pleasure boats, or giant aircraft carriers, every skipper was supposed to monitor that frequency for everything from maritime advisories to mayday calls. As the sun rose higher overhead, and he and Hank were having a little chat about what to have for lunch, the radio crackled to life. A pleasant female voice came on the radio. *Sort of sexy*, Matt thought, but maybe he'd already been at sea too long.

"To the vessel at 27.881 degrees north and 96.642 degrees west, cruising at a speed of five knots, on a compass heading of ninety degrees true, please come in on channel one-six, Captain. Over."

Matt wasn't sure if they were calling him or not, so he waited for a minute to see if someone else responded, while trying to reconcile the numbers that were called out with the slightly different ones currently displayed on his small GPS unit. The female voice came on a second time, this time sounding a bit more urgent.

"To the captain of the vessel at...cruising at a speed of five knots and on a heading of ninety degrees true, please halt your forward progress."

Still slightly unsure if he was the intended recipient of the call, Matt replied. "Sailing vessel Lonesome Dove here"—he listed his coordinates and added, using somewhat imperfect radio protocol—"Are you hailing me, ma'am?"

"Captain, this is the research ship *Victoria*. We're towing seven miles of seismic cable behind our vessel and you are currently on a heading that will cross our path. Captain, please halt your forward progress for thirty minutes to allow our line to pass. Over."

"Roger, this is the sailing vessel *Lonesome Dove*, heaving to, halting forward progress for thirty minutes. Over." Matt responded.

"Thank you, Captain. Research vessel *Victoria* clear and standing by on channel one-six," the pleasant voice replied.

Had Matt continued sailing forward, then *Lonesome Dove* really might have been towed along by a cable, rather than just seeming to be. He sprang immediately into action, and quickly "hove to"—backed the two sails in opposite directions. This was an old sailor's trick he'd learned that used the opposing forces of the wind on two sails to cause the boat to become almost "anchored" on the open ocean, remaining basically in the same spot for a short while. With a start, Matt realized this was the first time that he'd been called "Captain" outside of the army, and he recognized that he would have to call on his old skills to stay alert and ready for action. For his and his buddy's sake, he would have to be on the ball at all times if they were to make it safely across the Gulf of Mexico—and beyond.

After carefully placing the arm of the small electronic autopilot—a "tiller pilot" some called it—onto the long wooden tiller handle and setting it to a compass heading of almost due east, Matt ducked down into the cockpit to check the nautical charts. Passing his finger along the course he'd charted out; he observed that the depth of the water was now over eight thousand feet. He shuddered involuntarily. They were passing over an underwater feature called the Atwater Valley. It was a valley whose depths he didn't ever care to explore. He knew from harrowing stories heard back in his brief time as a rig worker that just a few miles to the east of this spot was where the Deepwater Horizon tragedy had occurred. The man-made disaster had caused the loss of eleven human lives and those of countless aquatic mammals, birds, fish, and crustaceans, after a massive offshore drilling rig exploded and released thousands of barrels of crude into the Gulf of Mexico. Just as in Julie's death, there was surely corporate greed and negligence involved, along with teams of corporate lawyers doing their best to sidestep moral and financial responsibility for the tragedy.

Behind *Lonesome Dove*'s transom, the water, which had for a while been a deep shade of blue, gradually turned inky black and ominous looking as they sailed farther and farther offshore. Just below the dark water in the boat's wake, Matt caught sight of an occasional flash of silver, blue, and green darting in and out beneath the hull. It was a school of curious dorado, or mahi-mahi that had come by to investigate the intruders. Matt wished he could invite at least one of them for dinner onboard, but unfortunately, his fishing gear was all stowed away for the voyage.

Never in his short sailing career had Matt seen an error message on the boat's depth finder, but there was one now, as only a series of dotted lines showed on the display. As they reached a distance of about sixty nautical miles offshore, off the starboard bow Matt could just barely make out the shapes of large offshore oil platforms appearing to slowly rise onto the horizon, some of them much larger than the massive Deepwater Horizon had been. As he studied his chart and plotted a course around them, the huge platforms seemed to grow taller and taller, towering over *Lonesome Dove* as he threaded his way nearer.

The last time he'd been anywhere near an offshore rig, his vantage point had been much different. He smiled wryly as he thought back to those days.

Way back when, he'd worked on some of those same offshore rigs during his brief stint as an oilfield worker. Before finding work as a lineman, Matt, fresh off the plane from Iraq, had struggled to find a decent-paying job, despite many employers claiming to be "veteran friendly." In the oilfield, which was commonly referred to as "the patch", companies were less discriminating, often hiring able-bodied workers as general laborers or roustabouts. The newest of these were the "worms", and they were often assigned to the most undesirable jobs. Those who couldn't cut it were quickly weeded out. While looking for work, Matt and his old army buddy, Miguel, had bypassed more conventional job-search techniques and simply driven up to a rig being set up in the middle of a dusty cotton field outside of Corpus Christi. A stern-looking rig boss, the toolpusher, had looked them up and down before asking,

"You boys druggies or runnin' from the law?" Side-eying Miguel, who was a fifth- generation American, the big redneck added "You hablay English, right?"

After demonstrating they could carry two sixty-pound sacks of cement at a time up a long flight of stairs to the rig floor, they'd both been hired on the spot. Matt chuckled to himself when he recalled the small, independent drilling company's new employee safety orientation. He'd been given a hard hat, gloves, and safety glasses which were to be worn only when OSHA inspectors showed up, and was directed to take note of a jar on a shelf above the "doghouse" door. Within the jar, what was clearly a human thumb, floated in murky liquid. "Worm thumb, dumb kid named Curt. Don't get hurt like Curt" was the sum total of the safety orientation.

Shrugging off the image of the pickled thumb, Matt recalled his first offshore hitch and being up on the rig floor on an offshore rig like the one above him. Once he'd been the poor sucker up there, looking down and seeing lucky people in various kinds of pleasure craft pass below while he was busy pulling twelve-hour shifts and wishing he were home.

Back then, it was enough to make anyone envious, especially when they'd been stuck out there, far from shore, for weeks on end. If there was any saving grace about offshore work, besides the money, it was that there was usually a good Cajun chef along for the ride. Along with the scent of diesel smoke from the rig's generators, Matt caught a whiff of something delicious cooking in the rig's galley and his mouth watered. Today was Saturday, which on some of the better offshore rigs meant the chef would be fixing thick, juicy steaks and fully loaded baked potatoes for the hungry hands.

Matt could see workers gathered around on the upper deck of one of the newer drilling platforms, where a helicopter had just landed at the helipad. A couple of the men waved down at him as his little boat slowly passed the massive rig, and as he waved back, he gave *Lonesome Dove*'s big brass bell a hard clang. The men were probably in an especially good mood because the newly arrived helicopter was taking them back to land and into the arms of their wives or girlfriends. Oilfield life was a hard one—and one that was also rough on relationships. The Cajun men would kid each other about the others' wives having a "Jody" or a "backdoor man" that visited them while the men were off at work. For the Spanish-speaking workers, the threat was a "Sancho." This kind of ribbing was all in good fun, but far too many times a rig worker, who may have been out at sea for a month or more, would return home to find someone else had taken his place.

Some of the old oil platforms, ones containing oil production equipment and tanks, were unmanned, and high on their decks sat piles of aging, rusty equipment. The ghostly, towering behemoths were covered with layer upon layer of seabird guano and festooned with yards of snagged fishing line. Hundreds of curious pelicans and seagulls, which seemed to occupy nearly every square inch of the rusty monstrosities, craned their long necks to watch Matt and Hank as they passed below. Many of the rusty old structures featured foghorns, which let out slow, mournful bellows every few seconds to warn off ships in foggy conditions.

Up on deck for another potty break, Hank kept a wary eye on the birds that lingered on the platforms, most certainly recalling his experience at Shamrock Cove, and erupting with furious barks when any of them flew too close to the boat.

As evening fell, and the sky turned from a soft blush to lavender, the old sloop entered a vast, seemingly empty stretch of open ocean beyond the area being probed for oil and gas. It appeared to Matt as if they were traversing a vast field of bluish-colored grass with patches of yellow sargasso weed dotted here and there. He knew sargasso was a kind of seaweed that grew in thick patches across much of the Atlantic and the Gulf of Mexico. Fed partly by fertilizer coming from factory farms in Brazil, huge mats of sargasso could stretch uninterrupted for hundreds of miles.

In the lowering light, he noticed a few floating coconut shells in the water, along with a flotsam of plastic debris. From what he'd read in his well-thumbed offshore sailing manual, *Chapman's Piloting*, the presence of the shells meant they were now crossing into the warm waters of the Gulf Stream. He'd learned that the name was a misnomer, because there were really many different "Gulf Streams"— wide rivers of warm water that flowed from the tropics, all the way up past Greenland—bringing the temperate currents that made the climate of places like Great Britain more tolerable. Glancing down at the water rushing by, he saw the plastic lid of a Clawson Chicken Tenders container, its label written in Spanish, drift by the hull, and felt his chest grow tight. He might be a long way away from the place he had called home, but he hadn't yet traveled far enough to outdistance the pain that clung to him like an unwelcome shadow.

CHAPTER 4

When darkness finally fell, and twinkling stars began spilling across the cloudless sky, Matt went below to study his charts and discovered that he and Hank had put more than sixty nautical miles between themselves and the entrance to Aransas Pass. The "four-to-six-foot seas" that the National Weather Service had forecast, never had materialized, and their first day at sea felt like an auspicious start to their journey. Still, there were 832 nautical miles lying between them and Key West, and Matt knocked on the glossy teak dinette table, hoping the gesture might secure their continuing good fortune.

Unfortunately, wood-knocking alone wasn't enough to alter the weather, and the winds began to shift restlessly, twisting around until they were "right on the nose," blowing in from the direction that Matt wanted to travel. Because sailboats couldn't travel straight into the wind, they were forced to tack from side to side, slowly zigging and zagging as they tried to make forward progress. Matt disengaged the tiller pilot and began steering by hand, maneuvering *Lonesome Dove* back and forth, tacking a half mile to port, then a half mile to starboard, until gradually the little boat began making headway along its charted course.

Finally, the winds shifted again, and now sailing on a "beam reach," with the wind coming across the side of the boat, he slowly eased out the sails, sending *Lonesome Dove* galloping along at a healthy clip of almost six knots—the upper end of the old sloop's top speed. What Matt initially failed to notice was that the boat's "knot meter" or speedometer—working off a small impeller underneath the boat—was feeding him false information. It wasn't until he checked the screen of the GPS, which gave a much more accurate reading, that he saw it displaying a speed of barely over zero miles per hour. They were caught up in one of the Gulf Stream's many eddies, currents that swirled around and ran counter to the main flow of water. If a boat got caught up in one of these eddies—flowing at the same speed as the vessel, but in the opposite direction—it caused it to stall and tread water, giving the illusion of sailing quickly forward as the bow skipped over the waves, yet went nowhere. Matt had learned that to escape from one of these eddies, he would have to sail at an angle across the current, similar to how a swimmer escapes a riptide along the shore. After a frustrating couple of hours of tacking, they were finally free of the current and back on track, making good time toward their next stop on the far side of the Gulf—the tiny islands of the Dry Tortugas, a U.S. territory just off the coast of Florida.

As night wore on, the biggest and brightest stars he'd ever seen, even bigger than those out in the desert of Big Bend National Park, covered the vast, clear seascape like a giant polka-dotted blanket. Head tilted back, Matt located the constellation Orion the Hunter, then traced a line downward from the three stars in the hunter's "belt" to Sirius, the Dog Star. He and Julie had chosen this as "their star" and they'd agreed to look for it and think of each other whenever they were apart. Like Orion's faithful dog, Hank sat in the cockpit at Matt's side, recently pottied and now cuddled up in a blanket, his head nodding and bobbing as he grew sleepy from sea air and adventure.

Matt switched off the brightly glowing GPS screen, which displayed a large arrow pointing toward Loggerhead Cay in the Dry Tortugas, and showed the remaining distance to be traveled: some 815 nautical miles. Choosing instead to navigate by the stars and *Lonesome Dove*'s trusty old compass, he drew the tiller handle toward him slightly to adjust his course so that Sirius shone just off the starboard side of the bow, setting them on the east-northeast course they would maintain throughout the night.

The cabin down below was warm and cozy, and a soft golden glow from the old brass wall sconces illuminated three brass porthole windows along each side of the vintage sloop, casting a dim light from each out onto the passing water. Matt reached an arm down into the companionway and fiddled with the dials on the stereo mounted just inside. All of the usual FM stations were now out of range, but after a few minutes of fruitless spinning, he could pull in a crackling AM station out of Havana, Cuba, which was playing a song by Buena Vista Social Club that he and Julie had both liked, called "Chan Chan."

"Cuando Juanica y Chan Chan
En el mar cernían arena
Como sacudía el jibe
A Chan Chan le daba pena."

Matt, who'd learned Spanish while spending summers working with the hands on his grandfather's ranch in New Mexico, knew it was a tale about a couple, Chan Chan and Juanica, who were gathering sand from the beach for a home they were building. As Juanica shook a sieve to separate the sand from shells, Chan Chan would become aroused by the sensuous motion of her body. Matt loved how Latin music could make almost anything—even sifting sand—sound erotic. The sexy beat of the music and the soft swish of the waves made Matt think of Julie and the way her cute little butt would sway whenever she'd crank up the tunes and get her groove on.

He wasn't sure what he believed in anymore, but at that moment, under the canopy of stars, wrapped up in the velvety night, he felt acutely aware of her presence, her *Julieness*. It wasn't the citrus scent of her warm skin, or the tickle of her breath on his neck he sensed, but a welling up in his chest that felt like hope—and a way forward. With sudden certainty he knew that, at least for now, she was out there, or up there or even *right there*, guiding him forward, watching over him. She'd never again make him Spam and grits, or wrap those long, strong legs around him, but Julie had loved him more than he'd ever been loved before and she had cared more for his happiness than she had, perhaps, for her own. Matt's eyes filled with tears and he brushed them away with the back of his hand, smiling just a little for the first time in a long while. Maybe instead of drowning in his memories, he could reach out a hand and grope for the lifeline he was sure Julie had just thrown him.

Climbing back up on deck, Matt placed the arm of the tiller pilot into a fitting on the long, varnished handle and pushed a button to let it take over the steering. Its tiny motors and gears buzzed to life and directed *Lonesome Dove* into a light breeze. Matt went down into the galley to fix a simple meal. This time the food was less ambitious than Spam and grits. Just a few fistfuls of stale Fritos corn chips topped by room-temperature bean dip and some canned Spanish olives. Hank got his usual dog food, with a few crumbled-up chips on top. Matt wouldn't trust the dog with bean dip, especially not now, outside of optimal dog-pooping conditions.

His appetite somewhat sated, Matt sailed on into the night, scanning the horizon and watching the glowing Furuno radar screen which would alert him to the presence of ships up to a distance of about eight miles. He sipped a little Jack Daniels from an old metal Pusser's Rum cup that he'd once got on a trip with Julie to the U.S. Virgin Islands. They'd first learned to sail—and caught the sailing bug—in the USVI. A poster tacked to a wall of a beach bar they'd been frequenting with more regularity than was perhaps healthy had piqued their interest. "Captain Bill's Sailing School," it was called, although "school" was a bit of an exaggeration. Captain Bill lived aboard an old Cape Dory sailboat in Cruz Bay, on the island of St. John. For forty

bucks apiece, he'd given them a day's worth of sailing instruction, as well as revealing closeups of his well-worn
Speedo bathing suit and everything it failed to cover as he
clambered nimbly about the boat. He'd taught them the
basics of sailing, and before they parted ways, Matt had
promised Captain Bill that one day he was going to surprise
him, and sail into Cruz Bay in his own boat, along with his
first mate, Julie. Taking a last hungry look at Julie's legs in
their cut-off denim shorts, Captain Bill had said he looked
forward to the day.

The music that the Cuban station was playing turned
plaintive and yearning, and so Matt switched off the radio,
preferring the sound of small waves breaking against the
boat's bow to the song of lost love. Looking back toward
the stern, he saw a trail of bioluminescence stretching out
to the horizon far behind them, as *Lonesome Dove* brushed
up against billions of tiny phosphorescent plankton in the
water. The luminous glow made the sea sparkle as if it had
swallowed some of the starlight from the blanketing night
sky.

The balmy Gulf breeze that had been blowing all day
had grown cooler with each minute past sundown. Realizing he was shivering, Matt shrugged on his prized red Helly
Hansen offshore sailing jacket and wrapped a small fuzzy
blanket around Hank, who was snuggled up against his side
in the cockpit.

The matching red his-and-hers sailing jackets he and Julie had given each other for Christmas were meant to be
worn together on weekend sailing trips, and finally, maybe,
around the world. Perhaps they could have eventually

saved up enough money to cast off *Lonesome Dove*'s lines to circumnavigate before they started a family. Or, maybe even afterward, once the kids were big enough—be home-schooled by Julie as many live-aboard sailing families had done before them. As his mind wandered, becoming lost in a sea of bittersweet memories, Matt cinched the thick cord on the jacket's hood tighter, imagining once more that she was there next to him, and wrapped his own arms tightly around himself. As comforting as it was, it was still no sub-stitute for Julie's sweet embrace.

Around midnight, Matt's head nodded and he decided to call it a night—or at least a couple of hours of shut-eye. Employing an age-old, solo sailor's low-tech trick, he wound up his manual egg timer, setting it to wake him every eight minutes so that he could scan the horizon for ships. Then, Matt set a guard alarm zone on the radar to alert him if any ships were within five miles. Arranging a cushion behind him, he leaned back, crossing his arms over his chest and drawing his knees up for warmth. The tiller pilot made a low buzzing noise as it moved the tiller handle slightly one way, then the other, to keep them on course. The soft sounds it made, along with the waves gently break-ing against *Lonesome Dove*'s bow, lulled him to sleep between each round of buzzing from the timer.

Seven minutes into what seemed like a hundredth call from the egg timer, Matt woke abruptly from a deep sleep. The wind slapped the sails as it picked up, and Matt feared the forecaster's predictions for higher seas might come true after all. As the wind increased, the waves swelled, growing to around eight feet in height. Soon, in all directions, the surface of the ocean was covered with huge dark waves topped with white sea foam. In the light of the full moon, the Gulf of Mexico's tranquil rolling blue fields of water had suddenly transformed into a ghostly landscape of angry dark hills stretching as far as the eye could see. Some of the "hills" that Matt sighted off in the distance appeared formidable, and his heartbeat raced. Tuning in the latest offshore weather forecast on the long-range marine radio channel, he learned that a low-pressure system had suddenly formed nearby, and that mariners could expect seas from fifteen to twenty feet in height. As long as waves in that range weren't breaking, as happened when they got too close together, he knew *Lonesome Dove* could still sail safely in seas like this. An approaching cloud bank dimmed the bright light of the full moon, and Matt knew he needed to ready the boat for some rough weather.

Matt quickly stowed away loose items, tucking his precious Pusser's Rum cup, as well as pots and pans, into the galley cabinets and securing his handheld GPS with a small bungee cord. He checked the buckles on Hank's safety harness and life jacket and prepared his "nest" in the V-berth at the front of the boat's cabin, fortifying his barricade with an additional wall of cushions and pillows. Mentally running through his safety list, he located his emergency parachute anchor, a safety device carried on many offshore sailboats. The anchor resembled an actual parachute, and during severe storms, he could pitch it off the bow of the boat, along with several hundred feet of heavy line, effectively creating an "anchor" that would hold the boat safely facing into oncoming seas. With the parachute anchor deployed, he could get some rest while they rode out the storm, rather than trying to fight the weather and waves by attempting to sail onward. As the seas continued to grow, increasing to over twenty feet high, and the waves broke closer and closer together, he knew he needed to deploy the sea anchor. *Lonesome Dove*'s bow was pitching and rolling up and down like a sea monster trying to shake them off its back. Matt double-checked the clip on his safety harness and began crabbing his way up the swaying deck toward the bow of the boat.

Recalling the instructional video and throwing in a prayer for the sea anchor's maiden voyage, Matt tossed the device off the bow into the dark surging water and briefly tried to check its status by shining a beam from his strong headlamp. It sank slowly under the surface, as if swallowed up by the waves, and then billowed out like a giant red man-o'-war jellyfish. After being hove to, he lowered the storm trysail that he'd put up earlier, and *Lonesome Dove* settled in to ride the sea anchor. When everything finally snugged up, the bow of the little boat jerked abruptly to attention, and remained there pointing toward the strong wind, riding up and down wildly on the growing waves like a wake boarder flying behind a ski boat.

Matt never would know for sure how huge the waves got that night, but way out there in the distance, he thought he could see some rising higher than *Lonesome Dove*'s thirty-seven-foot mast. He shuddered and ducked down to check on the cabin and Hank. After securing everything that he could, he slammed the two small companionway doors behind him, slid the hatch cover over his head, and latched it just before a huge wave lashed over the side, completely flooding the cockpit. Wedging himself between the companionway ladder and his large ice chest, the twin adrenaline rush of fear and exhilaration gripped Matt. He wasn't as concerned about the up- and-down motion as he was about broaching, which was what happened when a sailboat got knocked down on her side, often leading to capsizing or dismasting.

Down in the cabin felt safer—and drier—than being up on deck, but Matt knew that the safety of his cocoon was partly an illusion. Recalling a story he'd once heard about a similar-sized sailboat that had sunk offshore, he knew that should the mast ever break off, it would become a battering ram—one still tied to the hull by the rigging—which would bash holes in the boat's exterior with every motion of the waves. Thankfully, every time that *Lonesome Dove* was knocked sideways, she would go through a series of shuddering motions before slowly righting herself, issuing a few worrisome twanging sounds from her rigging. As the hull pitched and yawed, all sorts of things he hadn't expected to become airborne sailed across the cabin. A heavy brass barometer, which he'd carefully screwed to the cabin wall, came loose, and sailed past Matt's head, hitting the pantry's plexiglass cover with a loud thud. At the sound, Hank jolted awake, then burrowed himself deeper into his pile of pillows, probably wondering at his human's choice of their new home.

Clutching the VHF radio microphone in his hand and calling out his GPS position every few minutes to warn other ships that his vessel was in a stationary position, he eventually nodded off and fell exhausted into a deep dreamless sleep, the microphone slipping from his fingers to swing like a pendulum from its cord.

CHAPTER 5

When he awoke the next morning, his whole body ached, and through his sleep- bleary eyes, everything around him seemed strangely unfamiliar. The moment seemed frozen in time, devoid of noise and motion. For a second, he thought he might no longer be alive, and that he and his little boat might have passed on up to heaven. The foul scent of Hank's poop quickly brought Matt crashing back to reality. Tracing the source of the odor, he discovered several trash bags containing Hank's onboard waste had been tossed around the cabin during the storm and had leaked. The boat's shallow bilge was also overflowing, causing a foul slurry of bilge water, leftover food from an overturned cooker, and diesel fuel from a leaking jerry can to slosh across over the floorboards. It was all one hell of a mess, but he needed a cup of instant coffee before he could deal with any of it. But, first things first, and that meant taking care of his first mate, who stood up in the V-berth attached to his safety tether, wagging his tail as if nothing at all had

happened, clearly relieved that the boat was no longer rolling like a crazy carnival ride.

Matt had pulled off his diesel and water-soaked sailing
jacket and pants, T-shirt, and boxers, and was stark naked
as he went up on deck with his dog clutched under his arm.
At a distance of three hundred miles out to sea, he figured
there would be no need to worry about an audience. As he
waited for Hank up on deck to "do his business," Matt
gazed out at a sea which was as calm as a backyard swimming pool for as far as the horizon stretched in all
directions. It looked like a completely different ocean from
the one he had wrestled with only a few hours before. He
barely had time to process this thought when he looked up
to see the nose cone of a large orange-and-white Coast
Guard jet barreling straight down toward him out of the
clear sky. The jet flew so close by he could see the pilot's face
and the glimmer of his Ray Ban Aviators. The pilot pulled
out of the dive just a couple of hundred feet above *Lonesome Dove*'s mast before throttling the jet's afterburner
and shooting skyward, leaving the air heavy with the smell
of burned jet fuel.

"U.S. Coast Guard aircraft calling the sailing vessel at
position..." called a voice over the VHF radio.

Matt grabbed the cockpit radio mic and replied, "This
is sailing vessel *Lonesome Dove*. Over."

The pilot, on routine patrol out of New Orleans, had
seen Matt's big red sea anchor floating in the water, was
concerned that the storm had damaged his vessel and was
checking on his welfare. After quickly pulling on a pair of
gym shorts, Matt thanked the pilot for his concern and,

with a blush that traveled to the tips of his ears, assured the man that everything was just fine. The pilot circled back around, made one more pass, and upon acknowledgment that everything was okay, tipped the jet's wings from side to side and roared away across the blue sky.

Matt fixed a cup of instant coffee in his Pusser's cup, sprinkled powdered creamer over the filmy surface, and stirred it with his forefinger. He located Hank's kibble and fixed him a bowlful before proceeding to retrieve the parachute anchor, which was now bobbing alongside *Lonesome Dove* like a huge discarded red sock. Hauling the mass of wet fabric over the bow, he marveled at how such an insubstantial fabric could anchor a ten-thousand-pound boat.

Without a trace of wind to lift *Lonesome Dove*'s sails, Matt prepared to switch to motor power. He hit a switch, and after an irritated round of sputtering complaints, the boat's trusty Yanmar diesel came to life. At a meager pace of four knots, *Lonesome Dove* began carving out a long, broad wake across a vast expanse of glassy ocean as they inched toward the Dry Tortugas. Thanks to the sedate pace and autopilot, Matt was able to spend a couple of hours mopping up the mess on the cabin floor, reorganizing his supplies, and, most importantly, re-securing and stowing Hank's stinky poop collection. He even had time to fix a bowl of grits, marbled with a squirt of maple syrup. Belly filled, his eyes strayed to an overhead cabinet that miraculously had stayed secured during the storm. He figured this was as good a time as any. Before he had left Corpus Christi, his boat-slip neighbors from the marina, Ron and Dottie, had given him a package wrapped up in butcher paper, tied together with parachute cord, and labeled with the words "Open in case of emergency". Matt was exhausted and running low on good spirits and figured this was as good a time as any.

Pulling out the package, he ripped off the paper to reveal the contents. A handful of Hershey's Kisses, glinting in their silver wrappers, spilled out, along with a package of Dramamine, another of Alka-Seltzer, a few sticks of Juicy Fruit chewing gum, and a photo they'd taken of Hank at the prow of their rowing dinghy, brave and resplendent in his brand-new life vest.

At the bottom of the package was a postcard, with a rendering of St. Christopher on one side, and on the other, in Dottie's careful handwriting, the message, "May the Lord and all his angels protect you." Matt's eyes welled up. He unwrapped a bite of chocolate and popped it in his mouth, then carefully tucked the postcard, St. Christopher's image facing out, in the barometer's wooden frame. He would welcome the protection of the traveler's saint, as well as more earthly angels.

Later in the morning, when a light southerly breeze finally sprang up, Matt cut off the little auxiliary engine and *Lonesome Dove* surged forward in a lively galloping motion as they headed into the slightly choppy waves of a "head sea" that was coming straight toward them.

The next few days passed quickly, and for the most part, uneventfully as they slowly voyaged on toward the Dry Tortugas and Florida, their progress interrupted only by a couple of thunderstorms and the sighting of a lone whale which Matt could see spouting far off in the distance. During one of the small squalls, a waterspout—the first one Matt had ever seen—formed just off the starboard bow, and he had to do a quick bit of maneuvering to avoid crossing into its path.

Except for that nightmarish squall, most days on the ocean ended as quietly as they'd begun. Mornings were Matt's favorite time of day, though. He cherished the few minutes before sunrise when, for just a moment, it seemed that yesterday's imperfect world bloomed into something brighter. His hope was a little like the "false dawn" of which sailors speak, but it was hope, nonetheless. More than anything, he wished for one more chance to be better, to do better, and to right the wrongs that had stolen Julie's life, and forever changed his own.

By the eighth day, as dusk claimed the light, Matt heard a faint echo on his boat's radar pinging off something large about ten miles ahead. As the sailboat grew nearer, the faint image on the screen took on a geometric shape, and he realized he was seeing the massive hexagonal brick walls of Fort Jefferson rising into the darkening sky. An avid reader and history buff, Matt had learned that Fort Jefferson was built on Garden Key in the Dry Tortugas before the Civil War, out of thousands upon thousands of bricks, with cannons atop its walls to fend off any enemy ships that might come calling. With changing naval-warfare methods and munitions, the large fort slowly moved into obsolescence, eventually being converted into a U.S. military prison. Among the first to be incarcerated there was the Lakota chief Sitting Bull, who had bravely led his people as they

fought to keep their homeland, along with Dr. Samuel
Mudd, the doctor who treated the wounds of John Wilkes
Booth, President Lincoln's assassin. Although he claimed
to only be following his Hippocratic Oath, the fact that
he'd helped such a person was considered reprehensible by
some, and he was convicted of treason and imprisoned in
this far-flung place. As time went on, Dr. Mudd earned a
full pardon for the work he did during a terrible outbreak
of yellow fever at the prison, having saved the lives not only
of hundreds of Fort Jefferson's inmates but many of its
guards as well.

Matt couldn't wait to walk around the fort, feel the
heat of the bricks under his palms, and run his hands over
the names carved into its stone walls. Getting out his chart,
Matt navigated toward the entrance of the small harbor at
Loggerhead Cay, one of the smaller outlying islands beside
Garden Key, where the old fort was located. Then, he made
his way up to the bow and hauled out the best anchor for
the sandy bottom—a Danforth—and heaved it overboard.
He waited for the boat to settle back against the anchor and
made a mental note of a couple of fixed points on land to
reference so that he would be sure it wasn't dragging. As
soon as he was certain it was holding tight, he ducked back
into the cabin and crawled up into the V-berth with Hank
for the first proper sleep he'd had since leaving Shamrock
Cove.

CHAPTER 6

Matt awoke to a little dog standing firmly planted on his bare chest, filmy doggy eyes gazing lovingly into his own. Bright sunlight streamed in through the small windows of the V-berth, and he scratched Hank's apple-shaped head and checked the dial of his diving watch. It was just after ten, and Matt realized with a start he'd been asleep for over twelve hours. Pushing himself into a seated position, he caught Hank as the dog slid off his chest, then crawled out of the V-berth and climbed up into the cockpit. No sooner was Hank deposited up on deck than he ran barking toward the stern of the boat, where he stood up on his hind legs to get a better look at the action on the shore. On a nearby pier, a man was just landing a huge flopping fish, to the delight of a motley assortment of seabirds. Behind the man, the jetty stretched back to a large white lighthouse which seemed to rise directly out of the sea. *Lonesome Dove* bobbed gently in the little cove, her halyard tinkling in the soft breeze. The water was bright turquoise, a shade Matt had only ever seen before in the Caribbean, and a line of waving palm trees dotted the shoreline. He was only 878 nautical miles from Corpus Christi, and yet he felt reborn in this exotic landscape, ready to crawl out of his cocoon of self-isolation and stretch his adventuring wings.

After grabbing a hasty breakfast of a slightly crushed granola bar, and feeding Hank a handful of kibble, Matt popped the little dog into an old, drab olive backpack, leaving Hank's head poking out so he could still see. With the dog snugly secured against his back, Matt inflated his old gray dinghy and lowered it and the Yamaha outboard motor carefully over *Lonesome Dove*'s side. Then he climbed down the swim ladder with Hank, attached the dinghy's small outboard and cranked it to life. They putted slowly toward shore, the water cleaving in a foamy vee, the churning of the Yamaha a pleasant hum in the warm sunshine. As they neared the pier, Matt caught sight of a man and woman cleaning a large fish. The breeze ruffled their silver hair, and they raised their hands in greeting as they saw him approach.

"Throw me your line," called the man, reaching out for the bowline as Matt tossed the coil and he tied it off to a cleat on the dock. Matt scrambled out of the dinghy, trying not to jostle Hank, and then laughed as his feet contacted solid ground and the sensation of rocking, rising and dipping followed him onto land, causing him to stumble and nearly lose his balance.

"Been out for a while?" the man smiled, extending a broad, calloused hand. He introduced himself as "Charlie Mills, from Kansas City, Missouri," and called over the woman, whose smiling blue eyes caused creases in her deeply tanned face as she welcomed Matt to the National Park.

"Over a week," said Matt, smiling ruefully as he tried to shake off his sea legs.

"I'm Matt, and this is Hank," he added, pointing to his backpack, where the restless dog was wriggling to free himself.

"I'm Laney," she said, and waited for Matt to free Hank from his carrier before she continued her welcome speech. Charlie returned to his fish-cleaning task, but periodically tossed out a comment or two to add to Laney's informative recitation. Unleashed, Hank stretched out his back legs, and then trotted in circles around the dock, barking until he had cleared the immediate area of all bird-type threats.

It turned out that Charlie and Laney were the volunteer caretakers for this part of the National Park, and their job—which Matt thought mighty enviable—was to look after the large historic lighthouse that stood sentry over the harbor. Built back in 1856, this was thought to be the only beacon in the world built so far from the mainland. Once fitted with a huge, powerful kerosene light which was amplified by a Fresnel lens, its beam had reached almost all the way to Cuba. In more recent years, the light had been replaced with a much smaller solar-powered beacon, and its range intentionally decreased to discourage Cuban refugees from using it as a point of reference toward which to sail their rafts.

As they walked around the lighthouse, Charlie and Laney continued to chat about their life in the National Park, which struck Matt as a fascinating, if perhaps lonely, one. In an old shed behind the lighthouse, Charlie showed Matt a collection of homemade boats and rafts that had washed up over the years and been dragged up onto shore. Some of the old, heavily patched truck tires that had been strung together to make the craft bore sizable tears and holes. Sadly, not all the raft owners had survived, many of the craft washing ashore empty of all passengers. The thought of sharks crossed his mind, and it made Matt shudder to think of what may have happened to those unfortunate souls.

On several occasions, the couple had given aid to the refugees, yet were still required by law to call the authorities to report the landings. For many years now, a policy callously called "wet foot-dry foot," allowed any Cuban refugees who reached shore to remain in the U.S. and to receive expedited immigration processing, while swiftly deporting those who'd not yet reached land. Charlie shared that he'd seen more than one straggler refugee wading to shore to be apprehended, soon to be returned to Cuba, while the rest of their party stood on the sand and took their first steps toward freedom. It was hard to reconcile this tranquil shore as also being a bittersweet and terribly flawed path to freedom for refugees.

"Care to join us for lunch?" Charlie invited. "We've got some nice grouper fillets we can fry up..."

Laney cut him off with a raised hand and gentle admonishment.

"Oh honey, fish? Really? He's been out at sea for days. You remember how it was? All you wanted was a "cheeseburger in paradise" when we landed." She turned to Matt.

Would you like a hamburger, or maybe a chicken burger, Matt? I've got some ground chuck and some chicken patties in the deep freeze?"

Matt winced involuntarily at the mention of poultry, and his expression did not escape her keen gaze.

"Not a chicken fan?" she smiled. "Hamburger or fried grouper sandwiches? Which sounds the best to you?"

Matt nodded gratefully. "Anything would be great, but the grouper would be fantastic. I never get tired of fish."

Matt offered to help fix the meal, but Laney shooed both men off to an old wooden picnic table with the stern directive to "go visit." He suspected she was probably grateful to add someone to Charlie's social "circle" of just one and happy as well to have a little time for herself. The older man produced a trio of Bahamian beers from an ancient ice chest and, after running one up to Laney, came back to sip his cool beverage with his new friend.

The sun on Matt's skin was warm, the breeze pleasantly cool, and the Kalik smooth against his tongue. He stretched out his legs and leaned back against the table, shading his eyes and watching Hank running up and down the beach, chasing seagulls and looking much more like a puppy than a doggy octogenarian. The frantic scurry of a hermit crab caught the old dog's attention before he began poking at a hole in the sand where something delicious-smelling lay just out of reach. Then, he was trotting off to the dock, sniffing wildly at the lingering scents where Laney and Charlie had been cleaning fish only a short while ago.

It wasn't long before Laney returned, a heaped platter held high. Soon, Matt was biting into a crispy hot fish

sandwich, the fillet perfectly seasoned and snuggled between two thick slices of homemade bread. He moaned
involuntarily and Laney giggled, obviously pleased at the
unspoken compliment on her cooking. After a second
sandwich and another beer, Matt felt pleasantly full and relaxed in a way he had not for a very long time. So, when
Charlie's voice broke the silence, Matt's eyelids, which had
been drifting to half-mast, popped open.

"So, son...what's your story...what brings you down
this way?"

It was just a friendly question, an easy invitation. Over
the past couple of years, when any version of that question
had floated Matt's way, his answer would depend on his
level of sobriety and the darkness of his mood. Typically, he
kept his pain tightly buttoned up, freed only when too
much booze sent the room spinning and loosened his
tongue. But here, in the company of his new friends, with a
full belly and only the tiniest buzz, under the high-noon
sun and with the gracefully arching palm trees swaying in
the distance, sharing seemed like the natural thing to do.
And so he did.

Charlie and Laney were kind people and good listeners.
Maybe Matt told them a bit too much, but when Laney
leaned over, with tears in her eyes, and wrapped him up in
a big warm hug while Charlie roughly patted his knee, he
felt the weight of his heavy burden shift a little.

"Now I know why you weren't interested in having the
chicken," said Laney softly. Half a beat later, Charlie muttered gruffly, his shaggy head shaking slowly, "Poor Julie."

When Matt and Hank finally returned to *Lonesome Dove*, with new photos and contact information added to Matt's now seldom-used cell, they were both ready for a prolonged siesta. Matt had just crawled into the V-berth, opened the front hatch and switched on the twelve-volt fan, when the crackle of the VHF radio caught his attention. The voice that followed was a rich Cajun drawl.

"Hey y'all, this is the fishing boat, *Lady Rose,* anchored out here by the old fort. Anyone out there who can give some shrimpers a ride into shore? There's ten pounds of co-lossal gulf shrimp in it for any takers."

Matt heard some whooping noises in the background, a drunken catcall and a very belated "Over," all of which didn't fit conventional maritime radio protocol, but which certainly piqued his interest. Ten pounds was a lot of shrimp for someone without an onboard freezer, but he was running low on diesel and figured he might have a viable counteroffer for the *Lady Rose*. He grabbed the microphone.

"Fishing Boat *Lady Rose*, this is the sailing vessel *Lonesome Dove*. I can give you a ride, and if you can spare a couple gallons of diesel, that would be great. Over."

There was a pause, more raucous laughter, and then,

"Captain, you bring that ole boat of yours on over here and we'll fill her up for ya."

"Copy that, *Lady Rose*. On my way. Over."

Leaving Hank basking in a puddle of sunshine from one of the small portholes up in the V-berth, Matt went back up on deck, hauled up the anchor, then started up the diesel engine and steered *Lonesome Dove* toward what had to be the *Lady Rose*. As he drew closer, the sounds of revelry guided him toward his target. Approaching the large offshore fishing vessel, a ragtag crew of Cajun shrimpers gathered on the *Lady Rose*'s upper deck to greet him. There were half a dozen wild-looking men whose personal hygiene had clearly suffered while out at sea, and a couple of leathery, hard-looking women who looked like they might have been professionals—in some capacity or another.

Matt pulled up alongside, his own boat's deck a full six feet below that of the *Lady Rose*, and scanned the row of sun-beaten faces that peered down at him. A man with beefy, tattooed arms, ropey with muscle and popping with veins, shoved one of the onlookers aside and poked his head over the gunwale. "I'm Captain Marcel Boudreaux," he called, his Cajun accent slow and thick like molasses, "Toss me your line, Captain."

Matt tossed up a coil of line and one of the sailors tied *Lonesome Dove* alongside the fishing vessel next to a huge yellow fuel hose. It didn't take long for the crew to fill up the sailboat's small tank and a couple of Jerry cans. The scent of diesel, combined with the salt tang of sea air and briny, sweet aroma of marine life, was a heady perfume for Matt, and he felt strangely free and a little wild himself as his boat bumped up against the *Lady Rose*. Within minutes, and despite his protestations, a large five-gallon bucket filled to the brim with plump pink shrimp—the largest Matt had ever seen—was being passed over the side. Instead of the sixteen count-to-the-pound ones that passed for "colossal" at home, these were more like "five count," and some were as large as lobster tails. Before he could utter another refusal, the men were passing down buckets of crushed ice for his cooler and preparing to board *Lonesome Dove* for the trip over to Fort Jefferson.

As the deckhands clamored over the side of the *Lady Rose* and dropped onto *Lonesome Dove*'s deck, the cockpit filled up quickly with ripe body odor and a tangle of Cajun voices. It turned out that the big trawler had drawn too much water to make it safely into the fort's harbor. The men had been out at sea now for weeks and were eager to get to land to check out the National Park and its historic old fort. *Lonesome Dove* listed heavily to one side as the motley crew arranged themselves over her deck. Matt cranked on the Yanmar and eased slowly toward the fort, aware that his boat was sitting several inches lower in the water than usual. The day's drinking had apparently begun pretty early, as evidenced by the heady alcohol fumes and rowdy behavior of his passengers. One woman, obviously eager for a new audience, flipped her bleached mane of hair over her shoulder and began a colorful summary of life aboard the *Lady Rose*.

"We work hard but still like to pass a good time. We fish a little, we party a lot, and sometimes we go offshore and pick up a few bales of wee—"

A quick hand shot up a warning. "You best shut yer mouth!" roared Captain Boudreaux, as the flaxen-haired storyteller fell into a sullen silence, arms folded over untethered breasts. Matt cringed at the captain's warning and the resulting tension, turning his full attention to docking the sailboat. He cut the engine, stepped off, and set about tying *Lonesome Dove* to some rusty cleats on the side of the dock, then deploying a couple of bumpers to prevent her from scraping against the barnacle-encrusted concrete. In the few minutes this took, a new drama was unfolding in the cockpit. Now the two well-bronzed women had locked themselves in a tangle of brown limbs and brittle blonde hair, spitting and cursing unintelligibly until the words,

"He's my man, you damned bitch," followed by the snappy rebuttal, "No, he ain't, he's my man," rang out in bell-like tones that carried clearly over the long dock.

A fresh bunch of tourists, disembarking from a float-plane bobbing alongside the pier a short distance away, gawked openly at the display. A few grabbed their cell phones and aimed them in the kerfuffle's direction.

"Cat fight!" shouted one sailor, whooping drunkenly as the sound of clothing ripping accompanied the raised voices.

Then, Marcel's beefy forearms and Cajun fury reached into the fracas, sending the assailants to opposite ends of the small cockpit, where they adjusted their clothing and quelled their tempers. The motley crew began spilling out onto the deck, scattering like so many drunken ants.

"Whoo-eee," one of them shouted "A great big ole fort way out there in the Gulf 'a Mexico, whaddya know!"

Matt ducked his head and busied himself with securing the boat, eager to distance himself from the boisterous crew and their outrageous behavior. He had no interest in grabbing five minutes of fame via someone's cell phone footage. After checking on Hank and locking the companionway door, Matt headed off to explore the sprawling fort.

When he arrived back at the dock about a half hour later, a skinny park ranger was trying to herd a few tipsy crew members and their lady friends onto his patrol boat. Apparently, the sailors had managed to get themselves kicked off the island shortly after their arrival. Captain Boudreaux stood by *Lonesome Dove*, shaking his head.

"I'm sorry, Cap'n Matt. Shrimpers is good people, but sometimes we forget our manners."

This turned out to be a dramatic understatement, as the list of their lapsed manners had included public urination, a feeble attempt at flashing some fellow tourists, and a failed endeavor to break off and steal a brick from the fort. As Matt turned his gaze back toward the patrol boat, he noticed a lone escapee paddling slowly back toward the shrimp boat, partially supported by a life buoy he'd stolen from the ranger's vessel. Captain Boudreaux raised his eyes skyward and muttered something unintelligible. Whether prayer or curse, Matt would never know.

Matt divided up the shrimp with the park ranger, hopeful that this act would firmly establish him on the side of "Team Law & Order." He saved a handful to cook for supper, along with a couple pounds to offer Charlie and Laney, then headed on back to his anchoring spot at Loggerhead Cay, just offshore from the lighthouse. Shortly after Matt, exhausted from the afternoon's drama, had dropped anchor, Charlie paddled out in his kayak to meet him. Apparently the coconut telegraph was humming along nicely, as the older man was already up to date on the shrimpers' shenanigans at the Fort.

It turned out this was not the ranger's first go-around with the renegade band of shrimpers. The last time they'd attempted a visit to the fort, they had anchored so that their huge vessel blocked the harbor entrance, preventing the tourist boats and seaplanes from off-loading visitors. As they appeared to have settled in for the long haul, the ranger had been forced to pay them a visit in his patrol boat to politely request their immediate departure.

"I've got a funny story for you about the ranger, "Barney Fife" we call him" Charlie said, as Matt invited him onboard for a shot of Jim Beam. As the sun dropped low on the horizon like a big egg yolk dipping in the shimmering waves, Charlie told Matt how the ranger had once been one of the top officers in Yellowstone National Park. A famous senator from California was notorious for setting his own speed limits as he raced his Porsche through the park at his own discretion. The diligent ranger finally issued him one too many speeding citations, and the powerful senator pulled some strings, banishing the ranger to the Dry Tortugas for the rest of his career. Taking in the waving palm trees, picturesque lighthouse, and red brick fortress, all surrounded by a wash of brilliant turquoise water, Matt figured that there were probably worse places for one's expulsion.

CHAPTER 7

Early the following morning, Matt awoke to a soft pink light filtering through the old brass portholes. He was ready to move on, and eager for what was yet to come. Unsure if he were simply fleeing his nightmares or chasing a dream that had yet to fully form, Matt felt an irresistible pull toward his next destination. Julie always referred to his desire to keep moving as the "geographical fallacy of happiness," the belief that a change in location could magically solve his problems. If that were the case, Matt thought, he'd stay permanently in motion.

After fixing himself a quick cup of coffee and tending to Hank's needs, Matt stowed his loyal first mate away up in his snug nest in the V-berth, feeling like his repetitive daily routine was turning his life into a maritime version of the old movie, *Groundhog Day*. Bathed in the golden glow of the rising sun, Matt climbed up on deck and hauled up the heavy anchor, feeling the muscles along his spine stretch as each link slid through his fingers. After stowing the anchor in its locker, he went forward along the deck, untied the sail ties holding the mainsail to the boom, hoisted the main halyard, and let *Lonesome Dove* turn up into the wind. He gave the halyard winch a couple turns to snug the sail up against the mast before hurrying back to the cockpit to release the mainsheet, ducking as the boom slipped slowly over his head. After a few more adjustments to the sails, they were soon on their way.

The light breeze pushed the boat forward toward the long wooden pier, where Charlie and Laney were already out fishing. Matt raised a hand in farewell to the kind couple before tacking once more in the direction of the open ocean. *Lonesome Dove*'s crew of two was quiet this morning, as if reluctant to disturb the tranquil scene. The boat glided over the small waves as she rounded the old fort, its red brick walls bronzed by the rising sun. He caught sight of the banished ranger out on the dock, coffee cup in hand, no doubt enjoying a moment of peace before a fresh batch of tourists descended on his island. Matt took one last photo of the fort and its colorful, crumbling brick walls, then punched in the GPS coordinates for his next destination.

With a steady southerly breeze blowing in from the starboard side, they were making good time as they sailed on toward Key West. The blue-green ocean was translucent and *Lonesome Dove* sliced cleanly through the waves, leaving a trailing vee as she skipped along at a steady clip. As they glided along, idly scanning the water, something caught Matt's eye. A dark spot that looked like a rocky outcropping appeared to bloom in the crystal water. It was a large coral head standing tall in an otherwise vast expanse of shallow, white, sandy-bottomed ocean. While coral heads could spell disaster for the unwary sailor, Matt had a feeling that this one might be a good place to find lunch, as well as to try out some new diving gear. He headed up into the wind, which put the boat "in irons" and allowed *Lonesome Dove* to slow so he could drop anchor in the sandy bottom nearby.

After checking to see that the big Danforth anchor had dug into the sandy bottom and *Lonesome Dove* was good and secure, he pulled his scuba gear from the locker and headed back up on deck. He attached a full tank of air to his buoyancy control vest and checked the gauges and regulators twice just to make sure all was in order. Matt grabbed his Hawaiian sling fishing spear, then took a giant step off the deck and plunged into the gentle waves, feeling the cool water close over his head in a cloud of bubbles. He tilted his head back and quickly cleared his mask, then gathered his bearings and immediately spotted a large goliath grouper—a giant speckled monster—guarding the coral head. Just beyond, a couple of long spiny antennae protruded from the underside of the reef.

With his spear and catch bag clenched tightly, Matt began a stealthy, controlled descent, stopping once or twice to pinch his nose through the soft mask and equalize the pressure he felt in his ears. He was just about to go after the lobster when he saw a nice-sized yellowtail snapper off to his right and quickly impaled it. Suspended in the clear water, he paused to remove the fish from his spear and placed it in the mesh bag before he turned to see the spiny antennae quickly vanish beneath the coral head. He kicked lazily around the reef, entertained by the colorful darting fish, looking for the lobster's hiding place. Realizing he already had enough for lunch and not wanting to be greedy, he began his ascent, trailing slowly behind his own bubbles toward the surface.

Surfacing, he spun around in the water and suddenly realized he had made a grave error. No longer just a stone's throw away, *Lonesome Dove* now seemed to be traveling away from him, the gap between him and safety widening with every passing moment. During the brief time his pursuit of lunch had distracted him, the tide had shifted, and a strong offshore current had picked up. The current was now coming straight at him, right in the direction he needed to travel to get back to his boat. Even though he began kicking furiously toward *Lonesome Dove*, he felt like some strange force held him in place, unable to make any headway. He belatedly recalled the cardinal diving rules. *Never dive alone and always check the current before entering the water.* Matt had allowed the idyllic scene to seduce him, lure him from his floating home then cast him out to fight the wily ocean. As the tidal current held him in place, like a hand pushed firmly against his forehead, Matt imagined himself drifting further and further out to sea until he slipped beneath the waves for the very last time, and it was all over. It was almost tempting, the ease with which he could just let go…and for a moment, his fins ceased kicking, and he allowed himself to drift. He was just so damned tired.

Then he thought of Hank, and his filmy, hopeful eyes. Hank, who would wait forever, to suffer and ultimately to die for Matt's carelessness. He couldn't imagine facing Julie in the afterlife if he allowed anything to happen to Hank or to himself. Julie had always been the safety-conscious one—

the first to pull out an instruction manual, to follow directions, to remember and faithfully follow the rules. Matt felt a pang at the thought of his impatience as she'd check and recheck valves and pressure gauges, while he'd fidget around, barely masking his annoyance, just so eager to be in the water. He wished right then he could take back every second of snippiness and irritation. Julie would have checked the currents. And she would never have entered the water alone without taking the necessary precautions.

What now, Julie? The words were a thought, a surrender—a plea.

In reply, her voice threaded through the water, an otherworldly messenger, weaving into his ears and exploding in his motor cortex, impelling him with one word: *"Go!"* He renewed his efforts, pushing against the current with all the energy he could muster. Matt thought about ditching his scuba tank and buoyancy vest. Without the extra bulk, he could move more easily through the water, but if he still failed to reach the boat, he'd have lost the flotation device that could save his life. The life, he realized with a start, he wanted to reach for and cling to until some power higher than his own told him it was time to let go. He kicked harder and harder, the muscles in his legs burning with exertion, tears of frustration and desperation filling his eyes and his throat. For what felt like an eternity, he inched forward bit by bit into the increasingly powerful current, until finally his reaching fingers closed around the bottom rung of the swim ladder—and he was home.

CHAPTER 8

As he hauled himself up the dive ladder and flung his gear into the boat, Matt realized he still had the yellowtail snapper in his catch bag, which was connected to his dive belt. He could've swum much easier without it, but in his panic, he'd forgotten it was still attached. Setting the bag carefully on the deck, he flopped down on the bench, head cradled in his hands, breathing raggedly and staring off into space. Every muscle in his body ached and his lungs burned from his exertions. Matt was utterly alone and yet he no longer felt lonely. He was completely exhausted, wrung out like an old dishrag, and yet it felt like he'd come fully awake and alive, his every cell vibrating with vitality. Today he'd chosen life, fought the ocean current and his own dark undertow, and emerged into the sunlight feeling a sense of peace. Hope fluttered tiny wings inside his chest, but, as always, his feelings of happiness brought shadows of guilt.

Matt suddenly remembered an argument, or a minor disagreement, he'd had with Julie. A few years prior, one of her closest friends had lost her battle with breast cancer.

When Sarabeth had gotten news that the cancer had metastasized to her brain, she'd given her husband, Paul, a letter, making him promise not to read it until after she'd passed. Julie had learned of the contents of the letter after Sarabeth's funeral a few months later. In the letter, Sarabeth had told her husband that she wanted him to be happy, to keep on living, and to try, when he was ready, to find love. She'd even drafted an online dating profile for Paul that she'd included with the letter. When Julie told him the story, Matt had balked, struggling with the notion that Paul could ever be happy without Sarabeth. But Julie, being Julie, had shaken her head and told him gently that, if—and when— Paul again found love, it wouldn't mean his love for Sarabeth had died. Rather, her love for him lived on, in her intention that he live a happy life. They'd argued briefly, but when she forced Matt to put himself, figuratively, in Sarabeth's shoes, he had to admit that if anything ever happened to him, he'd want Julie to go on living. Even if that meant her loving another man, a thought that, even theoretically, made him a little jealous.

Hunger suddenly rumbled Matt's belly, cutting short his musings as he realized he was ravenous. He quickly filleted the snapper and headed down to the galley, where he poured himself a generous slug of Bacardi from a small bottle Charlie and Laney had given him as a farewell gift. Cutting several bite-sized chunks from the fillet, Matt dropped them into a plastic bag containing a bit of Zatarain's Cajun Fish Fry mix, and gave it a good shake. In a heavy cast-iron pan, he fried the tender morsels of fish until they were crunchy and golden. Hank's stubby tail wiggled furiously as he watched the process unfold. A dollop of ketchup and a handful of saltine crackers completed the meal. The fish was so fresh, Matt could taste the salt tang of the ocean in every bite. After what he'd just been through, the food was extra delicious, and his taste buds felt keenly alive.

As he and Hank shared the last bites of the fried fish, and Matt was making himself a final little saltine sandwich with a few crusty bits salvaged from the fry grease, a power-boat appeared on the horizon, looming larger and larger as it headed directly toward them. The pilot cut the motor as they pulled alongside. It was a large, broad- beamed aluminum workboat, heavily laden with dive gear. None of the crew looked thrilled—or friendly.

"These are restricted waters," said the skipper, sharply. "Y'all need to get on out of here. There's a recovery operation underway here, and there is no anchoring allowed."

The workboat stayed alongside, rocked by the waves, no one saying anything, as Matt found himself apologizing for breaking a rule of which he had been unaware.

Peeved at the man's curt directive and imperious manner, Matt hauled up the anchor and got underway, heading toward the main harbor in Key West, only a few miles away. As he motored into the calm harbor, Matt's nerves felt somewhat jangled by the reappearance of civilization after being "out at sea" for so long. Anchored boats of every kind dotted the harbor, from sleek million-dollar behemoths to dilapidated old sloops furred with moss and festooned with laundry. The color of the water had gone from crystalline turquoise to murky-green, but it was the next spot circled on his chart and Matt was eager to go exploring.

Anchoring near a mangrove grove, beside a cluttered old ketch named *Lucky Lady—more like Laundry Lady*, he thought—Matt took Hank up on deck to do his business. Afterward, he put out a big bowl of water and set the boat's twelve-volt fan on high to keep the little dog cool down in the cabin. Then Matt set about lowering the dinghy into the water and attaching its outboard motor.

Weaving between the strange assortment of watercraft that was moored in Key West's harbor, Matt *putt-putted* up to a long pier where he could tie up. The deck of the old Schooner Wharf Bar jutted out into the water, and the "Last Little Piece of Old Key West," as they advertised it, looked as quaint and, unfortunately, just as bustling as he'd imagined. But he was thirsty, his cooler was empty, and he'd stand all day in the scorching sun for a couple of cold beers if he had to. *Or, at least until Hank needed another potty break*, he thought ruefully. Once he knew the lay of the land, and which places were dog friendly, he'd bring his little buddy along for some well-deserved canine shore leave. Glancing further down the dock from where he'd tied off the dinghy, Matt spied the same workboat that had run him off earlier, unloading crates of rusted metal and what looked a lot like glittering bits of treasure among the sand and debris.

After only a brief wait, Matt found an empty seat at the long dockside bar and ordered a beer and a plate of conch fritters, the tasty morsels of fried mollusk being one of the restaurant's specialties. The beer was icy-cold and delicious and he was thankful there was only a short dinghy ride back to *Lonesome Dove*, as the first went down far too fast. While the second glass bottle sweated on the bar top, Matt fired off a few texts to friends back home, including some nice shots of the lighthouse to Eldon, just as he'd promised his old boss he would do. By his third beer, the crispy fried conch fritters were only a memory, and Matt had a pleasant buzz going on. He'd struck up a conversation with the bartender, Patrick, who was working his way through cooking school. Matt was learning the best way to fix conch salad and barely noticed when someone slid onto the stool beside him.

After Patrick went to serve another patron, Matt turned to look at his new neighbor, startled and somewhat put off to find it was the skipper of the workboat. The weathered-looking, wild-haired man extended a hand peaceably in Matt's direction, apologizing for their earlier encounter, and introduced himself as Dave. He explained his bosses got quite upset when anyone encroached on their treasure-hunting grounds, and that he had strict instructions to warn off any pleasure boats that got too close. After learning that Matt had sailed there all the way from Corpus Christi, he offered to buy him "a real Florida beer," a Swamp Ape Double IPA from Carib Brewing up in Cape Canaveral.

Matt willingly accepted the peace offering. "If I'd found treasure where I was anchored, I'm pretty sure *I'd* ask me to leave, too," he smiled, always quick to reconcile.

Patrick, obviously listening in on the conversation, wiped his hands on the bar mop, then cracked open two of the potent Swamp Apes, and pushed them across the counter to Matt and his new companion. Clearing his throat, he tossed in his own two cents.

"You better watch out, Matt. The natives, like Dave here, call themselves 'Conchs'—but I just call them rednecks."

Dave bristled a bit and tossed his chin back, half-jokingly, "At least I'm not a damn Yankee like Patrick here…"

Matt had heard that Conchs, the name given to those who were born here, were known to have a fiercely independent streak, and that during the Civil War, they favored whichever side allowed them to keep on smuggling and pirating. Back in the eighties, they had even declared their own country—the "Conch Republic"—made their own flag, and staged an "attack" on the US government by dropping water balloons on the Coast Guard's office from an ancient biplane. "We Seceded Where Others Failed" became the republic's official motto.

Shortly afterward, they demanded financial reparations from the US government for damages they'd suffered during "the war." Back then, the Feds were shutting down Highway 1 regularly to conduct drug searches, and many Conchs were feeling the hurt from the loss of both tourist trade and drug smuggling revenue.

As they drank their beers and shared another plate of conch fritters, "on the house" this time, Dave told Matt some stories about the wild days of the seventies and early eighties, when pot smuggling was going full throttle in the Keys.

"We used to unload bales of pot right over there...see, where our workboat is docked now." He pointed and continued. "Sometimes me and my friends would skip school and head down to the docks when we heard a load was in town. We'd run down there and offer to help 'em unload some bales in exchange for a little pocket weed. It was a 'win-win' situation, you know." Apparently feeling the effects of the strong IPA now, Dave drew a deep breath and sighed. "Man, those were some good times back then, before Pablo Escobar and the cocaine cowboys came and screwed it all up—with all their violence and shit." He took a long pull at his beer before continuing. "We do okay, though. I wouldn't want to live anywhere else in the world...although there's too many damn Yankees down here now," he said smiling, raising his voice at the last part and directing his words toward Patrick, before rising and wobbling off toward the men's room, muttering something about "freshwater conchs" as he walked away. Once Dave was out of sight, Patrick caught Matt's eye and hurriedly filled him in.

Apparently, his new friend had once been employed by the famous treasure hunter, Mel Fisher, who'd found, after years and years of searching, the wreck of the Spanish treasure ship, *Atocha*. Fisher had discovered an actual fortune under the waves, then further capitalized on it by building a Key West tourist attraction with a museum and shop where he sold tiny relics and coins at a handsome profit. A former chicken farmer from Indiana, Mel Fisher was apparently not destined to make his fortune by fowl exploitation as Clawson did, but by good old-fashioned hard work and perseverance—along with a bit of luck, and also apparently, a lot of misfortune.

Every day, for sixteen years, Fisher had started each morning off by uttering the words "today's the day," until finally it was, as a diver's gloved hand gently brushed away a thin layer of sand covering a cluster of emeralds, gold coins, and silver bars.

Like Matt, though, Mr. Fisher had suffered some enormous personal tragedies during his quest for the *Atocha*. Patrick told him that back in 1975, on the eve of another one of their treasure-hunting missions, Mel's oldest son, Dirk, and his daughter-in-law, Angel, along with one of his best divers, Rick Gage, had perished in the waters off Key West after a bilge pump failed and their vessel sank.

Despite this awful tragedy, Fisher recovered and pressed on in his quest, finally locating the wreck of the *Atocha*, along with part of the hundreds of millions of dollars' worth of treasure it held. It's believed that only about half of the ship's contents have been found, so the search for ever more treasure goes on unabated, a hunger unsated because that the sea continues, even now, to offer small amounts of gold coins and jewels, over four decades after the main wreck of the *Atocha* was first discovered.

Nursing what would be his last beer of the afternoon, Matt found himself half wishing that he could join the treasure hunters, chasing the dream of the next big discovery just around the corner. He was feeling pretty overwhelmed. The voyage across the Gulf . . . the exotic new tropical smells and flavors (conch fritters were pretty damn delicious, he discovered) . . . the sound of steel-drum island music drifting over, just down the dock from where Jimmy Buffett's old recording studio stood . . . it all seemed like a dream. He just wished that Julie was there to share it with him. He still felt lonely as dirt, but he also felt wild, free, and fully alive.

Matt set his empty beer bottle on the counter, tossed some bills on the bar, and bade farewell to his new friends. Alone once more, and weaving only slightly, he headed off toward Duval Street to check out the famous sights. First stop was Sloppy Joe's Bar, where Papa Hemingway once drank, back in the thirties when it was Joe Russell's place and had yet to be defiled by any barfing spring breakers. Then, he continued on further, past the galleries and restaurants and the Ripley's Believe It or Not Odditorium, which he gave a pass because of the steep entry fee. One bar Matt wandered into turned out to be, much to his surprise, "clothing optional." The phrase lent a whole new meaning to the question bartenders often asked when serving a Corona: "Would you like it dressed?"—referring to the optional addition of lime and salt, and not to the attire of patrons or staff.

Moving on in search of more conventional surroundings, Matt kept walking until he'd reached Mallory Square, and stopped for a few minutes to watch the fire eaters, stilt-walking jugglers, and sword swallowers perform. Then, realizing it was getting late, he headed toward the local marine hardware store where he found several nautical charts, which he purchased along with a new Cruising Guide to the Bahamas. His last stop was a grocery store, where he stocked up on a fifty-pound sack of Hank's favorite kibble, some tinned Spam, ground coffee, a couple ten-pound bags of ice, and a few bottles of cheap red wine. Laden down with his purchases, Matt hailed a passing pedicab to take him back to the pier where he'd tied the dinghy. The pedicab's owner, a skinny young kid who couldn't have weighed more than one hundred and twenty pounds soaking wet, wasn't entirely pleased when he saw the extra cargo. The poor kid struggled the whole way under the combined load of Matt and his purchases, but was happy in the end, after Matt offered him a generous tip. Realizing he'd been a bad doggy daddy for leaving Hank for a bit too long onboard, he hurried to get back to *Lonesome Dove* so he could take the little dog over to shore for a proper walk. The exercise, he thought, might also help him sober up.

As he untied his dinghy and took a last look around at the bustling harbor in the lowering late afternoon light, Matt turned his focus back toward his little home. Key West had been wonderful, but he had to keep going. He wanted to see it all: the Bahamas, the Virgin Islands, St. Lucia, Bonaire, Panama and the canal, and onward to the many islands of the South Pacific. He and Hank had miles to sail before their journey was done. The next morning, they'd make their way up toward the Middle Keys, to a more secluded spot. Perhaps even to see an elusive manatee, but if not, to relish a bit more of the peace and calm he was starting to find.

CHAPTER 9

The next morning, Matt woke and made a proper cup of coffee on the gimbaled stove. Julie had once schooled him in the ways of operating a French press, and the flavor of the product that it made far exceeded that of instant coffee. With the anchor retrieved and a full coffee cup in the captain's hand, they were soon underway. Just outside of Key West Harbor they caught a nice southeasterly breeze and Matt switched off the auxiliary engine and let the sails power *Lonesome Dove*. They followed a northeast course that ran parallel to Highway 1, of which they could just catch a glimpse, off in the distance. He and Hank spent the day watching the turquoise water gently slip by the hull, spotting an occasional sea turtle and being entertained by passing pods of dolphins as they frolicked off the bow.

Matt noted the wide swath of deep water on his chart, annotated with many warning indicators about strong currents and possible high seas, caused when winds ran counter to the flow of the massive Gulf Stream. Crossing the Florida Strait this time of year would be challenging, and countless small boats had been lost there over the years. If a north wind were to blow up and begin stacking the waves closer together, they'd become like thousands of massive tumbling blue boulders, easily able to crush a small sailboat like his. Matt knew he needed to find a quiet cove to sit and wait out the weather and try to cross only when the time was just right. As they sailed along, he spent the better part of the day thumbing through his new cruising guide, listening to marine weather forecasts, and plotting a course across the perilous Gulf Stream to a landfall at desolate Orange Cay in the Bahamas.

Matt and his trusty first mate finally found a small cove near a tiny, seemingly uninhabited island located near Big Pine Key. Eager for some downtime, he dropped the anchor in what looked like a suitable spot and gave a sigh of relief that he'd found such a tranquil place to call "home." Up on deck, lulled by the gentle rocking of the waves, they watched a fiery red sun drop over the mangroves. Fishing from his dinghy along the edge of the mangroves, he caught a nice-sized snapper, scaled it and scored it three times along each side, then dusted it with cornmeal and spices, and fried it up whole. He set aside some boneless chunks for Hank to enjoy along with his kibble.

His hunger sated by the fish dinner, and feeling festive, he opted for a little "hair of the dog." Matt opened one of the bottles of wine he'd just purchased, and began drinking multiple farewell toasts to Key West and to America herself. The following morning, if weather conditions were right, he planned to make the crossing across the Gulf Stream to the Bahamas. After putting a sleepy dog to bed, he remained sitting up in the cockpit, listening to an old Jimmy Buffett CD and finishing the last of the bottle. *Clean living could wait till next week*, Matt thought as his eyes grew heavy. As the boat's battery indicator dropped into the critical red zone, he finally turned off the player, stumbled down the companionway ladder and crashed out hard in the V-berth next to a slumbering Hank.

Around two in the morning, Matt was abruptly awakened by a loud crunching noise, which vibrated through the boat with a shudder. He instinctively knew this wasn't a good thing. Hauling himself up the ladder, head pounding and still half-drunk, he squinted into the moonlight and tried to make sense of what he was seeing. In his exhausted—and inebriated—state, he'd accidentally anchored too close to a large coral head, and with a change in the wind, the boat had swung on its anchor line until it rested right on top of it. Even though the tides in the Keys don't rise and fall very much, when it fell, it was enough to drop *Lonesome Dove* right onto the top of the coral head. As the old sloop rocked in the waves, she was accompanied by a cacophony of scraping, screeching and crunching, and, moments later and much to Matt's horror, the sound of running water underneath the floorboards.

In what seemed like only a few seconds the water had filled up the shallow bilge and was pouring out on top of the floorboards. Switching on a small electric bilge pump with one hand, and throwing open the cockpit door with the other, he ran up on deck and began hauling up the anchor while calling for Hank. The little dog, sensing danger, jumped from the V-berth and onto the step Matt kept beside the companionway ladder, out of reach of the rising water but still in need of a helping hand. He grabbed Hank, kicked on the auxiliary engine, and instinctively headed toward a line of white sand glowing in the moonlight where he could ground the boat if needed. As it turned out, it was the only option to keep her from fully sinking.

Motoring toward the beach, he felt the keel catch on the sandy bottom, then pivoted the boat broadside to the shore and began tying all the rubber fenders he could find along the side that faced land. A rush of adrenaline kicked Matt into high gear—all traces of fuzzy-headedness vanished—as he began hauling several hundred feet of coiled nylon line from the sea anchor stowed in the aft locker and threw it over his shoulder. Poor Hank knew that none of this boded well and let out a series of sharp barks to let his human know of his concerns.

Clutching the heavy coils of line with one arm, and holding Hank in the other, Matt stepped off into the dark waist-deep water, blind and barefoot. He didn't have time to worry about sea urchins or sleeping stingrays. His only thoughts were to get Hank safely to shore, then try to save his boat. Wading ashore, he released Hank, his ever-faithful shadow, who stuck close by. By the light of the moon, Matt located a large mangrove root near the water's edge. Quickly tying the heavy line to the root, he uncoiled the bundle as fast as he could and began paying it out toward *Lonesome Dove.*

With Hank's sharp barks echoing in the balmy night air, Matt splashed back through the water toward the boat, coiled the end of the line around the port side winch and began cranking as furiously as he could on the handle. As the line grew taut, he quickly realized that trying to haul a heavy old boat like this one ashore was going to take much more effort. In order to move her any closer to land, he'd somehow have to tilt the entire vessel over at an angle, so that less of its nearly five-foot-deep keel was touching the sandy bottom.

Without hesitating, he grabbed a second long line from the anchor locker, waded over to the shore and tied it off around another sturdy mangrove root, before returning to *Lonesome Dove* with the free end clenched in his hand. He cautiously mounted the mast steps to the spreader with the second line in tow, stopping about halfway up the mast to run it through a small pulley, allowing the loose end to fall to the deck. Quickly climbing down, Matt grabbed the free end, looped it around the starboard winch, and began cranking furiously until the line—and the boat's rigging—produced a variety of moaning, creaking, and twanging noises. Hank, hearing the commotion and growing very concerned about his human, ran back and forth on the shore barking in the boat's direction.

The second line was now pulling the mast, while the first was drawn against the side of the boat. Slowly, by alternating cranks of the two winch handles, Matt inched *Lonesome Dove* ever so slowly toward the sloping sandy shore. Matt knew that a sailboat's mast wasn't built to take this sort of strain, so he was careful to take it easy, jumping off into the water every so often to push against the bow and stern and ease the tension on the lines. Back and forth he went, cranking on the winch handles, careful to heed the metallic complaints the rigging emitted, warning him to back off on the tension on the lines. In slow motion, the heavy old boat slowly tilted, then half floated-half slid, inch by inch toward the island.

Head pounding and body aching, Matt pushed on, switching up tactics now and then, trying different combinations of lines and pulleys—some off the bow, others off the stern—until finally the hull of the heavy old Pearson neared the moonlit shore.

The angle of the boat had finally become too steep for him to stand on deck, and Matt had to drop into the dark, waist-deep water to crank on one winch. It was at this point that his luck, or what little was left of it, ran out. In the dark water, one foot landed on a sea urchin and a spine lodged in his heel. He reached down to pull it out, but the spine had broken off just under the skin. The pain was excruciating, making him gasp in shock, but the adrenaline coursing through his veins kept him moving. He shifted his weight to his other foot and labored on, cranking the winch with the last of his dwindling strength.

An occasional bark from over on the shore let him know Hank was still doing okay. As the sun rose slowly over the key, Matt, aided by the rising tide, finally got one side of the boat nudged high enough up on the sand to stop any more water from pouring in the hole, even as small waves still rocked the hull. The gash in the starboard side was ragged and ugly, but at least the injured portion of *Lonesome Dove*'s hull now sat safely above the water's surface.

Hours later, exhausted and nauseated from the pain in his heel and more than a little hungover, he surveyed the mess. *Lonesome Dove* was tilted over on her port side, looking strangely vulnerable—a giant's toy cast carelessly aside. The jagged scar, about two feet long, was visible amidships—a glaring reminder of the cost of letting his guard down, and for what? For a few hours of foolish self-indulgence. A small hermit crab scurried over the edge of the gunwale, then disappeared into the boat's cabin through an open porthole. *At least Hank will have something to play with*, Matt thought, laughing bitterly to himself.

He'd kept *Lonesome Dove* from sinking, sort of, yet she was now a semi-beached wreck, half full of water. Matt sank back onto his heels, dropping his head into his hands, feeling his dreams and all hope of continuing on his voyage fading away. The classic old Pearson Vanguard had been "too old for coverage," as the boat insurance agent had told him back in Texas, and his plan to *just be careful* had obviously failed. The cost of salvaging and repairing his only home would be entirely on his own dime, and Matt was getting a sickening feeling that his "around-the-world voyage" was now over before it had barely begun.

Glancing up at *Lonesome Dove*'s mast, which was now tilted at a crazy angle toward the beach, he caught sight of his dad's old eyeglasses, still snugly duct-taped in their original position. His Dad had intended them to help safely guide his voyage, and they'd worked pretty well so far—for obstacles above water. Matt chuckled wryly and, with a glance skyward, said: "Well Dad, I guess you didn't see that one coming, did you? My bad though, I really screwed up this time."

Thinking Matt was talking to him, Hank trotted over and nosed at his hand, asking to be picked up. Matt scooped up the little dog, wrapping his tired arms over the sturdy sun-warmed body, and began a long, heartfelt apology to his first mate. Hank seemed to understand and showed his forgiveness—or perhaps just his desire for breakfast—by licking Matt's face and wagging his stubby tail. Finally, sinking back into the sand, Matt pondered his next move, after Hank's breakfast of course, and barely noticed the appearance of a skiff on the horizon. As it came closer, he saw a grizzled old fisherman at the helm and a slim young girl with sun-bleached hair standing steadily up on the bow, keeping her balance as the boat lurched in the waves.

"You okay there?" called the man, piloting the skiff into the shallow water. The young girl jumped off the boat into the waist-high water, hauling the skiff toward shore with the bowline.

"I've been better," replied Matt ruefully.

"You've got yerself one fine mess there," uttered the old Conch fisherman, climbing out of the skiff and coming closer to survey the damage. *No truer words were ever spoken*, thought Matt. It was his mess to own, and every bit was his fault.

"We were heading out fishing when we saw you'd beached 'er." The old man leaned over to inspect the gash on *Lonesome Dove*'s starboard side. He ran his hand over his jaw, considering. "No way a barge can come in here and pick you up with a crane, too shallow. You're gonna have to fix 'er up and float 'er yourself. But, that ain't so bad though. You can put a patch on her at low tide that'll last till ya can get her back to the boatyard. The name's Kenny, do a bit of sailing myself" he said, slapping Matt on the back as he slowly shook his tangle of gray hair. "I've seen lots of boats get holed up on that reef over the years. You ain't the first, Cap'n, and you won't be the last."

His words offered little comfort and Matt cringed at the title of *Captain*, feeling it undeserved after making such a rookie mistake. Noticing Matt's limp, Kenny noted wryly, "Found yourself an urchin too, I see. Desiree..." called the old man, gesturing to the young girl who hovered by the skiff, "please bring the first aid kit."

"My granddaughter," he said proudly, smiling at the young girl. She ducked her head and smiled shyly at Matt, passing the kit to Kenny. Opening the metal box, the old man pulled out a razor, a pair of tweezers and a tiny tube containing antibiotic cream. "Gimme yer foot," he instructed. "This is gonna hurt, but it'll be over right quick."

Kenny was true to his word. It hurt like hell as the old man made a small incision with the razor, then dug the needle-nosed tweezers into his flesh, grabbing the end of the urchin's spine, and then slowly withdrawing an ugly-looking half-inch-long barb. The process might have been quick, but to the patient, it felt like an eternity. His wound clean and bandaged, Matt found he could put a little more weight on the tender foot and gratefully accepted Kenny's offer to shuttle him over to a nearby marina. "You're gonna need some spill pads, son. You gotta sop up any oil and diesel you got spilled inside the hull, before any leaks out. If any leaks out, it'll get ya' a helluva fine from the coasties, and/or the marine patrol," Kenny warned.

Over the drone of the skiff's outboard, Matt and Kenny swapped fishing stories while Hank, nestled in Matt's arms, panted in blistering hot sun, his pink tongue out and his lids at half mast. Desiree lost some of her shyness and, learning that Matt was from Texas, peppered him with funny questions about the Lone Star State. Like all folks who had yet to travel beyond their own backyard, she certainly had some strange ideas about other parts of her country. He patiently explained to her that not everyone there rode horses or lived on a ranch, and that just like Florida, there were even parts of the state with orange groves, swamps and deep pine forests.

While he and Kenny and Desiree strolled through the marina shop, buying spill pads, trash bags, epoxy, fiberglass matting, and mixing supplies, Matt told his new friends about sailing in Corpus Christi Bay, the rolling hill country with its spring bluebonnets, and the vast desert openness and jagged mountains of Big Bend National Park.

"Texas is big, sure, but the west just gets started there. There's even more amazing things to see beyond it...the Grand Canyon and Petrified Forest in Arizona, Carlsbad Caverns in New Mexico, the Rockies, Yellowstone...Maybe someday you and your family can take a trip out that way."

"I think you just gave us an excuse to plan a road trip out west, after next year's crabbing season," Kenny said, much to the girl's delight.

At the cash register, partly out of remorse for his
drunken blunder and also wanting to set a good example,
Matt made a last-minute decision to forgo his usual
choice—a cold beer—and opt instead for a can of Ting, a
grapefruit-flavored soda from Jamaica, to ease his thirst. He
bought drinks for Kenny and Desiree as well, along with a
large bag of cheese puffs, which he'd seen the girl eyeing in
the store. She was apparently thinking of a snack for Hank
as she immediately opened the bag and shared them with
the little dog, who had taken a shine to her and now followed closely at her heels.

Kenny and Matt swapped a few sailing stories on their
way back to Hidden Key, where *Lonesome Dove* was
beached. Desiree steered the skiff while the two men finally
got around to discussing the strategy for repairing the
sloop's damage. As they neared the shore, Matt's heart sank
a little as he surveyed his "fine mess." The task looked even
more daunting, closer up as the skiff pulled into shallow
water and Desiree cut the engine. Grabbing his bag of supplies, Matt stepped out into the knee-high water, this time
glancing down to be sure nothing spiny awaited his footfall.
Kenny promised to come back and check on Matt's progress, and after exchanging phone contacts, they said their
goodbyes.

Once more alone, Matt climbed aboard to take an in-
ventory of the damage. Below, the cabin resembled a
botched robbery. Overturned diesel cans, broken dishes,
pots and pans, and dirty wet clothes sloshed around in a
mucky mess, filmed with oil from the upturned diesel engine. Matt sighed heavily as he began the tedious process of

sopping up the oil, then cleaning up and transferring the necessities to his temporary camp on shore. Until he could complete the repairs to *Lonesome Dove*'s hull, he and Hank's home would be under a tarp that he'd stretched out between a couple of palm trees. When he'd first set out on his adventure, he'd fantasized about camping on pristine beaches like this one, but out of choice, not necessity.

Later that afternoon, to add insult to injury, a warden with the Florida Marine Patrol came ashore to pay him a visit. The man's chiseled jaw and tight-lipped, unsmiling face seemed even more expressionless, with his eyes hidden behind shiny mirrored lenses. Matt's heart sank to a new low as the warden issued him a five-hundred-dollar citation for damaging the coral head and for flattening the protected turtle grass growing along the shore where he'd half-beached the boat.

While writing out the citation, the tough-looking officer, who apparently possessed a deep knowledge of the marine ecosystem, explained how *Thalassia testudinum,* aka turtle grass, provided essential food and shelter for many species: sea turtles, naturally, but also manatees, crustaceans, conch, and fish. His voice becoming sterner as he continued to write and talk, the warden told Matt that Florida's sea grasses were faring poorly, and that runoff from large-scale sugar farms, rising sea levels, and last, but not least, careless boaters "like the recipient of this citation" were to blame for its demise.

Awash in shame, Matt promised the officer that he'd be much more careful next time.

"You've got five days to get this boat off the beach and be on your way," the warden said sternly, cutting off Matt's string of apologies with an upheld palm. He concluded with: "Just get her launched and be on your way, 'Tex'." Matt knew that because of his careless actions, and failure to educate himself on how to "tread lightly" as a boater in the Keys, he fully deserved the officer's scorn.

In many ways, he could relate to the officer's stern lesson about marine grasses. Back home, when hiking out in the vast expanse of the Chihuahuan desert, in the Big Bend Region, Matt always hated how some careless people ignored the *"Stay On Designated Trails Only"* signs, trampling across sensitive areas covered with BSC's—or Bacterial Soil Crusts. This complex, ancient layer of organisms—sometimes as thin as a Nacho Cheese Dorito and its composition just as mysterious—helped seal in valuable moisture and nutrients that countless desert creatures needed to survive, and which a few careless footsteps could destroy. Like the turtle grass, a "keystone species" in the Keys, the countless species of mosses, bacteria, lichens, and fungi that made up the soil crust could take years—decades even—to recover from the actions of careless humans.

As the ranger's boat powered away from shore, Matt breathed a little easier and vowed to do better in the future. As he resumed his cleanup, he crooned an old Bob Marley song to soothe his frazzled nerves. He'd reached the refrain, "Don't worry about a thing, 'cause every little thing gonna be all right," when he was startled to hear another voice.

"Well, hello there, Sailor . . . my, my, you've certainly made your little ole self at home, haven't you?"

Matt poked his head around from where he was stringing up a line of rumpled wet clothing. A bronzed, older man with a sculpted physique approached from the line of palm trees, wagging one long finger and shaking his shiny bald head. His other hand held a martini glass, the clear fluid within barely sloshing as he ambled closer.

"Oh Carlos, please. Give the man a break! Can't you see he just had a shipwreck?" said a second man, following close behind. He punctuated his words with a light slap on Carlos's massive shoulder.

The second man, shorter and pudgier, but just as deeply tanned, followed his slap with a playful shove to the bigger man and extended his hand in Matt's direction.

"I'm sorry. He can be a bit of a bitch." He side-eyed his muscle-bound companion and continued, "I'm Ricky, and this is my husband, Carlos." Carlos, clearly chastened, waved apologetically.

"Yeah, sorry, I can be a bit of a bitch. Ricky's right. You probably didn't even know this was our island."

At these words, Matt was speechless. He'd damaged a coral head, flattened turtle grass and now committed trespass—all in under twenty-four hours. He stammered, struggling to find the words to apologize and settled on, "I'm so sorry, I thought this was a deserted island."

Smacking his partner's backside playfully, Ricky giggled. "Ha! More like a *perverted* island." Catching sight of Matt's startled expression, he laughed again.

"Don't mind us, Sailor, we're just getting in the mood for the first night of fun. Welcome to our little slice of paradise: Hidden Key. We're heading down to Key West this evening for Fantasy Fest."

Matt knew that Fantasy Fest was a chance for the wildest of partygoers to let their freak flags fly, and was a little unsure how to respond, so he just smiled and nodded gamely. Hank chose this timely opportunity to trot by, wagging his tail excitedly at the prospect of the company. Carlos squealed and scooped the little dog up, laughing as Hank licked his face and made happy puppyish noises.

"Precious little man!" he cooed, as Ricky took careful sips of his own drink and strolled over to have a look at the shipwreck. He was shaking his head ruefully as he ambled back over to where Hank was now partaking of a belly rub, while Matt stood by, unsure if it was proper etiquette to continue hanging laundry on someone else's trees.

"You, sir, are in a mighty fine fix, and without a decent roof over your head at that. If you'd just be so kind as to clean up after yourself, you're welcome to come on up to the house, have a hot shower and use our heated pool while we're away. We'll be partying off-island for a few days and, in the meantime, you're free to have the run of the house." Carlos chimed in. "Also, you're welcome to tie your dinghy up around the corner at our dock and gas up if you need. We're taking our little boat over to Big Pine Key, where we keep a rusty old VW Beetle we use for trips to town. It's full of holes. Hell—half the floorboard is gone. We call her 'The Holey Roller,' which, of course, you're welcome to borrow when we get back."

The unexpected and extravagant generosity of these strangers took Matt completely off guard. With a lump in his throat, he thanked the men and promised he would "leave no trace" just like a good little camper, and stay no longer than absolutely necessary. He was relieved to have a quiet place to get properly cleaned up and a proper bed in which to sleep for a change. Matt had heard stories about the raucous adults-only extravaganza to which Carlos and Ricky were headed, and he'd decided to give Fantasy Fest a pass on this trip. He'd figured that it was probably one hell of a party for folks who were into those sorts of good times but decided he was in need of peace more than debauchery—although the current situation wasn't quite the island escape he'd envisioned.

Before departing for the festival, the kind couple stopped by with a key to the house, a stemmed glass and a cold metal cocktail shaker full of what Carlos declared was his "special" version of a Mexican martini. The tall muscular man was dressed in his finest, full-on Fantasy Fest regalia. His costume was an adult version of the Easter Bunny, the faux-fur-and-transparent-plastic garment featuring an integrated Easter basket at crotch height, where, under several brightly colored plastic ones, his own "special Easter eggs" were apparently nestled. Matt maintained steady eye contact as he accepted the key from Ricky's outstretched palm, wary of catching an unwelcome glimpse of another man's testicles. Ricky was dressed as Glinda the Good Witch, from *The Wizard of Oz*, holding a long, bejeweled wand tipped with a glittering star, and wearing a pair of large faux-diamond-encrusted stilettos which were proving to be less than practical for beach strolling.

"The house is all yours, Sailor. There are steaks in the fridge and some dog food for little Hankie on the counter," said Ricky, clearly already several drinks in and listing to one side as his heels sunk into the sand.

"If you leave before we get back, please have a safe voyage. Come back and see us anytime!" continued Carlos, smiling warmly.

"You guys are the best—thank you so much," Matt exclaimed, going in for an awkward combination backslap/hug, and winding up in an embrace full of glitter, faux fur, and spicy cologne.

Releasing Matt, Carlos steadied Ricky on his feet, and with a flurry of enthusiastic waves, they turned and made their way unsteadily back up the little path leading away from the beach. Matt chuckled to himself as he pictured the big men in their over-the-top costumes, crammed into the Holey Roller, a pair of high heels on the dash to avoid the holes in the floor, barreling south toward Key West. He hoped at least one of them was sober enough to drive.

Exhausted from an afternoon's work, Matt plopped down in the sand and lay back, feeling the warm sun filtering through the palms. So far on his voyage, aside from a grouchy treasure hunter and an understandably irate marine patrol officer, he'd been lucky to meet up with mostly kind and generous people, and from all walks of life. This fun-loving couple was no exception, and he could find no explanation for his good fortune. He pondered for a moment, then arrived at a conclusion that made sense to his exhausted, heat-addled self. *Maybe the old saying is true . . . Maybe God really does watch over fools, drunks, and sailors—even if in my case, they're all rolled into one.*

CHAPTER 10

For the next three days, the secluded cove on Hidden Key was a flurry of activity, with just one man behind it all. Matt threw himself, heart and soul, into work: salvaging what he could, bagging and storing what was beyond repair, and, in between tasks, focusing on the patch job for *Lonesome Dove*'s hull. He worked furiously when the tide was at its lowest, carefully layering fiberglass mat and West System epoxy, then patiently waiting for each coat to cure. Once *Lonesome Dove*'s cabin was clean and dry and he'd restored a degree of organization to the interior, Matt used the setting time between the final layers to take a dip in Carlos and Ricky's enormous pool. Floating on his back in the warm water, the sun overhead a sliver of brilliance against his lowered lids, Matt was relaxed and at peace, confident now that his journey had *not* yet come to an end.

As the sun dipped low over the horizon, Matt took a long, hot shower in the guest bath, then grilled up one of the thick rib eyes that Carlos and Ricky had left for him in their enormous Sub-Zero fridge, saving a nice chunk of lean meat for Hank. In a hammock stretched between two palms, with Hank snoring on his chest, Matt fell asleep before he could even make it to the comfy bed the couple had so generously offered. Finally clean, well-nourished and calm, his muscles felt loose and relaxed, and his mind drifted as peacefully as the gentle crawl of the waves on what was, for tonight at least, *their* beach.

The following morning, Matt went up to the big house, this time to ensure he was true to his word, making certain he'd swept the floors, cleaned and put away all the cooking utensils, and even squeegeed the huge walk-in shower. During his tidying up, Matt couldn't help but notice a few scattered clues in the couple's home that hinted at lives that differed greatly from what he'd narrow-mindedly imagined when he first caught sight of their Fantasy Fest finest. Matt barely recognized Carlos (though the mustache was the same) in a photo of a handsome young airline pilot in uniform, standing in front of a massive Boeing 737 aircraft. Below that photo, in a shiny silver frame, was one of Ricky seated behind an air traffic controller's console, looking very 1970-something, with a large afro cut and an equally wide floral tie. For a moment, Matt considered staying until they returned, just so he could hear what was most likely a very interesting story about how they'd first met.

He desperately wanted to repay Carlos and Ricky's generosity, and, looking around, couldn't think of a single thing the couple didn't already have, in duplicate and in triplicate. Then, he had it—a sudden bright burst of inspiration—and hurried back to *Lonesome Dove*, where he removed the big brass bell which he'd bought for his voyage back in Corpus Christi. Finding a nice, flat, smooth piece of driftwood, he gave it a good sanding, then carefully carved in some words and gave the whole thing a light coat of varnish. Once the piece had dried, he attached the brass bell to the wood base and carried his creation up to the house, where he attached it to a palm tree near the swimming pool. Standing back, he admired his work and the way the light caught the wording on the plaque: *"Martini Bell. Ring for Service."*

It was Matt's last day on the private island, and despite the beauty and solitude of the place, he was eager for a change of scenery, to resume his journey and to see what new adventures awaited him and his first mate. He rubbed his chin as he stood back and surveyed his patch job on *Lonesome Dove*'s hull. It wasn't pretty for sure, but he was confident that the crude repair would hold long enough to allow for safe travel to a real boatyard—a necessary detour—en route to their next destination. To properly repair the hull, Matt would need to get the old Pearson Vanguard to somewhere with a "travel lift" that would haul her clean out of the water and set her up in a proper repair yard. He figured it was time to call Kenny and to claim the offer to help him relaunch *Lonesome Dove*.

"If you reckon she'll float now, I think we can make that happen," said Kenny. "I'll be over there right after Desiree and I finish running our crab traps. High tide is one thirty p.m. That's our best window."

Later that afternoon, just as promised, Kenny returned to the beach with his crabbing boat, a large heavy vessel with a pair of powerful 200-horsepower Mercury outboard engines on its transom and a dozen or more crab traps stacked neatly up on the bow. Cutting through the waves behind him was his fishing skiff, piloted by a sturdy-looking older woman with a wild tangle of dark hair. As she had been when he first saw her, Desiree balanced on the bow, her skinny legs holding her steady despite the bounce of the boat as it clipped the waves. Both boats cut their engines almost in tandem and trimmed their props higher as they came closer to shore into the calm, shallow water of the cove.

Matt waved and came down to join them, followed by Hank, who trotted along at his heels, barking a friendly greeting. Matt waded out into the water to greet them and help pull the bows of their boats up onto the beach before tying a line from each to a mass of gnarled mangrove roots.

"This is my wife, Nelda," said Kenny, wrapping his arm around the shoulder of the older woman, who beamed up at her husband before reaching out to shake Matt's hand.

"Pleasure to meet you, ma'am. Your husband here darn-near saved my bacon. I really appreciate y'all coming out to help me yet again," Matt said with a warm smile.

"We sailors gotta stick together," Kenny replied, walking over to inspect Matt's repair job. "This oughta be good enough to getcha to port."

Standing back, the older man rubbed his chin, pondering for a moment, before outlining his plan to get *Lonesome Dove* off the beach and back in the sea where she belonged.

For the next half hour, the quartet worked together seamlessly, attaching lines to the sloop's bow and stern, and attaching these to a sturdy bollard on the transom of Kenny's crabbing boat. Matt attached another long line to a pulley placed just below the mast spreaders, then ran it a hundred feet out into the water to the skiff. He knew the relaunch would not be any more graceful than *Lonesome Dove*'s beaching, but he hoped it would be less destructive. With his friends' help, Matt closed off all the portholes and locked them down tight, then used waterproof tape to seal the companionway doors, hatch, and any cracks in the cockpit where water might potentially find an entry point as they pulled the sloop back out to sea. Using a shovel he'd found in Carlos and Ricky's garden shed, he dug something of a crude channel in the soft sand, leading from the deepest part of the keel and into deeper water, careful not to damage any more turtle grass than he already had.

"Are you ready?" called Kenny over his shoulder as he climbed back into the crabbing boat.

"Aye, Captain," yelled Matt, as he stood at his place half in the water beside *Lonesome Dove*'s bow.

"Then let's get this ole beached whale of yours back out where she can go for a swim." Kenny revved the throttle and the powerful dual outboard engines roared to life. Tension clamped down on the line leading to *Lonesome Dove*, the stern of the sturdy crab boat settling lower in the water, her bow rising sharply. He signaled to his wife and yelled, "Hit it, Nelda!"

Nelda reacted immediately, gunning the engine on the fishing skiff. With a low moan, accompanied by the twanging sound of tightening lines, *Lonesome Dove* rolled slowly over, like an enormous, grumpy old walrus awakened from slumbering in the hot sun. *Lonesome Dove*'s mast now pointed away from shore. Matt and Desiree pushed alternately on the bow and stern, their combined efforts helping wiggle the boat, inch by inch, free from the sand. The line to the skiff sang a rising hum, and just as Matt feared it might fray and snap, *Lonesome Dove* started to slide slowly on her side, out toward the freedom of deeper water. Then, at last, with a few more adjustments to lines and a dueling chorus of engines, the skiff and the crabbing boat finally tugged the old sloop to deep enough water for her to sit upright, where she now rested as she should, bobbing on the waves as if eager to be underway.

Matt let out a whoop, and Kenny, Nelda, and Desiree cheered and clapped. It only took a short time to remove all the lines and pulleys that they'd rigged up, and Matt found himself feeling a little forlorn that he'd soon be losing the trio's company. Kenny and his family had literally resurrected his dream, and he knew he would be forever in their debt.

As he prepared to say his farewells, Matt offered to send money to pay for their kind deeds, but Kenny would have none of it.

"Look here, Cap'n, my people were pirates—bona fide, honest-to-god pirates. My great,"—his brow wrinkled, and he squinted for a moment before continuing—"maybe great-*great*-grandfather, had a privateering license over in the Bahamas, issued by old King George himself. Allowed him to plunder any boat that wasn't flying the Union Jack, and he sure did his share of plundering back in the day. He was even known to 'relocate' a navigational marker or light now and then, just to get a few more 'customers.' I reckon it's high time I do a good deed or two to cancel out some of the mischief he did back then. You can pay me back by helping the next sailor you see in a fix like yours."

Matt promised him he would and extended his hand to seal the deal. As he clasped the weathered hand, he noticed a faded U.S. Army tattoo, bluish-grey, on the old man's deeply tanned forearm. It was like the one on Matt's own arm, though faded by time and hard living, much like his own would be one day. While Kenny's tale of pirate karma was a good story, Matt suspected there was something running deeper beneath his generosity: the unspoken brotherhood of those who'd served—and survived.

After saying their goodbyes, the family departed the snug cove, Matt waving until only the frothy vee from the twin wakes remained, swallowed up quickly by the lightly rolling waves. Matt spent another couple of hours ferrying all his belongings by dinghy back to *Lonesome Dove*, then shoveling and raking sand back into place until he'd wiped clean all traces of the relaunch. Back on board, Matt spent several knuckle-busting hours hunched over the steamy engine compartment, sweat pouring off his brow, wrench in hand as he bled air and water from diesel lines and injectors. After several minutes of cranking on it, just before the battery was completely exhausted, the old Yanmar engine coughed back to life once more. Finally, after he'd finished readying the boat for departure, he spent an hour carefully checking and rechecking his charts, making sure no shallow reefs or shoals lay in his path.

His chest was tight, and he tried to quash the rising tide of anxiety that threatened to overwhelm his confidence. He had to admit that his recent misadventure had made him question his judgment, if not his skill, and he made himself a promise right then and there to think more like Julie when it came to safety. " *WWJD*," he thought wryly, in this case ready to consult Julie rather than Jesus for sailing advice.

Cursing himself as a bit of a coward, Matt decided to motor instead of sail out of the anchorage in search of a deeper one in which to overnight. The hole in *Lonesome Dove*'s side was along one of her more critical structural areas, where the stringers—or boat's bones, were located. He knew that with such a deep wound, his superficial patch job was hardly sturdy enough for serious offshore sailing. For the time being, they'd have to stick to calmer coastal waters until he could put her up in a boatyard for a more thorough repair job.

A few hours later, *Lonesome Dove*'s anchor safely nestled in a sandy bottom blessedly free of coral heads, Matt piloted his little inflatable dinghy a couple of miles across the bay to a small fishing marina to inquire after the availability of local boatyards. It seemed like everyone he talked to had only a pessimistic headshake or shrug to offer in response. One crusty old Conch fisherman, cheek bulging with a plug of tobacco, informed him that nearly every boatyard from here, past Miami and up to St. Augustine, was full of busted-up boats, courtesy of last year's hurricane. He informed Matt that his best chance would be to keep going to where there were fewer pleasure boats: somewhere like Mobile, Alabama, where there were several large boatyards serving the needs of the offshore drilling industry. With the recent slump in oil prices, they were probably hurting for work, and might be able to help him.

Feeling a stab of despair at the naysayers, Matt decided to cover all his bases. He found a bench in the sun and settled Hank at his feet before pulling out his cell and starting the onerous task of Googling and calling the number of every boatyard he could find along the Keys and around Miami. Sure enough, the waiting list to even have someone take a look at *Lonesome Dove*, much less do any repairs at all, would be a minimum of several weeks.

Even though his boat was still salvageable, and both he and Hank had survived the near-sinking, Matt struggled to find much to be happy about. On the far side of the dockside bar, a band called Casey and the Cajuns had set up, and a pretty, raven-haired singer was belting out her version of Linda Ronstadt's "Blue Bayou." Her voice made Matt smile for a second, something about her rich tones reminding him of Julie and how beautifully she would sing "Amazing Grace" in their church's choir. Yes, grace had "saved a wretch like him," but after what had happened to Julie, his faith had waned a bit.

Matt set his phone down, and with his elbows resting on the table, he cradled his weary head in his hands, feeling once again downtrodden and hopeless.

A well-groomed older couple in natty, crisp white sailing garb, seated at a table nearby, appeared to have been paying close attention to Matt's string of dead-end phone calls. When the man ambled over to talk to him, Matt felt a slight irritation at the invasion of his privacy and tried to tamp it down, knowing that he was about to be on the receiving end of an attempt to offer helpful advice.

"Sounds like you've got yourself one heck of a predicament," the man said, his bright blue eyes keen, his expression sympathetic. Matt nodded slowly in agreement.

"I'm Jim, and this here"—the woman waved from her seat before rising to join them—"is Clara."

"Nice to meet you," Matt offered politely, standing to shake first Jim's, then Clara's offered hands.

The man continued, "That's our boat out there, the *Charleston Clipper*. We're from Charleston, as you might have guessed. I'm a barber and Clara is a hairdresser. Both of us are semiretired, but we still do haircuts and 'dos aboard if you need one. To keep it legal in Florida, we only accept the barber barter system—drinks, food, and even just good company—as payment, you know."

Matt laughed ruefully, nodding as he brushed away the bushy blonde tangle that now hung ever-present in front of his eyes.

"Anyway...we suffered a bit of damage from Hurricane Frances back in our home port before sailing down here. *Bullfrog's Boatyard*, if your patch is good enough to get you there, is where you need to be. They have the best fiberglass man in the South: Roy is his name. He's a big guy—some folks call him "Tiny"—and he patched our Clipper like it was brand new."

Hope bloomed in Matt's chest. After the nearly fifty phone calls he'd already made, to boatyards up and down both sides of Florida, Matt figured that Charleston, even though it was five hundred miles away, might be his best bet for getting the repairs he needed done in a reasonable amount of time. His crude patch job would likely hold, but he would have to stick to sailing and motoring in the protected waters of the Intracoastal Waterway, which ran all the way from Brownsville, Texas, up to Maine.

After chatting for a few more minutes, Matt reluctantly agreed to a haircut onboard the *Charleston Clipper*. The couple had come ashore in a beautifully restored vintage rowboat that his outboard would easily outpace, so Matt agreed to give them a few minutes' head start as the couple rowed out toward a stately ketch moored a couple of hundred yards offshore from the marina. With Hank in his usual place up on the bow, proudly sporting his yellow life vest, Matt fired up the outboard and slowly motored over to join them.

"Permission to come aboard?" he called up to Clara.

"Please, come on up, both of you!" she beckoned with a friendly wave. As Matt lifted Hank up on the gleaming deck, Clara ducked down inside the galley, coming back up on deck with a fresh bowl of water for Hank and a cold can of beer for Matt. Jim called from below, inviting Matt to join them in the cabin. The big ketch was a Morgan Out Island, a spacious, fifty-one-foot sailboat whose interior appeared large enough to fit two *Lonesome Doves* inside. Right smack-dab in the middle of the cabin was a barber's chair, something that Matt had never seen onboard any other sailboat. Before Matt could ask about the chair, Jim explained,

"I tried to retire, and Clara did too, but we just missed talking to folks and plying our trade. Now, if you don't mind, Clara here is going to cut your hair this time. I've had about one too many rum runners, and you might not be too happy with my work right now."

His wife carefully placed a barber's cape around Matt's neck, and after inquiring as to his preferred length, started clipping away at his thick mane.

"Ah, I see you found a bit of sea tar along your way," she commented, as she snipped away at a gummy clot of what Matt assumed was West System epoxy.

They'd outfitted the spacious old boat with every modern convenience, and its surfaces gleamed with cost and care.

"Are you a baseball fan? Astros versus the Rays?" Jim inquired with a note of hope in his voice.

"Sure, I'll watch just about anything. I've only got an AM-FM radio onboard, so this is the lap of luxury for me," Matt replied as Jim switched on the satellite TV. They continued to chat, half watching the game as Clara finished up with Matt's haircut. Finally, their conversation turned more personal and Matt swapped an abbreviated version of his latest adventures with Jim's own. The older man concluded with a sigh.

"At one time we were going to sail around the world, but now, at this stage of our lives, the Florida Keys is about as far as we're comfortable going. Not to mention, this chunky old girl is a handful for two old people like us to sail in blue water." Clara winced and scolded Jim not to talk about their "baby" like that. "But you, you're still a young man, and I hope you get to make your around-the-world voyage." Jim reached for his cell phone and began scrolling through his contacts. "Now, let me give Roy a call and see if we can't get your boat all fixed up." He found the number he was looking for and connected, setting the call to speaker mode.

There were a couple of rings, then a slow, deep voice answered,

"Bullfrog's...This is Roy speaking. How may I help you?"

"Hello Roy, this is Jim, from the Charleston Clipper. I'm just talking to a nice young man down here in the Keys in need of your fine fiberglass work. Do you have room for one more injured sailboat in your yard?"

Jim explained Matt's situation and the lack of available repairmen anywhere in the vicinity. There was a brief pause on the other end of the line and then Roy replied.

"It's a pretty long sail for a busted-up boat with a patch, but sure, you tell him we'll be waitin' for him—we got lots of room. Tell him to take his time and we'll see him when he gets here. Also, have him make sure his bilge pump is working, plus have a spare . . . Oh, and he should stick to the Intracoastal, no offshore!"

As Matt prepared to head back to *Lonesome Dove*, he was overcome with gratitude for the kindness of the couple who had been strangers only hours before but with whom he now parted as friends. He'd lost his precious Julie, been forced to sell his home, and more than once, almost gotten himself killed. His tangle with Clawson had caused him to nearly lose his mind. He could have drowned in the Gulf Stream, came close to losing his boat to a coral head, and nearly had to cut short his journey before it began. And yet, at every turn, a helping hand had pulled him out of the darkness and back on his feet. It reminded him of Julie's favorite holiday movie, *It's a Wonderful Life*, that they watched faithfully every Christmas, Matt half dozing and Julie sniffling softly, until the very end where they both got misty-eyed and held each other close. Matt felt now a lot like the beleaguered George Bailey who questions his own good fortune throughout the entire film, only realizing, as he's about to lose everything, that he has the love and support of his family and entire community. Matt nodded to himself as he recalled his favorite quote from the movie, "No man is a failure who has friends." As he turned the dinghy back toward home, Matt felt those words deep in his heart, seeing his future with fresh eyes and a dawning understanding that he was finally going to be okay.

CHAPTER 11

Rather than deal with the hassle of going through Miami, and all the busy tangle of shipping traffic that route would entail, Matt decided to backtrack. He would return to Key West and continue on up to Fort Myers, where he could then journey up the Okeechobee Waterway, cut straight across the lower half of Florida, pass through Lake Okeechobee, head toward the port city of Stuart, and then— finally—ease northward up the Intracoastal Waterway.

Trying hard to quell his frustration at having to double back on his route, Matt steered *Lonesome Dove* slowly and cautiously back up the Keys, stopping briefly in Key West for one last cold beer at the Schooner Wharf Bar and to replenish his supplies. After picking up some more of Hank's favorite liver treats, along with a large bag of Nacho Cheese Doritos that he'd been craving, Matt dropped in at the local marine chandlery to look for a new ship's bell and a secondary bilge pump that he might need if his patch job sprang a leak. The manager recommended a three-thousand-five-

hundred-gallon-per-hour model as a backup, and Matt grimaced when he saw the price tag on the dusty box.

Matt figured that the costly little device might just save
his bacon though. He recalled the fatal tragedy that had be-
fallen Mel Fisher's boat which was caused in part by a faulty
pump, and Matt gladly made the purchase then resigned
himself to eating a few more meals of beans and rice, and
taking fewer trips to shore for overpriced beers and burgers.

As he was strolling back along Elizabeth Street, purchases clutched under one arm and Hank's leash in his free
hand, he heard familiar voices calling from behind.

"Yoo-hoo! Ahoy Matey!"

It was Carlos and Ricky, this time dressed in much
more typical street attire than when he had last seen them,
both apparently in full-on hangover-recovery mode yet still
bubbling over with good will and merriment.

Carlos was the first to come in for a hug, with Ricky
following right behind, and Matt soon found himself sand-
wiched in a tight, awkward embrace.

Ricky sang out, "We just adore the bell you made us!
You shouldn't have, but we sure are glad you did!. Thank
you so much for being so kind—and for leaving everything
spotless. You're welcome to come back anytime!"

Carlos chimed in with a wicked look.

"We have a little Morse code system for our special bell.
One ring of the bell means 'bring me a martini,' but two
rings mean 'I want a blow job.'"

"He means the *shot*, you know," Ricky interjected in a
stagey voice, adding a naughty wink. He poked Carlos in
the ribs before giving Matt a final affectionate squeeze and

waving goodbye. The pair weaved a bit, unsteady on their feet, before disappearing into a nearby bar for a fresh alcohol infusion. Key West was certainly a fun place, but Matt's head wasn't yet in that space. He yearned for the solitude that he knew he could find offshore, along the quiet backwaters and bays of the coast, where colorful birds and wildlife were still more plentiful than colorful humans.

Early the next morning, Matt sailed northwest from the Keys, tailed by a bright red ball of a morning sun that gradually faded to orangey-yellow and warmed the back of his body in the cool fall air. This time they steered well clear of Mel Fisher's old treasure-hunting grounds, and Matt carefully checked his charts to avoid any environmentally sensitive areas.

For the next few days, Matt stuck to a course within sight of the shore, just in case his patch job failed and he was forced to ground the boat again. Having learned his lesson about acting rashly, Matt took his time, stopping whenever he could find a suitable spot to anchor: to fish, maybe snorkel, and finally spend an uneventful night before resuming his journey.

On day five, *Lonesome Dove* nosed into the Caloosahatchee River, the first part of the Okeechobee Waterway. Just as Matt ripped open the bag of Nacho Cheese Doritos he'd been saving since Key West, and was savoring the first of the tasty morsels, the crunch of the chips was drowned out by the steady *thump-thump-thump* of a big ship's diesel engine. Matt glanced back and saw a familiar boat gaining on him, its wheelhouse towering high above his little boat. It was the *Lady Rose*, her ship's horn honking wildly as she edged up behind him, the captain playfully reversing the boat's powerful engines just in time to give *Lonesome Dove* a gentle kiss, which was cushioned by a couple of large truck tires draped across its bow.

From way up on the bow of the shrimp boat, one of the crew's companions lifted the hem of her T-shirt and saucily flashed her breasts before her girlfriend yanked it down and gave her a shove. Recalling the wild shenanigans that had transpired back at Fort Jefferson, Matt grimaced, hoping the shrimpers had played out most of their antics back in the Dry Tortugas.

"What the hell are ya doin' out here, Cap'n?" shouted Captain Boudreaux from the boat's bridge. "Thought you was headed off to the Bahamas to chase them island girls?"

"Slight change of plans," Matt yelled back, and gave him and the crew a summary of his latest misadventure as the two boats, engines off, bobbed in the gentle waves alongside the canal.

"You ain't no sailor unless you run into a few things first," was Marcel's reply, and Matt laughed heartily, finally far enough removed from his near-disaster to see the humor in the situation.

"So, where ya headed now?" called the captain.

"A boatyard in Charleston," replied Matt.

"Charleston? Son! That a long, *long* ways from here in a blow boat! C'mon, me and the crew can help you get on up there a little bit faster." Then, without waiting for a response from Matt, Captain Boudreaux kicked on the *Lady Rose*'s powerful diesel engines and edged the huge shrimp boat around the sloop, directing a crew member to toss

Matt a line. The heavy tow line was so thick that Matt barely managed to fit it around his little boat's bow cleat. Before he could get back to the cockpit to mind the tiller handle, the line snapped taut, and *Lonesome Dove* launched forward, rising as high in the water as her weight and deep keel would allow, like an ungainly water skier unable to get all the way up on their skis. He worried for a second about the speed they were now traveling and his patch job, but then decided that whatever was going to be, was just damned well going to be.

For miles and miles, the mismatched pair of vessels cruised effortlessly along the Intracoastal Waterway, passing slow-moving barges, scores of lumbering alligators, billowing flocks of roseate spoonbills, and a few wise-looking old gray herons, each of which earned a loud bark from Hank when they dared to pass close enough to his spot up on the bow.

Taking full advantage of a lazy "sailing day," Matt relaxed with Hank up on the bow, dipping Doritos in cold bean dip and listening to the sounds of the boat's AM-FM radio which was tuned to a classic reggae station out of Miami. The mellow sounds of Bob Marley and Peter Tosh were occasionally interrupted by commercials, which Matt didn't really mind that much until he heard one in particular. It featured a female voice extolling the virtues of Clawson Chicken in a cringeworthy, fake-Jamaican accent that was hell on the ears. *"Clawson chicken, betta dan me own momma's dat she cook in da islands, mon!"* singsonged the faux islander with maximum cloy and minimal conviction. At that point, Matt got up and switched off the radio, preferring instead to listen to the low hum of the shrimp boat's diesel engine.

When they finally reached the other side of Florida, thankfully without drama and with only an occasional flash of bare butts and boobies from the female passengers on the *Lady Rose,* it was time for them to say farewell once more. They were off for some more "fishing" somewhere way off-shore, and although he was truly grateful for the tow, Matt was a little wary of getting caught up unawares in some-thing shady. Before they parted ways, Marcel again topped off *Lonesome Dove*'s diesel tank and dropped down a bucketful of "super-colossal" shrimp—this time, plump and juicy Gulf "browns."

Leaning down from the wheelhouse, one of the women called down in an ostentatious whisper: "We got to make some room in the freezer so we can pick up something off-sho—" before Captain Boudreaux silenced her with a wag of his finger and a fake throat-clearing. "*Ahem* . . . remem-ber what we talk about, Cher?"

After a quiet night in a calm anchorage just off the ICW near Sailfish Point, Matt and Hank caught a nice following breeze. He hoisted the spinnaker and *Lonesome Dove* zipped through the waves, carrying them past Melbourne to a small island near Cape Canaveral. Here, they anchored for the night and Matt began cleaning the shrimp for a gen-erous evening meal. He removed the tasty crustaceans' little translucent jackets, cut along their backsides to "butterfly" them and then washed them off in a bucket of seawater be-fore dusting them with a seasoned mixture of cornmeal and flour. As always, when human food preparations were underway, Hank gazed with rapt attention to the proceedings. Just as Matt finished pouring a glistening stream of oil into the skillet on the gimbaled Force 10 stove, he heard something and, attention piqued, climbed up the companionway ladder. The roar was louder than any jet he'd ever heard and accompanied by a towering column of white smoke that stretched from near the shore to as far up in the sky as he could see.

Matt then recalled hearing, just a few days earlier, that a rocket carrying a new Mars probe, would take off from Cape Canaveral today. Seeing the thick column of smoke from the shuttle's ascent cast him sickeningly back to the Challenger disaster. Like many American children of his age, he'd witnessed the tragedy unfold on a classroom television set. His teacher had rushed to turn off the picture as he and his little schoolmates watched in shock, unsure of what they'd just seen. Just like his own schoolteacher wife, Julie, Christa McAuliffe—another teacher—had her life cut tragically short because of the shortcomings of a huge corporation. In McAuliffe's case, the negligence was on the part of a large aerospace contractor who had supplied a faulty part in the shuttle's engine. He remembered his mother explaining to him how "sometimes bad things happened to good people," yet this explanation never sat right with him. Someone was to blame for McAuliffe's death, those of the men on the Deepwater Horizon, and for Julie's.

He was again swamped with guilt that he could not seem to find her any justice. Whenever he'd bellyached about some shortfall or small injustice, he felt he'd suffered,

Julie always told him to keep his head up, that living well was the best "revenge." He knew without a trace of doubt that she would want him to go on living his best life, but he continued to struggle with his conscience. The Clawson Corporation had not only gotten off scot-free but would continue to cause suffering with their negligence and criminality until someone pulled the plug on their operation. He sighed, feeling powerless. Maybe someday, an answer would reveal itself, but for now, all he could do was keep moving.

Since the wind was wily and uncooperative and because it was almost impossible to tack inside the Intracoastal Waterway, Matt motored much of the way, meaning frequent stops at local marinas to fill up his small tank and plastic jugs with diesel fuel, grab an occasional cold beer, a fresh bag of ice for the cooler, and of course treats for him and Hank to share.

As they traveled farther and farther north, the water in the Intracoastal waterway took on a muddy brown color. Every color change from clear turquoise to milky chocolate meant putting that many more miles between where he was and the dream of sailing in clear tropical waters, a fact that made his spirits droop a little. Nearing Mobile, Alabama, the ship traffic along the waterway grew steadily, and the challenge of navigating between the many large barges—some towed along in twos and threes and up to nearly half a mile long—kicked Matt's attention into full gear. On one occasion, the wake from one of these behemoths, whose towboat captain probably had little sympathy for "yachties," threw *Lonesome Dove* up and on top of a "spoil bank" alongside the waterway. The Corps of Engineers were notorious for creating large, randomly placed piles of mud as they dredged. These were seldom marked by warning buoys and lay just under the surface for sailboats with deep keels to find. Unfortunately, his old sloop was one of those with a fairly deep keel, and for several frustrating hours, *Lonesome Dove* was stuck fast.

Aware of the real chance he could rip off his patch job, sinking them right there, he took his time, slowly reversing his engine back and forth, yet to no avail. Matt despaired of ever rocking her free from the spoil bank, but suddenly had the bright idea to raise his mainsail. A gust of wind, combined with the thrust from the Yanmar diesel gave him just enough propulsion to push off the mud so that *Lonesome Dove* was finally floating free. Back on their way, Matt motored on to a sheltered cove along the Intracoastal Waterway where they could safely anchor for the night. ICW "sailing," which consisted mostly of motoring, wasn't his favorite, but with his boat held together with a crudely made epoxy patch, it was a much safer option than being offshore in unpredictable seas.

It took a little over two weeks to make the journey up from South Florida. By early afternoon on the fifteenth day, Matt finally entered Charleston Harbor from the Intracoastal Waterway route and felt an immediate wave of relief. The patch job had somehow held, and he and Hank had arrived safely. Their current route, passing boatyards like the one they'd soon be visiting—scores of old rusty barges and a few badly aging yet stately homes—was safest for his injured boat, but did not feature the serene and scenic views he yearned to see. When not dodging countless towboats and barges on his long journey north from the Keys, he'd scanned through a well-worn copy of *Cruising Guide to Coastal South Carolina and Georgia* that he'd picked up from a sailor's book swap in the Keys. From it, Matt learned that going the usual route in from the ocean would have led him past the historic site of Fort Sumter, where the horror that was the Civil War had begun in 1861, after the Confederacy fired on the U.S. garrison stationed there. Matt grew contemplative and mused to himself: *So many needless deaths...640,000 soldiers—men, and a surprising number of women for the time—all gone. All those lives lost... just like in so many wars.*

Matt shook off thoughts of war, both long ago and far too recent, took a deep swig of coffee from his rusty Pussers Rum mug, and welcomed Hank up on deck to greet Charleston Harbor. By now Matt was having long, serious conversations with his little canine sailing companion, and the rat-terrier mix seemed to be hyper-focused on his human's every word. It probably helped that he fed Hank small treats now and then during their chats. The dog's love affair with food was probably a much better explanation for his rapt attention than was a deeper understanding of his human's mind. But, one never could know for certain, and Hank really did a good job of posing as a sympathetic listener, especially during those long days at sea.

Matt's most fervent hope was that Bullfrog's could soon return *Lonesome Dove* to "bluewater" sailing status, and that the next time they ventured this way, they'd be easing past the welcoming, clanging bell of the bright red

"R24" buoy as they entered Charleston Harbor, its red light flashing every 2.5 seconds. "Red right returning," the saying goes. Matt knew that here, as in most of North America at least, keeping a red buoy on the right of your vessel meant you were staying on course and in safe depths when returning to most harbors from out at sea.

Sailing, though it had been a childhood dream, didn't come naturally to Matt, and he had had to resort to learning little memory tricks for the most critical stuff, like differentiating between "port" and "starboard." "Port" and "left" both had four letters, so they went together, and by default, "starboard" meant the right-hand side of the boat.

Another trick was remembering the saying: "port wine is red, it's red to port," red being the color of the boat's navigation light on that side of the bow. This one helped Matt determine if a vessel was coming toward him, or moving away from him at night, depending on which color of light he could see. Matt laughed to himself as he thought of a new one: "Anchor only in good light, with no coral heads in sight," which he would definitely add to his list of nautical mnemonics.

The owner of Bullfrog's Boatyard had asked Matt to call him just before their arrival so that he could direct him to a free mooring buoy, one to which the owner normally kept his own fancy private yacht tied. Here, he and Hank could tie up easily without needing to drop an anchor, before motoring up the Stono River to Bullfrog's Boatyard the next morning. There, a crew would haul *Lonesome Dove* out of the water with a travel lift, and set her up on blocks and jack stands for the long-needed fiberglass work to begin.

After taking the dinghy to shore for a brisk walk, the pair returned to *Lonesome Dove* to do some housekeeping. Matt spent the next few hours making a list of needed supplies, sorting trash and recycling to take ashore, and scrubbing and cleaning the boat's interior. His last task was plotting a future course that led them out past Fort Sumter and back across open ocean toward the tip of Florida, then hopefully, this time, on toward the idyllic clear waters of the Bahamas. As darkness fell across the harbor, the lights of Charleston sparkled brightly, casting hundreds of twinkling, multicolored polka dots across the surface of the calm water.

Their home for the night was definitely more convenient than having to "drop the hook," but unfortunately, it was located just offshore from a hopping dockside bar. The familiar notes of one of the many requisite Jimmy Buffett cover bands drifted across the water. Matt liked the song, whoever was playing it, and the free-spirited, beachy island vibe of Jimmy's musical styling had been at least partly responsible for his desire to sail to the Caribbean. *But*, he thought, *If I have to listen to one more bad rendition of "Margaritaville"*...

"Check, check, one-two, one-two," boomed across the water, so loud that Matt could feel the vibration in the boat's hull.

"Loud and clear over here," he muttered to himself, as he set about making his final preparations before turning in for the night. Just as he was heading up to the bow to check the anchor line one last time and admiring what was otherwise a tranquil scene—minus the noise—an enormous motor yacht came barreling by, ablaze with gaudy lighting, and throwing up a huge wake that sent the old sloop wildly rocking. As they zipped past, Matt caught sight of a half dozen or more scantily clad young women lounging around on the deck, while over the large yacht's ornate wooden wheel presided a corpulent older man who was chomping on a huge cigar and clutching a cocktail in his free hand. Before Matt even had time to flip him the bird, the yacht had rocketed into the "no wake zone" and he squinted to make out the vessel's name. Emblazoned on the vast transom was the moniker *Colonel's Mistress*. Matt's heart pounded. It wasn't . . . yes it was! *That motherfu...Colonel Clawson!*

Matt barely slept that night, tossing and turning as his thoughts raced. Seeing the object of his darkest, most vengeful thoughts, alive, well and clearly living *his* best life, filled Matt with a fury he thought had gone dormant. By the next morning, however, he'd tamped that anger down in the place it usually lived, undeniably there, but locked up and waiting—a sleeping giant. They went through their usual drill of coffee first, then a potty break and breakfast for Hank, then the same for the captain, followed by preparing *Lonesome Dove* for castoff.

Continuing on up the river, passing an odd mixture of stately homes with fancy yachts docked just out front, and rusty, half-sunken barges anchored alongside the channel beside moss-draped trees, they arrived at the docks down below the boatyard just before noon. Tying *Lonesome*

Dove up at the long dock, Matt, with Hank following along at his heels, trudged up the path toward the boatyard office. There, from behind a cluttered desk piled high with parts catalogs, under a blanketing cloud of cigar smoke, they were greeted by a stout middle-aged man with pouchy, froglike cheeks who introduced himself as Billy, the owner of Bullfrog's. A friendly little dog whose collar bore the name "Ranger"—apparently the boatyard's unofficial mascot—darted out from under his owner's desk and circled Matt's feet, then trotted over to engage in the age-old dance of "sniff and be sniffed" with Hank. Billy escorted them outside to discuss the procedure of lifting *Lonesome Dove* up out of the water and putting her "up on the hard" so that his best fiberglass man, Roy, could assess the damage and begin the repairs.

As the dogs ran and played around the assortment of boats (some of which looked as if they'd seen their last days on the water years ago) the boat-lift team took *Lonesome Dove* by her bowline and guided her into a narrow channel and underneath the overhanging frame of the travel lift. The travel lift was an odd-looking machine, built for no other purpose than to drive out over a narrow slip with its wide frame and pick up and transfer boats to and from dry land. After Billy and a couple of other workers wrestled a pair of of enormous nylon bands underneath *Lonesome Dove*'s keel, the winch motors began to grind and whir, ever so slowly raising the sloop up and out of the water. As soon as the boat's hull was clear of the sloping bottom, the travel lift, which was fitted with four huge tires, drove slowly back up into the boatyard, carrying *Lonesome Dove* suspended in her sling like a lumbering, leggy stork carrying an oversized, diapered baby.

Matt walked slowly alongside as the lift wound farther and farther back into the sprawling boatyard, carrying the little turtle shell that was his only home, past rows and rows of every imaginable sort of vessel: from large catamarans, to sleek ocean-racing yachts to old houseboats with hull shapes that had long ago gone out of style. Every one of them had once been someone's dream, and whether those dreams had ever been fulfilled or not, the fact these boats could still be restored and put back in the water made their plight seem a little less forlorn. Finally, the lift ground to a stop at an empty space in a far corner of the yard that bloomed with tall weeds. This would be where *Lonesome Dove* was to be secured within the embrace of a team of jack stands and old railroad ties. Here, far from the shore and the sound of waves lapping against the hull to which Matt had grown accustomed, they would spend the next couple of weeks living aboard while the boatyard crew completed the needed repairs.

For the next hour, a crew of workers quickly arranged the blocks and stands that would support *Lonesome Dove* until she could stand perfectly steady and still on her "land legs," and the travel lift returned to the water's edge to pick up another boat. Matt scratched his head, pondering his next move. Then, from between the many rows of boats, a large muscular man emerged, his ebony skin powdered with a coating of fine white dust. He smiled broadly and came toward Matt with an outstretched hand.

"I'm Roy," he said, "my friends call me 'Tiny.'" His voice was deep and resonant, the accent thick and rolling––Southern––but in some ways similar to what Matt had heard in parts of the Caribbean. "I'm the "glass man", I'll be fixing your boat up as good as new," he concluded.

Matt shook the big man's hand firmly and explained the damage—and with more than a trace of embarrassment—the cause. Roy walked over to *Lonesome Dove* to inspect the damage more closely, carefully running a small electronic device over the surface of the hull to check for moisture damage. Ranger, the little Australian Shepherd-mix dog that was now Hank's newfound friend, followed closely at his heels as Roy ran his big hand over the patch. Taking a chisel from his tool belt, he began tapping away at the edges of Matt's temporary patch work, loosening the fiberglass chunks which fell in chunks at their feet. Witnessing this exciting development, Ranger snatched up a mouthful of fiberglass, lay down, guarding his treasure between his paws, and began a tentative investigation with his teeth. Roy immediately scolded the little dog, who looked ashamed as he spat the chunk of fiberglass out at the human's feet.

"'*E got long eye* - anything looks like bone," he said. Matt would later learn that the phrase was from Gullah Geechee, a Creole language based on a handful of African and European languages, now spoken only in a few places in the Lowcountry. Tiny, obviously concerned that Matt had missed the gist of his words, translated: "That little dog is greedy for anything looking like a bone." Glancing over at Hank, who also loved to chew on anything that made a crunching noise, Matt said that he could totally relate.

Later, a quick Google search informed Matt that this unique language still survived in several places along the Sea Islands of South Carolina, where the people were mostly called Gullah, on down to Georgia, where they were more often called Geechee, possibly since some had settled along the Ogeechee River. These proud descendants of escaped and emancipated African slaves settled in this hard country and preserved a unique language and rich culture. They'd survived countless hurricanes and thrived for many years with little Western medicine or modern technology, farming small plots of land and living off what they could grow or gather from the sea and swamps around them.

Matt didn't know it yet, but this new acquaintance-ship—what would become a fast and enduring friendship—would dramatically alter the course of his journey. From this point on, there would be no turning back.

CHAPTER 12

As work progressed slowly on *Lonesome Dove*'s repairs, Matt spent his days reading, sanding, varnishing some of the topside teak, and polishing the old brass work around her interior. Roy came by a couple of times a day to add fresh layers of woven fiberglass mat to the patch that was gradually knitting together the ragged hole in the boat's side. Matt found himself looking forward to the daily visits, enjoying the colorful stories Roy shared about life in the boatyard, as well as his curiosity about Matt's adventures. After discovering that Matt was genuinely intrigued by his deep roots in the Gullah culture, he began to teach him a few words of the language and to tell him a little of his childhood on Jasmine Island. Unlike many people, the big man seemed as interested in learning about others as he was in telling about himself, a quality Matt found refreshing.

Aside from the ragtag shrimper crew and his brief, albeit pleasant encounters with others along the way, Matt hadn't had a lot of opportunities to socialize. Yet here, in the hot, dusty boatyard, filled with the smells of resin, sawdust, and varnish, he finally had the time and energy for something as uncomplicated as a new friendship. While Roy worked, and Matt assisted where he could, they talked about the usual things, trading stories of their foolish younger selves, of girls, and travel, and wild pipe dreams. Matt talked at length about Julie, but for the first time in the telling, found himself pushing aside the weight of her accident and all that had followed, focusing instead on the adventures they'd had, the life they'd built, and the love they'd shared.

Roy had served as well, as a diesel mechanic in the Navy. Although he'd seen much of the world, he had returned to coastal South Carolina to put his skills to use closer to home and his large extended family. Roy also had loved and lost, but didn't elaborate on how his wife, Marie had passed, and Matt, sensing pain that needed no probing, didn't press for details. During one break from work, Roy pulled his phone from his pocket and began scrolling, stopping when he found what he was looking for. He passed the device over to Matt, who studied the picture of a slender, dark-haired woman with a thick coil of braids flipped over her shoulder. She smiled brightly into the camera, full lips stretched widely over glossy white teeth. Matt nodded as he handed the phone back to Roy.

"You're a lucky man, Roy. She was a beautiful woman," he said simply, smiling at his friend as he reached for his own phone so he could share a picture of Julie. Matt scrolled through his gallery until he found his favorite picture: Julie standing at the bow of the boat, her skin golden-brown from the sun, her long, dark hair tangled by the wind and the water, the lens perfectly capturing the way she looked past the camera—deep into the heart of the photographer.

Roy smiled at the photo and back at Matt.

"You too, you've been very lucky. Julie was also a beautiful woman. But please, Matt. I think we can safely say we are now friends. So, please, call me Tiny."

With the Thanksgiving holiday approaching, and his own family and network of friends far away, Matt was feeling a little blue. He knew that Roy—"Tiny," like the rest of the employees, would leave for home while the boatyard closed down in observance of the festivities. He and Hank would likely be spending the holiday sitting "on the hard" in *Lonesome Dove*, celebrating with some canned turkey and peas. Maybe even with the ancient can of cranberry jelly he'd uncovered in his stores, if he was feeling really ambitious.

Realizing that his new friend would likely spend Thanksgiving alone, Tiny asked Matt to join him and his family for the holidays. When he wasn't staying in a small trailer behind the boatyard office, Tiny lived with his large extended family, down in the Sea Islands—a chain that stretched from the Carolinas down to Georgia. Tiny told him that in his fast Carolina Skiff, Jasmine Island was only about an hour's boat ride away, and that he'd see some beautiful scenery along the way. At first, Matt resisted, not wanting to impose, but Tiny insisted that his Nana B would be delighted to make room for one more at her table. Finally, Matt relented, grateful for the company and excited to check out the island—a place that Tiny had spoken of so many times, and in such detail, Matt thought he could instantly feel at home there.

Late the next morning, as the big yellow ball of sun had nearly climbed to its zenith, Matt and Hank boarded Tiny's sturdily built 24' Carolina Skiff. With all the time Tiny spent working on other people's boats, the glossy surfaces and meticulously organized interior of the skiff showed that this vessel was the big man's pride and joy. With Hank secured, Matt untied and stowed the lines and Tiny pressed down on the throttle. The boat's big Yamaha outboard roared to life, pushing the heavy skiff up out of the water so it almost seemed to fly atop the small waves. It wasn't long before they had left the crowded Charleston Harbor behind and were carving a wide wake across the nearly empty sea before them. As they drew closer to some of the small islands and the depth became much shallower, Tiny skillfully maneuvered the craft through a watery obstacle course of oyster reefs, crab traps and shoals as if he'd done so countless times before.

Nearly an hour later, and just within sight of Jasmine Island, Tiny suddenly cut the engine. The boat's hull settled down into the waves and glided to a crawl through the water, stopping near a spot where half a dozen pelicans were diving and feeding on something in the water.

"Those pelicans are feeding on little bait fish." Tiny remarked, peering over the boat's gunwale. "Where there are little fish, there should be big fish too!"

Just off the boat's bow in the nearly clear, aqua-hued water, they could see the top of a swirling vortex of tiny fish extending deep down in the water. Hovering at the periphery of the large school were several larger dark shadows betraying the presence of bigger fish, rapidly darting in and out of the swirling mass. Grabbing a rod, Tiny cast a shiny metallic lure just off to the side of the school where some of the larger shadows lurked just under the surface. He allowed the lure to drift leisurely into the water before slowly cranking on the reel. Within seconds, the tip of his rod tilted forward, and the reel hummed as a fish ran with the lure. Tiny quickly yanked the rod tip backward to set the hook and began a game of tug-of-war that lasted for several exhilarating minutes, finally scooping a nice twenty-two-inch red drum or "redfish" into his dip net.

Passing the rod to Matt, he said, "Here you go—your turn to catch dinner."

Matt cast the shiny lure just to the side of the silvery swirling ball of fish and a dark shadow shot toward it like a bullet. The reel sang its siren tune once more, and Matt yanked back hard on the rod to set the hook. Apparently, the fish had not fully swallowed the lure though, because as he arched backward with the rod, the lure came whizzing out of the water, whistled just past Tiny's ear, and landed in the water on the opposite side of the boat. Just as Matt was apologizing and cursing his rotten luck, the rod tip doubled forward again, almost ripping the pole out of his hands. The reel hummed again as another fish ran with the line. This time he hesitated for a little longer, firmly setting the hook - or so he thought. Matt cranked hard on the reel's handle and finally pulled the heavy fish alongside the boat where Tiny scooped up into his large dip net, just as the big redfish spat out the lure.

Tiny slowly shook his head. "I've seen a lot of fishing styles, but that one...I've never seen that one before! Is that how you boys from Texas catch fish?"

As the two large redfish flopped heavily on the floor of the boat, and Hank barked nervously, Tiny quickly reached under the boat's seat and pulled out a bottle of aged Bacardi rum. Matt watched curiously as Tiny opened the bottle and poured a couple of shots into an old metal cup. "My Auntie, Nana B, she don't approve, but it's for the fish," Tiny explained.

Matt's brow furrowed as he leaned over to see what his friend was talking about. With gentle hands, Tiny drizzled a bit of the rum onto each of the fish's gills. Within seconds, they had ceased to flop, and lay still. Tiny offered the cup to Matt, whose face reddened and eyes widened as he swallowed a too-big gulp of the potent rum. Tiny took a more modest sip for himself, then tossed the small amount that remained, over his shoulder, into the water.

"Some for the fish, some for us, some for the sea," he explained. "It's just something I do, kills them quick, so that way they don't suffer long. There's enough suffering." Tiny paused for a second, and as a hint of sadness came over his face, he added, "Nothing in this world should suffer that doesn't have to."

In all the excitement of landing the two redfish, neither Tiny nor Matt had noticed that they were about to have company. Seemingly out of nowhere, a sleek patrol boat materialized and came up alongside the skiff. A pair of mammoth-sized men, their eyes hidden behind dark wraparound sunglasses, regarded them with disdain and brusquely demanded that they leave the area at once, declaring that they had crossed into a "gas pipeline construction area." Both men wore quasi-military looking uniforms and were carrying sidearms .and military style AR-15 rifles, and Matt felt instantly uneasy. He'd seen their type before over in Iraq, working for one of the larger corporate outfits which were euphemistically referred to as "private security contractors," but in were really private armies, and he knew they lived outside of any laws. Typically thick-necked and brimming with toxic masculinity, fond of the worst parts of war, these men were lured back to work as mercenaries after they were discharged—honorably or dishonorably— from service. In Iraq and Afghanistan, guys like these two would have been hired by Uncle Sam to do the really dirty work: assassination, torture, killing civilians—all with little accountability to the Geneva Convention, or any other so-called "rules of engagement."

Tiny immediately held up his palms in a placatory gesture. "Sorry, we're just fishing, don't want to make no trouble," he said, gunning the heavy skiff's big outboard engine, intentionally leaving behind a generous-sized wake that rocked the guards' smaller boat as the Carolina carved a path toward his home island. As they zipped along, he told Matt that these waters, as familiar as the back of his hand, were not home to any natural-gas drilling or pipeline-construction projects of which he was aware. Matt agreed the encounter felt suspicious, if not outright wrong. He knew that most of these waters were protected by state conservation laws, enacted to protect several endangered species of birds which nested there, and that it was damn near impossible that any kind of construction would be allowed here.

"I bet you those are some of Clawson's boys," commented Tiny.

"You mean the *'Clawson Chicken'* Clawson? Matt asked, incredulously.

"Yep, he owns half of the damn islands around here now, stinking up the air with chicken manure, and polluting all our water. They killed my sweet Marie, you know, in his chicken plant," Tiny said, a look of fury contorting his usually placid face. Matt recoiled in disbelief. *Clawson, again? What the hell?*

As they approached the curving shoreline, Tiny cut the engine, allowing the craft to drift lazily on the waves. His soft voice turned to steel as, gazing off into the distance, he told his own Clawson tale. Tiny's Marie had worked at the local chicken processing plant, putting in long days for minimal compensation. There were few opportunities for employment in the area, and she'd been grateful for the job. Tiny said that they'd both been working hard to save money so that they could build their own home next to Nana B's on Jasmine Island, where they planned to raise a family one day. One fateful afternoon, as she toiled on the chicken processing line, Marie's arm had become ensnared in the teeth of a meat grinder. While waiting the seemingly interminable time it took for an ambulance to arrive, Marie had died because of massive blood loss.

"All because that monster Clawson made the workers remove all the safety guards from the machines to speed up processing and make more money," Roy said, his face creased with anguish and pain. "*Birds per hour...*yeah, *birds per hour* is what he'd go on about. My wife died because he wanted to process more birds per hour. And that's not the worst of it. I know they delayed calling for help on purpose. Marie bled out there on the plant floor while they ran around putting the safety guards back on the machines."

Tiny paused for a moment, running his palms down his face. Then, he shook his head and said, "He's an evil, evil man, you know, the Devil himself."

Matt nodded vehemently. "I know, Tiny I know. Let me tell you, I know." Then, little by little, Matt unspooled the tangled fibers of his own tragic tale, weaving the patchwork of details, and stitching it all together with the one ugly fat thread that ran through everything: "Colonel" Clyde Clawson.

For a long time, the two men sat silent, the quiet slosh of the waves and occasional cry of a gull the only sounds. Then Tiny spoke, pointing a finger up toward the bright, cloudless sky.

"I don't know, Matt, but I think the good Lord put us here together on this little boat for some kind of reason. I try to forgive and forget, be a good Christian, you know...but sometimes I'd just like to see him get what's coming to him." Tiny gazed into the distance. "He calls it 'Clawson Island'—where the new plant is—but we call it Salt Pond Island. It used to be our family's home before he took it from us." Pointing toward to the string of small islands ahead of the boat, he continued. "Jasmine, Salt Pond...all those islands over there are what they call "heirs' property." All of it is, or was, our land, passed down through the generations, since we got it back after the Civil War. It's owned by a lot of folks—hundreds sometimes—shared equally among them, but all it takes is one heir to agree to sell out, and then things can get all messed up. The Colonel got one of his lawyers to visit an old uncle of mine. They claimed that he'd signed some papers agreeing to sell. I know for a fact the poor man wasn't up for signing anything because he was in a coma. That's how Clawson got our land. So, not only did he take my Marie, he took my home as well. But what can you do, you know? You just got to go on and hope the good Lord will deal with people like him...someday."

He switched on the ignition, and the outboard bubbled to life. They motored on toward Tiny's home, both men silent as they reflected on their combined losses—and thirst for justice.

CHAPTER 13

The skiff finally coasted into a protected little harbor lined on one side by a high, root-filled bank with overhanging loblolly pine trees, and on the other, by a large clearing on which stood several outbuildings, including a small cottage with a column of white smoke slowly rising from its chimney.

Tiny sighed with obvious pleasure, turning to Matt and declaring, "This is still the best place in the world to me, but as they say down here, "*Evry frog praise 'e own pond.*""

It was a beautiful place indeed, and Matt imagined that if he'd ever had a "pond of his own" to praise, it might have been his and Julie's little home and farm in the Texas hill country. It was just far enough away from the bright lights of Austin that they could still see "their" stars at night, yet not so far away that they couldn't spend a lazy day down at "Blues on The Green" on the shores of Lady Bird Lake, or maybe have a dip in the cool waters of Barton Springs. Like the treasure hunter he'd met in the Keys, who longed for the "good old days," Matt suspected that his best times

were in the rearview—back in the hill country with Julie—
before Clawson snatched away his everything.

After they had tied off the skiff at the long creaking
dock, Matt grabbed the two redfish and followed Tiny up
toward the house, Hank trailing along behind, his twitching black nose fixed on the fishy aroma. As they
approached, the door to the cottage opened and a small,
stooped woman emerged. Catching sight of Tiny and his
companions, she waved enthusiastically and, with a long-
handled spoon, began striking a large bell that hung beside
the front door. Reaching his auntie, Tiny scooped her into
a tight hug, her slight figure dwarfed by his bulky frame. He
released her, and turned toward Matt, who hung back
slightly, carefully placing the two fish he carried on the deck
rail and wiping his palms discreetly on the seat of his chinos.

"Auntie, this is Matt, my friend from Chucktown. He
came all the way here from Texas on his boat." Tiny con
tinued the introductions:

"Matt, this is my Auntie Betsy. Our family call her
'Nana B.'"

Flustered, unsure how to address the elderly lady, he
reached for one of her small wrinkled hands, taking it in his
two and settled on:

"Pleasure to meet you, Miz Betsy."

She shook Matt's hand with a firm grip that he hadn't
expected, then tilted her head back to regard him, birdlike,
her dark brown eyes missing nothing.

"My goodness, all the way from Texas? How'd you get
so lost you ended up down here in the Lowcountry?" she
asked as she continued to size him up.

Matt smiled. "It's a long story, ma'am, but I'm sure glad to be here now. Thank you for having me."

"Well, young man, any friend of Tiny's is welcome at our table." She nodded to herself. "Hmm...I see you got those sad eyes. You got a story to tell me. I just know it," she said. "We'll talk more later, young man." Catching sight of the redfish, she clapped her hands with pleasure. "Fish tonight, Matt," she declared happily, beckoning them to follow her inside. "Him too," she said, smiling down at Hank, who trotted in at her heels.

They followed Nana B as she slowly climbed up the steps to the cottage, crossing a long, white front porch with a ceiling painted a pretty, greenish shade of blue. Matt would later learn that this color, "haint blue", common throughout the Lowcountry, was thought to keep a home free of evil spirits.

The family had furnished the well-kept home with sturdy pine furniture and covered its wide plank flooring with colorful braided rugs. Crisp white curtains fluttered at the open windows. They followed Nana B through to the kitchen at the back of the house, where several savory-smelling pots bubbled on the stove and a dozen or more pies and cakes sat cooling on the counters. Matt's mouth watered at the delicious aromas mingling in the air.

The room was uncomfortably warm from the heat of all the cooking, so Nana B ushered them through a door that led off the kitchen to a lengthy, screened-in porch that ran the length of the cottage and was dominated by a long table that looked like it could seat at least thirty people. Along the side of the long, screened porch, up against the wall, there were several large chest-type freezers where, Tiny explained that the family stored the fish they caught, venison, pork from the hogs they raised, and vegetables they'd grown in their gardens. He went on to describe how, back when LBJ was president, a handful of the Sea Islands had first gotten electricity after an underwater cable had been laid from the mainland, as part of a Rural Electrification Administration project.

"One good thing he did, I guess, after all that mess over in Vietnam," Tiny added.

"That don't mean Nana B's going to let the kids get away with making ice cream with any electric machine though," he laughed, pointing to a young boy and girl who were taking turns cheerlessly grinding away on a hand-cranked ice cream machine.

As the boy, the smaller of the two, struggled to turn the rusty old handle, his sister, glad for a moment to have the better job, was gazing off in a daydream as she halfheartedly poured a bit of rock salt onto the ice as the machine turned. The question, *"Is it done now?"* was asked often enough that they began to try the old woman's patience. Sensing she was preoccupied, one of them tried to sneak a taste of the contents and was quickly scolded by Nana B. "Don't you be peek'n inside! Salt in the cream'll spoil the whole batch!"

Soon, Nana B's home was crowded with members of Tiny's large extended family, drawn by the clanging of their matriarch's bell from their own homes, which he explained were scattered across the small island. Matt, who'd never been good with names, nodded and smiled, trying to fix the

different faces and relationships in his memory, as each new
person was introduced. The gathering included Tiny's five
siblings, a handful of aunties and uncles, a dozen or more
cousins of all ages, and a young woman whose baggy olive
cargo shorts, plain white tee and loosely laced hiking boots
did little to hide her natural beauty. Tiny introduced the
last as Hannah, a long-lost second cousin from "the big
city," who was visiting the Sea Islands to study the Gullah
Geechee culture and language. Matt blushed beet-red after
he realized his eyes had lingered for a beat too long while
glancing down at the young woman's long, caramel-
skinned legs. "Nice to meet you ma'am," he uttered clum-
sily and was relieved to receive a wide smile and
outstretched hand, despite what he thought was an obvious
transgression.

While Nana B continued to bustle around the tiny
kitchen, an auntie recruited several of the younger family
members into assisting, and everyone squeezed around
each other in the tight space, laughing and chatting as they
grabbed cutlery, plates, and platters and laid the table for
the big family. Tiny picked up the two redfish and laid
them out on a large wooden cable spool outside that served
as the fish-cleaning station. Matt and two of Tiny's cousins
headed back to the skiff, where they grabbed the remaining
ice chests full of food. As they made their way back up to
the house, Matt could see that Tiny had already cut four
perfect, long fillets from the redfish and was handing them
off to Nana B. Brimming with pleasure, the old woman
hustled the fish off to the old gas stove, where a large cast-
iron skillet full of oil was just beginning to crackle.

Tomorrow would be Thanksgiving and Matt had heard all about the delicious Lowcountry delicacies they would be enjoying. Tonight, the table seemed to sag under platters of fresh, fried fish and shrimp, soup bunch—leafy greens combined with root vegetables—and Gullah red rice and cornbread. Someone had set out a row of desserts on a side table: pecan pie and a delectable-looking Lowcountry treat Hannah told him was called "hummingbird cake," a moist spice cake made with bananas and tinned pineapple.

The long table on the back porch practically groaned under the many platters of food as Matt and the family found their places. After the family was seated, Nana B bowed her head, waiting until even the smallest child had fallen silent, and said a simple blessing. She'd barely raised her head and reached for her fork when Tiny tapped on his mason-jar glass to ensure his audience's continued attention, then gave a quick play-by-play of how Matt had so unexpectedly "hooked" the last fish. He ended with a hearty laugh, saying, "And you know how sailors all want to go and pierce their ears? He almost did that to me, too!"

Matt felt his face heat up again, yet took pleasure in Tiny's good-natured ribbing. Unable to muster a snappy response, he grinned awkwardly and filled his mouth with a large crunchy bite of the fish that had traveled from Tiny's tall tale to the heaping platter in front of him.

Nana B smiled, wagging a small gnarled finger at Tiny and declared, "Don't matter how 'e get caught, long as 'e ends up in the pot—fish that get away never feed anybody!"

Everyone laughed, and just as if someone had suddenly cranked up the dial on a radio, multiple conversations sprang up all around him, voices fading and rising as everyone battled to be heard over the din. Tiny had explained that most of his family had been educated, at one time or the other on the mainland, but Gullah Geechee was the language most commonly used, and the more excited the chatter became, the more it became prevalent. Matt struggled to understand a word anyone was saying, except for Tiny and Hannah, who switched effortlessly back and forth to translate news and gossip. Hannah was still a "comya"—or newcomer, but had learned enough of the dialect spoken by the "binyas"—or locals, to understand at least the gist of the conversation.

As the platters of food gradually emptied, and the rising tide of conversation continued to swell, Hannah, seated to Matt's right, leaned over, caught his attention with the touch of her warm hand on his arm, and asked how he and Tiny had met. Matt told her briefly about the wreck that had led him to Bullfrog's, and in turn, to their new friendship. In exchange, Hannah shared about her studies, which turned out to be part of a cultural preservation project sponsored by the Smithsonian Institute. She explained she had graduated a few years back from the University of South Carolina with a master's degree in linguistic anthropology and had been unsure what path to pursue. Her mother, a French-Canadian, had also attended the same university and had married a man from South Carolina, a great-uncle of Tiny's, it seemed, who was originally from the Lowcountry. Her curiosity about her family's heritage, along with a desire to help preserve its language and traditions, had inspired Hannah to join the research project and to spend a few weeks each year in the Sea Islands, visiting with elders and recording the stories and traditions of the people and their culture.

Hannah described how the art of oral storytelling was the backbone of Gullah Geechee culture, and it was only by this means that many of the old tales had survived. The stories had been passed down faithfully from generation to generation, since the time of the first slave ships that had stolen their ancestors from their homes in West Africa. Her lively brown eyes sparkling with passion, Hannah described her devotion to recording as many tales as she was able while the elders who knew them best were still alive. Sadly, she'd found that many of the younger generation, with all the new distractions of media and technology, had lost interest in hearing the same old stories told and retold by their elders.

"You know the song *Kumbaya*, that everyone sings by the campfire at church camp? It means '*come by here–my Lord*,' and it originated right here on these islands." Hannah called excitedly to Matt over the din of conversations bubbling up all around them.

As much as Matt enjoyed talking with Hannah, he tried to keep an ear tuned as well to the general conversation, latching on to some of the newer tales being told, some of them seeming too far-fetched and disturbing for a place that appeared so tranquil and idyllic. With Hannah's help, he heard, and began to make sense of, some strange goings-on near Jasmine Island.

The fish on which many of the families depended for food and a source of income were disappearing at an alarming rate. Big "reds" like the one they'd caught and just eaten were becoming increasingly rare, and not because of overfishing. From what Tiny had told him, Matt knew that like most Lowcountry residents, the Gullah people were good stewards of their waterways, taking only what they needed and closely adhering to state size restrictions to allow for a healthy population of fish to reproduce.

Besides the declining numbers of fish, anglers were finding strange anomalies on some of their catches. Odd ulcerations cropped up on scaly backs, and some folks even reported hauling up fish with curious deformities: a malformed jaw, a stumpy extra tail fin, a fissure in the flesh. One of Tiny's young cousins had even pulled up a flounder with a third eye sprouting from its flat head.

The strange stories continued over platefuls of rich dessert. Matt learned that two of Roy's cousins had gone missing the previous year, only months apart from each other, while fishing out among the islands. Their bodies were never recovered, and no trace of their fishing boats had been located. Some locals blamed their disappearance on "haints"—witchlike spirits, while others suspected much more earthly demons to be responsible. The authorities had come up empty-handed, and had quickly closed both cases, although the chronology and similarity of the disappearances rendered them beyond suspicious. Hearing about the vanishings gave Matt a chill, gooseflesh crawling up his arms as he thought back to the patrol boat that had stopped Tiny's skiff on their way to Jasmine Island. Just as Matt thought he'd heard everything there was to hear, Tiny leaned across the table and spoke in a low tone.

"And you know, Matt, that bastard Clawson? Across the bay from here is his chicken farm and processing plant where my Marie lost her life. It once was beautiful, but now it's the most disgusting and inhumane place on this earth. Every time the wind blows from the north—the stench! Enough to make you sick. "Smells like death.""

Matt was struggling to process all this information. After he'd helped with the clearing up and Nana B finally shooed him out of her kitchen with a flap of her dishtowel, he slipped away to be with his thoughts. With Hank at his heels, he headed toward the water's edge, where several Adirondack-style chairs were arranged around a fire pit. He'd only been there for a few minutes, listening to the rustle of the waves as they threaded through the pebbles on the beach, when Hannah plopped down in a chair opposite his.

"I hope you don't mind, but I wanted a chance to talk to you away from . . . all that," she said with an apologetic smile, waving vaguely overhead toward Nana B's house.

"Yeah, that's cool," replied Matt, sitting up a little straighter and self-consciously running a hand through his tangled hair. It had been a long time since he'd been alone with any woman other than Julie, and without the rest of Tiny's family there to run interference, he felt tongue-tied and a little shy.

He needn't have worried, however, as Hannah didn't seem to expect anything other than casual conversation and a listening ear. She had a keen gaze and ready grin, and her body language betrayed her natural curiosity and enthusiasm, peppering her stories and responses with demonstrative hand gestures as she scooted forward on her chair, emotions playing out on her expressive face. The warmth of her smile, which sometimes featured a mischievous twist at one corner, accompanied by a generous wink, made him feel like he could tell her anything, but out of a longtime habit, he held back a bit.

The slanting rays of the late afternoon sun gilded the light as Matt told Hannah a very condensed version of his journey from lineman to vagabond sailor and his plans to sail around the world. It turned out she was a bit of an adventurer herself, having spent several summers backpacking across Europe, Australia, and South America, where she'd once caught a ride from Cartagena, Colombia across to Panama on a small sailboat much like *Lonesome Dove.*

"I guess wanderlust runs in our family. My mom should have retired by now, but oh no, she's off somewhere in North Africa, studying the languages of Bedouin tribes."

Hannah told Matt how her parents had met at college while taking the same anthropology class, ultimately graduating with degrees in the same field, then later taking off to the far corners of the globe to study ancient cultures.

"After I was born, they moved up to Toronto for a few years. Back then, you didn't see many mixed couples around here and I think they just felt more comfortable up there. Dad taught at the University of Toronto, then they resumed their travels after I was about five years old. We went everywhere, up the Amazon River, to remote villages in India, West Africa...to study the roots of the Gullah Geechee language...Hell, by the time I was ten, I had more stamps on my passports than most diplomats! After we moved back to South Carolina, "Doctor Dad" received tenure at the university just in time to be my professor of Linguistic Anthropology 101—no pressure there!" Hannah laughed, but her voice was thick, and her eyes shone. *With unshed tears?*

"Your dad, is he..." Matt hesitated, not knowing quite how to phrase the question.

Hannah smiled sadly. "It's okay. My dad died several years ago, on a trip to East Timor with a couple of his graduate students. Rebels mistook their bush plane for a military aircraft and shot it down. He was on his way to meet my mom, who'd arrived at the field camp the day before. She was understandably devastated and had a really tough time finding her way after he passed. To cope, she did the only thing she knew how to, which was to throw herself even harder into her work." Hannah took a deep breath and continued. "He was a great dad, a really good man, and I still miss him every day, but I know he lived his life to the fullest. For someone with humble beginnings in the Lowcountry, he got to see a helluva lot of the world and experience things others only dream about."

"But enough about me...you seem to have been bitten by the wanderlust bug as well. Where to next?"

Matt sketched out his plans to sail Lonesome Dove to all the Caribbean islands before crossing the Panama Canal and heading to the South Pacific and beyond. Hannah seemed fascinated with his planned journey, drawing up her knees and hugging them to her chest as she leaned in to listen. Matt paused for a moment, shaking his head slowly.

"I don't know, Hannah. I'm wondering if this plan of mine isn't *too* crazy. I mean, you haven't heard all my wild stories yet, but it's only been a little over a month, and I've already had one shipwreck too many..."

Hannah laughed before her expression turned grave. She leaned forward and laid one steady hand on Matt's knee.

"No, Matt. Just go for it. *Seriously.* Man, I wish I could go with you."

Immediately, her face blushed crimson and she clapped a hand over her mouth.

"Sorry...sorry, I didn't mean it that way. Me and my big mouth."

Bending over, she scooped up Hank, who was nosing around in the pebbles at her feet and buried her blush in his furry back. Hank squirmed around with pleasure, as always, loving being held close to a soft, warm body. For one fleeting moment, Matt envied his little dog.

CHAPTER 14

The awkward moment quickly passed, and the conversation resumed, their words flowing along smoothly, occasionally branching off as they got sidetracked and began exploring yet another new topic. They talked on, comfortable silences filling in the occasional gaps, as the sun dropped lower and lower on the horizon and the sounds of music from the clearing drifted down to the water. Finally, Hannah mentioned her recent split with her ex-boyfriend, Mitch, a fellow graduate of the University of South Carolina ("the real USC," she added with a wink) who was now a biologist specializing in genetic engineering and something called "cellular agriculture." She approached the topic tentatively, as if she were feeling Matt out, and to his surprise, the mention of a boyfriend—even one she described as an *ex*—made him feel strangely unsettled.

"So, what happened? Why did you guys break up?" he blurted out.

Hannah broke eye contact for a moment, gazing off into the distance beyond Matt's shoulder. Then, she gave a sardonic laugh, seemingly out of character with her easy-going persona.

"Are you sure you have the time?" she asked, the words tinged with what sounded like bitterness.

"Nothing but," replied Matt, leaning back in his chair and stretching out his long legs.

Hannah took a deep breath, as if bracing herself for a challenge, and ventured,

"So...you know Colonel Clawson...of Clawson Chicken?" Matt grimaced and swallowed hard, unsure where this story would lead, but already fearing the worst. Hannah continued. "Well, Mitch, my ex, he worked for him. The big processing plant that Tiny told you about? Mitch helped design the plant and...other things." She paused for a long moment. "I wasn't sure exactly what he was up to until one day when my laptop died and I couldn't get my charger to work. So...I borrowed Mitch's."

Hannah looked down at her hands where her fingers were tightly laced together.

"And?" prompted Matt gently.

She sighed heavily. "And, I opened something I shouldn't have. I didn't understand everything at first—I'm not a scientist—but it made sense to me the more I read. And, I'm embarrassed to say that, once I looked at the first file, I kept looking for more until I thought I understood...well...everything."

Hannah gazed down at her lap, where Hank dozed in blissful slumber. The rhythmic *thump* of music floated down to the water from the clearing.

"I meant what I said, Matt...literally. Do you have the time? This is going to be a lot and you're the first person I've told. I've wanted to say something to someone but, honestly, I didn't know who to burden with my story. My friends back home are mostly Mitch's friends, and the family here was so torn up after Marie died that I didn't want to open up old wounds. You just strike me as someone...I dunno...I can trust. And maybe if I walk you through everything, it will help me sort things out for myself and figure out what to do next."

Matt's brow furrowed. He wasn't sure why Hannah suddenly seemed so uncomfortable, almost afraid, but he felt a little swell of pride that she'd chosen to confide in him. "Tell *me*, Hannah," he said, his voice quiet and earnest, his heart dipping as he caught sight of the tears making her eyes shine in the lowering light. And so, with a tremor in her voice, she began.

"So, Mitch was initially hired to improve chicken genetics to get them to produce more plentiful meat in a shorter amount of time, while at the same time consuming less food. But he didn't stop there. He continued to manipulate their genetic code until finally he pioneered a bioengineering technique that could produce living animals whose flesh was already infused with the flavor of other species."

"Okay..." said Matt, grimacing. "That's a little...creepy."

"Oh yeah," Hannah agreed, "But it gets even weirder. So...now the Colonel could breed chickens with genetic material from other animals. This meant that the birds could have all kinds of exotic flavors, from beef to pork and even fish. It's like they created a "Swiss Army bird" that they could process to fill every other meat product niche that the Colonel didn't already control. So now, thanks to Mitch's bioengineering expertise, Clawson is able to make 'pork nuggets,' 'beef chunkies,' and even 'alligator poppers.' His new 'secret recipe' is just a mix of genetically engineered chicken, artificial chemical fillers, synthetic flavorings, and mystery meat by-products. Creepy and gross and now legal, thanks to food safety laws his own people helped to re-write."

Matt nodded, eyes fixed on Hannah, encouraging her to continue.

"And that's not even the worst of it," said Hannah "wait till you hear this." But, *this* would have to wait, as Tiny, who had left them alone for a suspiciously long time, appeared with a couple of cold beers—which he suggested they all enjoy well out of sight of Nana B before heading on up to join the singing and dancing that was picking up pace at the house.

Later that night, after Nana B had slipped off to bed and some of the older aunties and uncles drifted back to their own homes, Tiny and a couple of his cousins headed down to the long dock to do some night fishing.

"You care to join us, or...?" Tiny invited Matt, his eyes flitting between his cousin and Matt, with a trace of a smile twitching his lips.

Matt shifted self-consciously before replying.

"I'd love to...but..." he trailed off, glancing at Hannah, who poked Tiny in one of his big biceps and spoke up, in-terrupting.

"I'm borrowing Matt for a bit. I need to finish telling him my life story."

Tiny laughed, shaking his head, and ruffled Hannah's curls with obvious affection.

"Girl, I just knew you'd be chattering his ear off the first chance you got. Matt, fair warning—she's a talker," he said, tossing a sly wink in his friend's direction as he headed off toward the dock.

Matt followed Hannah, carrying a sleepy Hank, as they made their way back down to the little beach and settled in the creaking wooden chairs. For a few minutes, they said little, allowing the silence to stretch out as they gazed out over the calm bay. A full moon was just beginning to rise, making the small ripples across the water look like thousands of softly glittering diamonds.

"Well..." Hannah drawled, pausing as she turned her gaze back to Matt. "So, you sure don't mind me rambling on a bit longer?"

"Of course not," Matt assured her. "You've got me intrigued."

"Okay," she began, "So when Mitch first got hired to work for the Colonel, he was invited to stay for a while in the servants' quarters of his mansion. Clawson has this crazy, sprawling antebellum palace over on the windward side of his private island. Believe me, that's one place around here where the wind doesn't carry the stink of his factory...Anyway, Mitch made friends with some of the staff there, and that included the family butler, who'd worked for the Clawson family for decades. This old man—'Jeremiah Jones,' but they call him Hopkins—knows

Clawson better than anyone. He basically raised Clawson after his parents died of malaria back in New Guinea.

"Well, Mitch got pretty friendly with old Hopkins. He seemed really interested in his stories, and for a while I didn't really understand why. I mean, here's the thing: Hopkins had a fascinating history. He was the first of his family to graduate from any school. He had a degree in English Literature and graduated with honors from historically black Tuskegee University in Alabama, yet returned as a young man to the Lowcountry to work as an elementary school teacher for several years.

Being a butler to a rich white family probably wasn't his dream job, but he'd always wanted to become a writer, so the opportunity to travel the world with the Clawson family was one he couldn't turn down. But Mitch wasn't into literature or history, so what was the deal? Was he really interested in Hopkins? No...what he wanted from Hopkins was to find out everything he could about Clawson's backstory. I'm not really sure why...unless to have some leverage over the old man?"

Matt leaned forward, resting his chin in his palm, unsure where all this was leading as Hannah continued.

"Okay, remember how I told you about the Colonel's genetic hybrid creation? Well, once I figured out he was creating some kind of gross, cross-species meat abomination mixed up with chemicals and by-products, I knew that Mitch was caught up in something terrible. So...I kept snooping. I went through all the files on his laptop and I found one buried within his old taxes. It was obviously a manuscript, even though Mitch was never much of a writer. The title was, or *is, My Life as the 'Cannibal's' Butler"*—Hannah paused, making air quotes around the words—"and the author's name was Jeremiah H. Jones." Hannah leaned toward Matt, dropping her voice to a whisper.

"I made a copy and I read every word. Matt, you're not going to believe this, but the 'cannibal' in Hopkin's manuscript? The wanna-be cannibal was...is...Colonel Clawson."

CHAPTER 15

Matt struggled to process Hannah's latest revelation as he followed Tiny up the footpath and back to the boathouse by the long dock. The sleeping loft where he was to spend the night was small and cozy, accessed by a sturdy wooden ladder. While Hannah had been occupying the space doing her research on Jasmine Island, she'd moved up to Nana B's place, and the old couch—to give Matt a bed for the weekend. Bidding Tiny good night and thanking him profusely for his hospitality, Matt hauled himself up into the loft one-handed, the other cradling Hank and a fat manila envelope containing Hannah's secret copy of the butler's manuscript. Hannah had concealed the latter in a stack of fluffy towels she'd asked him to return to the boathouse. As he'd reached for the stack, she'd leaned in close and whispered, "The manuscript is in there. Look for yourself and tell me he's not a monster."

Matt stripped down to his boxers and climbed onto the low platform bed, laying his old sweatshirt on the cover to keep Hank's sandy paws from dirtying up the duvet. The snowy white sheets were clean and soft as he pulled them up to his waist, and he sighed with pleasure as he stacked the fluffy down pillows behind him so he could get into a comfy reading position. At the foot of the bed was a small window through which moonlight glittered off the bay. He leaned over and switched on a small brass sconce beside the bed, angling the light, the better by which to examine the manuscript. Drawing the envelope toward him, he pulled out a stack of papers, bound with a large black binder clip. He flipped past the cover page and read.

Dear Reader,

If you are reading these words, then either I, or the subject of my tale, have likely passed into the great beyond. The story within these pages, as horrible and convoluted as it may seem, is completely true, yet I could never dare to publish it without placing the lives of my dear family, and my own, in grave danger.

A life lived in service is one of invisibility, of subjugating one's own needs while living always in anticipation of another's. It is through this lens that I have observed, often undetected, the downward spiral into depravity - the loss of all humanity. Indeed, the very creation of a monster.

For the past four decades, I have called this abomination by many names: Clyde, Young Master Clawson, Sir, and most recently, Colonel Clawson. The story I am about to tell you is based upon my observations, family tales overheard during my service, and the bourbon-laced ramblings of the Colonel himself.

The roots of my tale run deep, all the way back to far-flung, exotic places. Clyde Clawson's parents were God-fearing people, Christian missionaries who traveled far from their homes to spread the gospel. Although their life in the field serving the Lord was a far cry from the luxury of life in their well-appointed old Southern mansion, they believed it was their calling and pursued their mission with a fervor that sometimes blinded them to the truths that lay coiled like poisonous snakes at their own doorstep.

The Clawson clan first departed the United States in 1958 with six-year-old Clyde, leaving their staff—except for me and a ladies' maid—to care for their sprawling estate. For the next ten years, they, that is, we, traveled to faraway jungles across the world to convert isolated societies to Christianity. Some of these people, even then, still observed the ancient practice of killing and consuming their rivals for reasons that ranged from spiritual to nutritional.

Although his parents were decent, hardworking folks, they carried a blind spot for their only son. Despite the hardships of life in the jungle, they had always spoiled their boy. Everywhere they went, they carried an ample supply of his favorite butterscotch hard candy, never required him to pitch in or to carry any of his own things, and catered to his every whim, especially during their annual visits back to the plantation where they did everything in their power to compensate for the deprivations they believed young Clyde suffered while traveling. He wanted a pony? The loveliest little gray trotter was delivered the next day. He wanted a circus? They hired one to come to the plantation. All of this indulgence created first a little, then a much bigger devil. By the time he became "The Colonel," his massive wealth meant that he could indulge his every desire, no matter how depraved.

Matt paused and blew out a breath, raising his eyes from Hopkins's manuscript and fixing his gaze on the rectangle of moonlight that glowed over the foot of the bed, shedding a little beauty on the ugliness of the words on the page. Then, with a sigh, he continued.

The Colonel's strange desires were developed early on, shaped by his parents' overindulgence, his own innate greed, and experiences he was yet too young to fully understand.

It was 1964, and deep in the remote New Guinea highlands, the elder Clawsons were preparing to give a sermon, fervent in their belief that they were about to deliver yet another remote village from Satan's clutches. Young Clyde was now twelve and had heard literally hundreds of his parents' sermons. He was bored and jaded and yawned openly as his father held a Bible over his head and gesticulated toward it. The Indigenous people looked on bewildered, uncertain if he was extolling the virtues of the thing for wiping bottoms—as they'd seen the white people do with paper instead of with leaves—or something else more powerful. Whatever it was, the white man thought it important enough to come all this way, so many of the villagers gathered around to watch. Mostly they just enjoyed the entertainment, along with the things that the missionaries carried with them, such as toothbrushes, which, when carved and sharpened, made acceptable points for their blowguns' darts. And the hard butterscotch candy that

Clyde's parents kept on hand for him and occasionally shared with the more agitated audience members.

Seeing that his father was about to begin the same lengthy monologue, Clyde slipped away from the group, deeper into the jungle, where he came upon a small group of men gathered in a circle around a smoldering fire, clasping hands and chanting as an elder shaman intoned in a rhythmic, low-toned voice. He recognized from the cadence of the man's voice that it was some kind of sermon, or religious ritual, not unlike one of his father's, yet this one was much more compelling.

Unable to resist, Clyde crept closer and closer to the men, moving as stealthily as his stocky frame would allow, curious eyes fixed on the ceremony. Suddenly, one participant noticed his presence and pointed in his direction. Heads turned. Clyde's first instinct was to run, yet he could not seem to stop his feet as they shuffled him forward toward the ring of men. The wrinkled face of the shaman opened in a devious smile, and he beckoned for the boy to join them. Young Clyde wriggled his way amongst the adult men, feeling the vibration from their bodies as they continued to chant in unison. After a few minutes, they passed around a large green banana leaf, in which some kind of tender-looking roasted meat was wrapped. Each man took a piece with his fingers and held it until every person had received their own. The shaman's words, incomprehensible to young Clyde, grew louder and faster, rising to a feverish pitch before dropping into sudden silence. He beckoned for the men to eat the morsels of meat that they were *holding, and each one slowly placed them into their mouths. Clyde immediately copied their actions.*

As he placed the meat on his tongue, he was overcome with sensuous pleasure, every taste bud suddenly alive as if for the first time in his young life. Back home at the mansion, his indulgent parents allowed young master Clawson to have filet mignon whenever he wanted—when he wasn't dining on the ice cream, chocolate cake, or cookies that the kitchen staff had at the ready to satisfy his constant demands. He hadn't tasted good meat now for months, and this was far superior to even the finest cuts of steaks he'd sampled. Besides the exquisite flavor, which pleased him mightily, he was flooded with a sense of strength and power far beyond that ever experienced by his stocky, pimply twelve-year-old self.

After they had finished consuming the last of the meat, passed around once more on the banana leaf, and young Clyde was furtively sucking the juice from his fat fingers, he realized the sermon had by now wrapped up and that his parents would be looking for him. He tried to communicate his thanks with vague hand gestures and then hurried back through the jungle to find his parents.

As the Clawsons made their way back down the long winding path to the village where they were staying, the boy felt confident that he'd been chosen to be part of something very special. Intuitively, he knew to keep his experience a secret from his parents, and he told them nothing of his time in the jungle, revisiting the moments again and again in privacy as the most cherished memory of his young life. The tantalizing flavor of the meat and the sense of power it bestowed left a craving deep inside that would haunt him for the rest of his life - a hunger he would go to any length to satisfy.

Sometime later, as he learned more of the ancient ways of the local people, he came to believe that what he had consumed that day was human flesh. Once upon a time, eating part of their enemies was the means by which warriors could gain strength, courage and power. Believing that he'd unearthed the truth of what he'd experienced did not come as that much of a shock to twelve-year-old Clawson. Perhaps he'd suspected what he was eating from the very first and didn't really mind. Or perhaps he saw his awakening desire as a tool to rebel against his devoutly religious parents. Whatever the motive, it really didn't matter that much. From his first bite of what he believed to be forbidden, Clyde wanted only to possess it again.

I believe that Clawson, fool that he was, had eaten nothing more exotic than pit roasted wild pig, cannibalism no longer being actively practiced among the people of the highlands. But we are driven, not by truth, but by belief, and Clawson's first bite of the forbidden set him on a misguided and avaricious path. I have asked myself many times why I remained in his employ and reasoned that it was, perhaps, solely to keep a watchful eye on his darker tendencies. There was just the one time...but I will never know for sure. The elder Clawsons passed away before Clyde's sixteenth birthday and he promptly returned with me to the plantation where he became master of the entire estate. Rumors swirled among the staff, none ever proven, but none ever refuted. Shortly after Clawson's return, a young boy from

Moss Landing disappeared suddenly while out fishing on the river that ran near the Clawson plantation. Folks had seen young Clyde near where the boy was last seen, very close to a still smoldering fire pit....

Matt dropped the manuscript, his belly twisting in unease. He thought of the two men who'd recently gone missing and imagined what could have become of them. He placed a hand on the curve of Hank's spine, drawing comfort from the rise and fall of the little dog's breath. Matt's eyes were gritty from fatigue, and he'd read enough for one night. He already knew the truth. Clawson *was* a monster.

Rearranging the stack of pillows and switching off the lamp, he shifted his body down under the covers, and with a last look at the starry night, closed his eyes.

Although the bed was comfortable and he was tired from a long day, Matt struggled to fall asleep, visions of cannibals and secret labs scrolling through his head. When, toward morning, he did finally fall into a deep slumber, he dreamed of men dancing wildly around a fire, gnawed bones clenched in their hands. They all chanted in unison, some dancers dressed in ancient-looking garb and others wearing modern business suits. One man looked a lot like Colonel Clawson.

CHAPTER 16

Matt awoke to the sonorous and continued clanging of Nana B's mealtime bell a few hundred feet away. Hank stirred at his side, roused from his little nest in the rumpled bedding, and sniffed the air as the scent of bacon wafted through the open window. Moments later, a voice called from just outside the boathouse door: "Coffee's on...Breakfast time, come and get it!"

Rubbing the drowsiness from his eyes, Matt yawned and stretched, still tired from his late night and restless sleep. He ran his hand through his unruly tangle of hair, pushing the strands back from his face, then ruefully rubbed his day's growth of beard. Grabbing his backpack, he pulled out clean chinos and a slightly rumpled polo shirt, which he donned quickly before grabbing a sleepy Hank and climbing back down the ladder from the sleeping loft. He pushed his feet into his old leather flip-flops, then headed back up to the house, his little dog tagging along behind.

Today was Thanksgiving, and Matt hadn't had a good one for a long while now. Somehow, he knew this one would be different. He was pretty sure he was the only sailor from Texas within fifty miles of Jasmine Island, but he had never felt as welcomed and at home as he did now, waved on up to the cottage by Nana B herself, and greeted by warm smiles and friendly voices that drew him right into the heart of the home. Matt lingered in the kitchen for a moment, hoping to help with some chore to show his gratitude for his inclusion in the family gathering, but Nana just laughed and shooed him out onto the porch.

Breakfast was apparently to be a quick, casual "come and go," with food already laid out, as before, on the long wooden table. A big urn of rich-smelling coffee and a platter of bacon and scrambled eggs awaited hungry guests, and warm biscuits peeped from under checked tea towels. Fresh whipped butter and various preserves were set out nearby. Tiny was already seated at the table with Hannah and a couple of older gentlemen that Matt recognized as Tiny's uncles. Most of the action—and family—seemed to be in the kitchen, where preparations for the noontime feast were already well underway. Mingling with the breakfast smells of coffee and bacon were the distinctive holiday notes of roasting meat and savory herbs.

"Matt...good morning! How'd you sleep?" asked Tiny. Then, before Matt had a chance to respond, his friend waxed on, nostalgically: "Like a baby, right? Out over the water, the sound of the waves...the ocean breeze..."

Matt nodded and smiled, hoping that his bleary eyes did not betray his fatigue. "It was great—thank you. And thank y'all for the hospitality. This is the best holiday I've had in a long time."

"You are so welcome, my friend. And today, get ready to eat and rest and eat some more. Nana's Thanksgiving feasts are legendary. You'll go home dreaming of the juicy roast turkey she's famous for—'locally sourced,' as the city folks say—from the front yard!" replied Tiny.

Hannah caught Matt's eye and raised her eyebrows. He could tell she was eager to talk to him about the manuscript, and he himself was eager to resume their conversation from the night before. But, sensing that she wished to keep her secrets between the two of them, Matt merely smiled and, noting that Tiny was momentarily distracted by a conversation between the two uncles, gave her a tiny nod and tapped his watch, mouthing the word "later."

Filling his plate with eggs, bacon and a fluffy biscuit topped with butter and what looked like fresh blackberry preserves, Matt tucked into his breakfast and listened to the banter of the two old men, though he struggled with the unique language they spoke to each other. From Hannah, he'd learned that the Gullah Geechee people had a long and rich history, mostly preserved through the tradition of the oral story—passed one to another over hundreds of years. From the conversation that Tiny's uncles were having, Matt could only make out an occasional word here and there, along with a name that he recognized all too well: "Clahsssssn," spoken low and slowly with heavy emphasis on the "s" as if they were talking about some kind of a snakelike demon that dare not be named. Matt was now more certain than ever that the man might be precisely that.

He tried to distract himself from thoughts of "Cannibal Colonel," not wanting to let the monster ruin what had so far been a perfect holiday, so he petted Hank under the table and focused his efforts on finishing the last few bites of biscuit.

Despite Matt's halfhearted attempts to shoo Hank away from the dining area, his little sailing buddy remained stubbornly in place. The canine had whined a little at all the delicious smells and was being bribed into silence with bacon crumbs and bits of unbuttered biscuit. Hannah, having finished her own meal, scooped up the little dog and took him off in search of a bowl of actual dog food. By now, everyone else had cleaned their plates and idly sipped coffee as they traded island gossip. Tiny finally set down his mug and leaned across the table toward Matt.

"I need to go get cleaned up and do a couple of quick chores. Then, would you like to do a little fishing before the big feast?" he invited.

Matt nodded enthusiastically.

"Yes, I'd love to."

"Okay, I'll meet you back here in, say...an hour?"

Matt agreed and Tiny left, followed a moment later by the two uncles. Helping himself to another cup of coffee and lacing it with heavy cream, Matt sipped the rich brew and reflected on all the strange things he had learned from his late-night reading. Only moments into his reverie, the screen door banged and Hannah came back out onto the porch with Hank at her heels. Matt reached down and lifted the little dog onto his lap, where he made a single circle, then curled up.

"Nana B says I'm 'in her way'"—Hannah made air quotes—"and told me to come out and keep 'that nice boy from Texas' company." She winked and plopped down opposite him, leaning both elbows on the table and lowering her voice conspiratorially.

"Which is great, because I've been dying to know what you thought of the manuscript, and to tell you...well, everything else." She exhaled heavily.

Matt rubbed his temple as he slowly shook his head.

"This is some crazy shit, Hannah...the butler, the manuscript...Clawson? I'm worried you're mixed up in something really bad."

"You're right, Matt, it's really bad...and you don't even know the half of it yet."

"Then tell me—what's going on?"

Hannah's hands were now in her hair, gripping her scalp as if struggling to hold in her thoughts. Matt reached across the table and touched her elbow lightly. She lowered her hands to the table and raised one palm face up. Matt clasped her hand and gave it a brief squeeze.

"What is it, Hannah?"

Hannah raised her gaze to his and smiled wryly. "Okay, buckle up. Here's where things get really weird."

Matt cocked his head. "Weirder than wanna-be cannibal kids? You've got my interest now."

"Yeah...definitely weirder than that. So . . . first, the manuscript. When I found it—and the rest—I stupidly confronted Mitch. I mean, what kind of monster would . . ." She held up her hand. "Sorry, sorry, I'm getting way ahead of myself."

Matt smiled reassuringly. "Go ahead. Take your time."

"Okay, so the manuscript...that asshole actually admitted he'd copied it from the old man's laptop and was holding on to it until Hopkins died. The butler wasn't in the best of health, and Mitch figured the old guy didn't have that long to live. Mitch was planning to sell the story anonymously and apparently told himself—and me—that since Hopkins didn't have a family of his own, *he* was the closest thing to it."

Matt rolled his eyes.

"Your ex sounds like a total jerk."

Hannah's curls bobbed as she nodded enthusiastically. "I know, I know...I was a total idiot, you don't have to say it..."

Matt protested, but she rolled her eyes and held up her hand.

"No, really, I'm so pissed at myself, but *anyway*," she said, emphasizing the last word as if to close the subject of her poor choice in men, and continued. "Anyway...Mitch spilled, and I mean *spilled,* the whole damn thing. Honestly, in retrospect, I should have been scared about what he'd do to me after I uncovered all his top-secret shit, but I wasn't. I just...had to know. And he may be an a-hole, but he's a cowardly one and honestly pretty naive, because when I told him we were finished, all he was worried about was if I would tell anyone. When I swore, hand to heart, that I wouldn't tell a soul, he believed me. I headed out to Jasmine the next day and blocked him from my contacts." Hannah winked. "Now here's the part where you find out that I'm not great at keeping secrets, because I'm going to tell you everything that Mitch told me. So, I know I told you about Mitch and his nasty hybrid meat 'nuggets.' Well, before he went to work for the Colonel, he'd just finished his doctorate in animal tissue engineering, or what some people call 'test tube meat.'"

Matt nodded, and Hannah continued.

"So the Colonel had learned that some of his overseas competitors were about to market lab-grown 'chicken' and decided if he wanted to stay on top of the market, that he should invest in this new technology before all of his nasty chicken farms became obsolete. He bumped Mitch's salary up to the high six figures and put him in charge of his new pet project. After a few months, Mitch had developed—and the Colonel had patented—a process for growing vats of chicken cell cultures that, in only a few days, produced vast quantities of nearly perfect white flesh for his nuggets. This cell-cultured meat, or 'cultivated meat,' as Mitch preferred to call it, could be grown using a slurry made from leftover chicken waste, industrial detergents, and whatever else they scraped off the floor of the processing plant."

Matt made a disgusted face.

"So, with their new technology, the Colonel could still keep up the disgusting and inhumane farming practices he was used to, and make his entire operation even more competitive by growing his 'other' chicken with what was, essentially, toxic waste."

Then, catching sight of Matt's expression, she said, "Agreed. Disgusting. But, about to become so much more so." She glanced across the table at his empty plate. "The next bit goes down best on an empty stomach." Hannah passed a hand over her mouth and grimaced. "This is the part I didn't ask Mitch about. It was just too"—her words trailed off—"too much. You'll know what I mean in a minute."

She paused for a moment, gazing over Matt's shoulder as if gathering her thoughts.

"Okay...so I'm a little embarrassed about how nosy I actually was...because the last file I discovered was hidden within a file that was within another file that contained an old and *very* personal diary from Mitch's high school days...so I really did some digging to find it."

At this, Hannah blushed, the color pinking her cheeks.

"I get it," Matt laughed. "I'd have done the same thing in your shoes. Well, maybe not fallen for Mitch. He doesn't sound like my type."

Hannah giggled. "It turns out he wasn't my type, either. But seriously, this was where the shit gets crazy. Crazier than crazy, if that's possible." Hannah again lowered her voice, although it was just the two of them there. "It turns out that the meat the Colonel was most interested in growing was...human."

Matt recoiled inadvertently and as Hannah continued, couldn't help but recall the words a horrified Charlton Heston had uttered, after learning of a similar diabolical plot in the old sci-fi movie *Soylent Green*: *"It's people!"*

"Apparently, Clawson's bizarre perversion was something he shared with other deranged sickos all over the world. He'd found a secret site on the dark web called the "Circle of Tantalus." It's a society for uber-rich, modern-day 'enthusiasts' and named after a son of Zeus who, according to Google, wasn't actually a cannibal but had tried to feed his own son to the gods at a feast. To punish Tantalus for this, and other things, the gods placed him in a pool of water from which he couldn't drink, and kept him just out of reach of a tree laden with delicious fruit. The myth is where the word 'tantalize' originated. Anyway, according to Mitch's files, the members of the Circle of Tantalus apparently believe the same thing as Clawson...that if you consume – or even just just possess a bit of your enemy - you will in turn become more powerfu...

"Wait a sec," interrupted Matt. "So the Colonel was trying to grow human...whatever... in a lab. But whose...oh God, um...*where* was he getting the—"

"I'm getting to that...just hang on. So the Colonel thought that by using lab-grown 'tissue', he was giving these sickos what they craved while doing 'God's work' by saving actual people from being consumed. And of course, profiting from a fresh market that would pay top dollar for this new product."

Matt nodded impatiently. "Okay, so then how..."

Hannah rolled her eyes. "Patience...I'm going to tell you. Mitch always talked about how vain the Colonel was. There was this super-exclusive plastic surgery clinic in Charleston he'd visit for an occasional "touch-up," which catered to Hollywood stars and country music royalty, as well as to some of the world's most powerful business executives and world leaders. Well, the Colonel began dating a nurse who worked there. He'd fly her in on his fancy helicopter and spend hours locked away with her in his suite. I realized, from reading Mitch's files, that she must be his...source. Her boss, a Doctor Hoffmann, kept a secret collection of frozen tissue samples from all of his patients, and *she* would have had access to his high-tech cryo-freezing chamber. So, via his girlfriend, the Colonel then had access to little bits of everyone, from dead celebrities like Elvis and Marilyn Monroe, to living ones like that country singer Polly Darton, even though they always kept her visits to the clinic hush-hush. Dr. Hoffman had little souvenirs from some of the world's biggest movers and shakers, even that genius who started his own space program after getting bored with making electric cars. Every time someone rich and famous came into his clinic for a little nip and tuck, no matter how small, Dr. Hoffman took a souvenir. So, the Colonel—"

"Had access to all the cell samples he needed," interrupted Matt.

"Right? Not only could he make lab-grown 'bits' of people from these samples, but he could also offer his clients—literally—a taste of stardom." Hannah concluded.

Matt sat back, mind reeling. He remembered reading that several cultures, including the original inhabitants of Samoa, once believed they could gain "mana" or spiritual power by consuming a part of their enemy. Not only had the Colonel trampled on his life and Tiny's, but now he was playing God. As this bizarre tale permeated Matt's brain, he wondered how such a nice girl could have become mixed up with her twisted creep of an ex, and how all of this related back to the events that had taken Tiny's wife from his life and Julie from his own.

"He's a sick bastard," he said finally. "A sick, twisted excuse for a son of a bitch who cares no more about human life than he does for something growing out of a test tube."

"Who . . . Mitch or Clawson? asked Hannah, tilting her head.

"Both of them. They deserve each other," said Matt. He pondered a moment, unsure of the direction he was about to take. Maybe it was too soon, or too much... *But no.* His journey had brought him here: to Jasmine Island, to Tiny's story and now Hannah's. It seemed only right to share his own. And so, he did, filling in the gaps of the story he'd begun earlier, telling her first of Julie's death, then the long court battle and, finally, his legal and personal defeat. Hannah's eyes grew wet with tears as Matt's voice, thick with emotion, poured out his tale. She reached across the table for his hand, and this time, he didn't let go.

He had barely finished speaking when the screen door slammed once more and Tiny came out onto the porch. His deep brown eyes crinkled as he caught sight of the joined hands on the table, and he smiled knowingly at the couple. The long, slow nod that followed looked a lot like a seal of approval.

Later that Thanksgiving Day, at the same long table, they feasted on everything from peas and rice to roast turkey. Also cornbread-oyster dressing, mashed sweet potatoes, roast pork, shrimp and grits (*much better than Spam and grits,* decided Matt), okra and hot fried corn cakes, which were passed around the table in a wide sweet-grass basket, along with a big bowl of homemade butter. Nana B even took a big pork bone with lots of meat still clinging to it out to little Hank, who was sitting on his bottom just outside the porch's screen door, furiously wiggling his stubby tail.

Matt was mostly quiet during the meal, enjoying the friendly clamor of voices and the delicious food, but still consumed both by everything he'd just learned and by feelings at once familiar and yet strangely new, which grew inside him like seedlings bursting through soil in search of light. Some crazy collision of forces had guided him to this mossy little cluster of islands, and he was both terrified and excited to find out what their purpose was.

CHAPTER 17

The sun was low on the horizon as Tiny's skiff carved a path through the waves on the way back to "Chucktown." They'd departed Jasmine Island bearing bags of neatly packed leftovers, unforgettable memories, and, in Matt's case, Hannah's cell phone number stored in his contacts.

Nana B had wrapped him in a tight hug as they said their farewells, then leaned back as she released him, fixing her warm brown eyes on his and smiling.

"May the good Lord watch over you, young man. Come back and see us on your way out. Who knows? I might even put you to work. I can't afford to pay you much, but I promise to feed you, and feed you well. And I'm sure you'll find some good company if you're back this way. Here, Matt, take this, something to protect you," she added, and handed Matt a small bundle of what felt like seeds and dried herbs, wrapped in burlap, and tied with a ribbon. "Mojo," was all she said. Matt would later learn that besides being a devout Christian, Nana B was also well-versed in the art of hoodoo, also known as rootwork or "low-country magic."

She gave an exaggerated wink and inclined her head in Hannah's direction. Hannah was grinning, looking pointedly away. They'd already said their goodbyes in private earlier that morning, out on the porch, and when she asked if they could keep in touch, Matt had squeezed her hand and promised that they would. Even though it would mean a significant detour en route to Florida, Matt was hoping to return to Jasmine Island before picking up the thread of his journey.

Matt and Tiny chatted idly, each of them recalling how much they'd missed good old home cooking while serving overseas, then finally lapsing into a comfortable silence. Having traveled so far from home with only his own thoughts and a small dog for company, the recent flurry of social interaction had left Matt with a lot to digest—physically and mentally.

After the delicious Thanksgiving feast, they'd helped Nana B clear the table on the back porch and had taken the scraps down to feed to the family's pigs, which were housed behind the barn. Matt was astonished to find that almost everything they'd eaten had come from the little farm, and that nothing seemed to be wasted. Even though he'd grown up in the country, most of his family's food had come from the grocery store, and he realized that he, like most Americans, didn't really know where most of the food he ate came from. Watching the chickens running around outside, pecking at bugs and plants, he felt sickened at the thought of all the animals pumped up with chemicals, hormones, and antibiotics, and forced to live in cages for the entirety of their miserable lives.

Everyone in Tiny's family, from his little cousins to octogenarian Nana B, was vital and active, and even the cranky uncles didn't complain of aches and ailments like many of his own elderly relatives. Matt rubbed his belly and resolved at that moment to eat a more natural diet, drink less alcohol, consume fewer helpings of canned mystery meats, and generally get himself whipped into shape for his round-the-world voyage. He gazed out over the stretch of silvery water. It wasn't the ideal time of year to head off to sail the Caribbean, but if Tiny were able to finish the repairs to *Lonesome Dove* soon, Matt could sail short hops offshore between cold fronts, and duck into the shelter of the Intracoastal Waterway when he had to, until he reached the tip of Florida. From there, he'd sail across the Gulf Stream, on to Bimini, then the Berry Islands and Great Abaco Island, maybe stopping for a while to snorkel in the pristine waters of the Exumas before heading on to the Dominican Republic, and from there...

"Sorry, what was that?" he asked, aware that he'd become lost in his musings and missed Tiny's question.

Tiny laughed and shook his head.

"I asked if you were going to see Hannah again. I can tell that girl likes you."

Matt felt his face flush, feeling ludicrously like a teenager getting ribbed by his buddies for a not-so-secret crush.

"Yeah, I like her too," he admitted. " I dunno, I guess I just have to see how everything...works out," he said lamely.

Tiny paused a moment before speaking again, glancing at Matt's flushed face before turning his eyes back toward the rapidly approaching shoreline and marina.

"It was hard for me too...after I lost Marie. I kind of gave up on being happy—like my being happy meant I was forgetting." His fingers tightened on the wheel.

"You won't ever stop remembering Julie. But I think you can be happy again without feeling like you've forgotten. You'll see."

With those words, Tiny eased back on the throttle and cut the wheel, preparing to dock the Carolina Skiff, while Matt flipped out the fenders and grabbed the lines, ready to assist. Busying themselves with docking and then unloading the boat allowed Tiny's small kindness—just those few words—to linger for an instant, like the scent of a woman's perfume stolen by the breeze.

While Hank, obviously relieved to be free from the jud dering bounce of the skiff, trotted along the dock toward the boatyard, the two men said their goodbyes. Then, Matt followed his dog, clutching a bag that contained some of Nana B's roast turkey and dressing, as well as a slice of her mouthwatering pecan pie, and made his way back through the rows of boats to *Lonesome Dove*.

The old boat smelled musty after two days of being closed up on the hard, and he opened up all the sliders to catch some of the fresh air coming in from the ocean. It was only dusk, but he grew unaccountably sleepy and yawned widely as he crawled into the V-berth with Hank. Despite his fatigue, his thoughts kept spiraling back to Hannah and the wild tangle of the story she'd spun. Matt didn't doubt that she was telling him the truth, but he was still wary of the reach of the Clawson undertow, always there, ready to pull him under. The details of that perverse tale squirmed around in his gray matter, though, and he found he just couldn't let them go. He didn't know if it was his involvement with the corrupt corporation, or Tiny's or Hannah's, but he felt that maybe his part of the story was not yet over. In the end, curiosity won out and he pulled out his phone, swiping the spiderweb cracks in its glossy surface to pull it to life. He clicked the message icon first, finding himself unaccountably disappointed that there was nothing new—or, at least, nothing from Hannah.

Then, fingers clumsy on the tiny screen, he typed "Circle of Tantalus" into the search bar. The screen bloomed with options: links referencing Greek mythology, tourism, geology, art and a couple that sounded fringe and New Age. As he scrolled down further, he finally found one that looked promising, clicked and waited. The black page bled, top to bottom, deep crimson blossoming over the small screen. Then, in the upper right-hand corner, a tiny skull-shaped icon appeared, with the words *"Only Those Who Are Worthy May Enter"* immediately under it. Matt clicked on the link, and a message from his browser popped up. *"Hmm, we're having trouble finding this site..."* it read. Noticing that the ominous link had a suffix he'd never seen before—".onion"—he did a quick Google search and soon learned he needed a special browser, called *Tor*, to visit this address on the dark web.

Matt's better instincts told him to just stop right there, to close the page and call it a night, but his sense of curiosity

got the best of him. Pulling the cushions off the settee, he
opened up the under-seat storage and unearthed his old laptop, connecting the cable and plugging it into the long
extension cord that Tiny had been using for his power
tools. After waiting for it to boot up, and then tethering it
to the hotspot from his phone, he was ready. It wasn't long
before the download of the Tor browser was complete and
installed on his laptop. He returned to the ominous-look-
ing Tantalus website and clicked the link. Now, instead of
an error message, he was looking at a simple black-and-
white screen displaying the words "*This is a Private Website
for Members of the Circle of Tantalus Only. Authorized
Users Must Present Biometric ID To Proceed.*"

Matt flopped back on the bed, frustrated. What was all
this about "biometric ID" and what people had their own
secret website requiring CIA-level skullduggery to even access it? Although he wasn't much of a computer guy, he
knew enough to be wary of messing around with the dark
web, the deep underbelly of the Internet, where one could
order anything from cocaine or meth, to a hitman, and pay
for it anonymously with Bitcoin or some other cryptocur-
rency. But...behind this virtual steel door could be the
answers he was looking for, answers that might help finally
bring down Colonel Clawson.

Threading his fingers behind his head, he gazed out the
slider at the darkening sky. From the beginning, Hannah's
story had sounded a bit like something from a Carl Hiaasen
novel, ringing with truth and more than a touch of over-
the-top, but the creepy login page really plopped the proverbial cherry on top. He needed to know more and,

maybe, just maybe, find something like justice—not just for him, or Julie—but for all of Clawson's victims: past, present, and future. Closing his eyes and breathing in the peculiar scent of salt, fiberglass, wood, and must, he thought back to what Tiny had said about remembering and not forgetting, and then of happiness. He made a mental note to reach out to an old friend back in Austin who had been a hacker in the good old days...then, moments later, he was fast asleep.

The next few days were a flurry of activity. Matt made several trips to town to replenish his food stores and do laundry. At a local marine supply store, he purchased waterproof containers to store food, clothing, and spare parts, and even one in which to store Hank's poop bags. He wasn't eager for a repeat of what had happened on his voyage across the Gulf of Mexico. Tiny worked on finishing up the last of the fiberglass repairs: sanding the final coat of resin until it was silky smooth, before spraying on several coats of smelly marine epoxy, and following this up with several coats of antifouling paint to discourage barnacles from attempting to hitch a free ride.

A strong cold front was blowing in and Matt needed to wait for the weather to settle down before anchoring out in the bay. Tiny loaned him a small electric space heater, which he secured safely up on the gimbaled cooking stove. It made hunkering down in the cramped quarters during the nasty weather a bit more tolerable. That night, a steady rain mixed with sleet fell, and the north wind howled relentlessly. Matt could actually feel his boat moving a bit with each gust, despite her being tied down to the heavy jack stands and wooden braces. At one point, the wind blowing through the rigging moaned—a low, sad, eerily human sound. Matt had heard that sailors called this sound the "death moan," for when you heard it out on the open ocean, it was like the call of the Grim Reaper. At this point in his voyage, he was actually glad that his boat was sitting up on dry land and not anchored out in the bay.

He and Hank survived the night, and by dawn the wind had subsided a little, but not enough to stop the sound of dozens of halyards clanking against sailboat masts up and down the rows of boats in the yard. Once the sun was fully up, Matt finally emerged from the warmth of *Lonesome Dove*'s snug little cocoon, braced himself against the chilly morning air, donned the prized Helly Hansen sailing jacket Julie had once bought him, and made his way down to the office to settle his account. After extracting what seemed like an endless stream of paper from a noisy old track feed printer, Billy presented Matt with the final invoice. The bill was much less than he'd expected but would still put a dent in his already tight sailing budget. He thanked Billy for the prompt turnaround, for the use of his private mooring ball, and lastly threw in a generous word of praise in for his best employee, Tiny, who'd done the lion's share of the work.

Back at the boat, after Matt had ensured that he'd stowed everything neatly away, Tiny drove up in the big travel-lift machine, and with the help of several yard workers, wrestled *Lonesome Dove* up into the massive sling, and then carried her slowly down to the boat ramp and lowered her gently back into the sea. She rocked enthusiastically on the waves, as if grateful to be returned to her element. A classy-looking old boat, she'd looked ungainly perched up on jack stands, and Matt was relieved to see her back in the water. Now, he and Hank could resume their travels.

Although adventure beckoned him in most of his waking thoughts, he was a little blue. He knew that the next leg of his journey meant turning the page on this one, and he'd enjoyed visiting with Tiny, especially knowing that they shared the unique kinship of Clawson victims. Over the past couple of years, waves of sadness and a feeling of being alone and lost in the world had come over him when he wasn't keeping busy, but the past few weeks had given him a new sense of belonging and contentment. It wasn't as though he'd forgotten or misplaced his misery—it would always be there, tucked away in a drawer in his mind—but he felt lighter than he had in a long time and he found he felt okay about letting happiness back into his life and edging the door closed on its flip side: guilt.

Later that afternoon, seated at the dinette in *Lonesome Dove*'s galley, Matt pulled his large nautical chart toward him, smoothed out the folds, and placed his new Weems & Plath nautical protractor upon it. He traced a couple of potential routes lightly in pencil. One of them, a couple of days out of the way, would take him on to Jasmine Island where he could see Hannah again and fulfill his promise to visit Nana B's. As if guided by a force stronger than his will, the pencil seemed to help make the decision for him, and his hand pressed more firmly when he traced a line along the edge of the protractor toward Jasmine Island.

That night Matt slept fitfully, as changing winds blew across Charleston Harbor. No longer tied securely to

Bullfrog's owner's mooring ball, he was now hanging out "on the hook," relying solely on a length of strong line leading to *Lonesome Dove*'s heavy plow anchor, which he hoped was securely dug into the mud at the bottom of the harbor. The wind continued to pick up, and several times, he woke to check the anchor line as *Lonesome Dove* tilted on the waves like a seesaw. Throughout the long night he slept only a few minutes at a time, tossing and turning up in the V-berth, wrestling with his decision to return to Jasmine Island, knowing that doing so would open the door on another crazy Clawson nightmare. An alternate route would take him toward Florida and on to the Bahamas, leaving the past behind. From his time in Iraq, to the months spent battling Clawson's lawyers in court, maybe he'd seen enough conflict to last for this lifetime.

Around 5:00 a.m., Matt awoke abruptly and glanced at his phone. He'd failed to turn off his notifications, and a text had just come in with its distinctive chime. He squinted at the tiny screen, then sat bolt upright.

Sorry to bother you, but I could use a friend. There's trouble in paradise. Will you please call me when you get this? Thx.

Seeing that Hannah had just sent the text, Matt figured it was okay to call this early. Rubbing the sleep from his eyes, he clicked the phone icon above her message. She must have been in the sleeping loft, where she had a signal, because she answered on the first ring.

Her voice sounded keyed up and electric, as though she hadn't slept at all.

"Hey Matt, thank you so much for calling me back. I hope I didn't wake you, but I couldn't sleep. I didn't know what to do, and you're the only one who knows the entire story. Do you have time to talk?"

Matt smiled, even though he knew she couldn't see him.

"No worries, it's all good. What's up, Hannah?"

He could hear Hannah draw a deep breath, as if steeling herself for what was to come.

"Okay, so when you guys left—that smell I told you about? The awful smell from the Clawson plant? It got really bad. And you know why?" She didn't wait for an answer, but plunged in. "They've parked four barges just offshore from Jasmine. They're piled high with manure and slaughterhouse waste. When I called the state Department of Health and Environmental Control, they told me that Clawson has permission for a special permanent anchorage for their waste barges. They must have bribed some state officials because there is no way that's legit."

"What the hell—?" Matt muttered before Hannah cut him off.

"But here's the worst part: Clawson is sending teams of lawyers to visit families on all the islands, offering to purchase their property at rock-bottom prices and issuing vague warnings if they refuse to sell. Matt, it's not enough that he has the largest island in the area—he wants them all!"

She took a breath, and Matt chimed in. "What is he up to? What does he need all that land for?"

"Well," she responded, "I've been calling around and talking to friends and family to figure it out. It sounds like he wants to expand his factory farming operations...or maybe to build more processing plants? I think he wants to be somewhere with no oversight—far from the prying eyes of government regulators."

"So he can continue with his disgusting experiments as well," added Matt.

"Exactly!" said Hannah. "Not only that, but I found out that on one island, on heirs property that he basically stole from my relatives, he's built several rows of shoddy apartment buildings, which he rents out to his own employees at ridiculously high prices. Now some of these people are having to pay nearly half a month's wages to live on the island where their own, paid-for homes once stood. He's putting in 'Clawson's Mini Marts' as well, selling everything at hugely inflated prices, just like those "company stores" that mining companies once forced workers to buy from in the coal towns of Appalachia. And get this—he's planning to buy up all the local gas stations, which will drive up fuel prices, so it's too expensive to drive to Charleston for groceries. Now the workers will have no choice but to shop at his crappy 'Mini Marts.'"

Matt could almost visualize her making angry air quotes.

"He can't keep doing this. Not with more land, not on more islands. Matt, what can we do? We have to do *something*!"

Matt took a long breath, looking from the peacefully slumbering Hank coiled up on his pillow to the gray morning outside.

"I'm not sure, Hannah, but yeah, we've got to do something. Sit tight, I'm gonna head your way."

And with those words, his course was set. He was on his way back to Jasmine Island.

CHAPTER 18

Matt dumped out the last tepid sip of instant coffee from his metal Pussers' Rum cup. He was so eager to be underway that he hadn't bothered to heat the water, and the cost of the quick caffeination was a mouthful of brownish water and coffee-flavored sludge. Hastily, he tidied up the galley, fed Hank and secured him in his little doggy life jacket, then went above deck and hauled up the anchor. He would text Tiny later that morning, knowing beyond certainty that their paths would soon cross again. Motoring up into the wind, he went through the process of hoisting and trimming sails, a task he was now much faster at completing than when he'd first departed Texas. He killed the engine and set out on a tack toward the mouth of the harbor.

Glancing at the large-scale navigational chart, he noted the obstacles and shoals that he'd have to avoid, and in pencil scrawled several GPS waypoints that would take him on to Jasmine Island. Although he and Tiny had made the trip in only about an hour, the slower gait of the sailboat meant it would take him almost until evening to make the journey.

Setting his course out of Charleston Harbor, they glided slowly past the looming stone fortress of Ft. Sumter, then once clear of the shipping lanes, steered Southeast, passing by the stately silhouette of the Morris Island Lighthouse. For several hours, they sailed parallel to the distant shoreline until finally sighting the mouth of the channel that would lead him toward Jasmine Island.

The sea was choppy, as was usual for this time of year, but he and Hank made good time, *Lonesome Dove* bouncing along at a nice clip. Just as the sun was dipping below the horizon, they arrived at their destination, dropping anchor with a splash in the middle of the protected harbor. The sight of a thin plume of smoke gently rising from Nana B's chimney filled Matt with a sense of calm. Strangely, he felt almost like this was a homecoming. The wind shifted then, and he caught a whiff of something foul—a smell of death and decay. It must have been coming from the barge Hannah had mentioned. He hadn't caught sight of them as he entered the harbor, so he realized they'd been stationed on the windward side of the land, causing the odor to have maximum potency as the prevailing winds swept it over Jasmine Island. He sighed in disgust, his hand involuntarily moving to cover his nose.

Hannah must have seen him sailing into the harbor, because as he turned to go below deck, he caught sight of her head of wild curls and her huge smile as she paddled out to meet him in one of the kid's battered plastic kayaks.

He waited for her, watching her paddle dip from side to side, water splashing silver in the early evening light. A smile spread across his face, and his pulse quickened.

"Long time no see, Sailor!" she called up as she pulled alongside.

"Too long," laughed Matt.

"Permission to come aboard, Captain?"

Matt grabbed her hand as Hannah struggled to make the long step up from the low kayak and onto *Lonesome Dove*'s higher deck. She tied the kayak's bowline quickly to one of the boat's side cleats and kneeled to greet little Hank, whose stubby tail was now beating a furious tattoo against the cockpit's fiberglass sidewall.

Their linked hands formed an awkward handshake, which turned into a tight hug, which turned into a kiss that lingered. Then, Hannah pulled away and flopped down onto the cockpit bench, her wide smile slowly fading. She sighed, long and loud.

"I've spent most of today calling around to find out everything I can about what's going on. Nana B's called some of her old friends and I recruited some aunties and uncles to reach out to our neighbors. This is a mess, Matt."

"I want to hear everything. Can I grab you a beer?"

"Yes, please," Hannah agreed.

Matt ducked below and grabbed a couple of cold cans, emerging topside and handing one to Hannah. She popped the top and took a long swallow.

"So, I know I told you about Clawson's people wanting to gobble up more land by basically stealing heirs property from local families?" Matt nodded as she continued. "Well, apparently it's not just about rock-bottom offers…his people are actually threatening us. They're telling us that the waste barges are never going away, and that our best—our *only*—choice is to sell to Clawson before even more of them are docked in the 'newly authorized' anchoring zone. They're only offering a quarter of the land's value!"

Matt shook his head. "That's bullshit. It's just a new twist on an old scheme. I watched a YouTube documentary the other night about the land grab for Gullah Geechee-owned property. Developers are desperate to get their hands on land, and some people are desperate enough that they will sell. They also use dirty little tricks, like paying back taxes to the county before the rightful owners even know they owe anything. Greedy folk have been trying to get their hands on this land since after the Civil War, when families finally got deeds for some of the land from the U.S. government. The amount of black-owned land is now just a fraction of what it was fifty years ago. Many families wind up being forced to sell because of hard times, or because of pressure from wealthy landowners who want to annex their small farms to their sprawling plantations. Enter Clawson as the next contender."

Hannah sat up, gesturing wildly. "Yes! That's exactly what's happening! Damn, look at you, learning stuff on YouTube," she said, winking before her face once again turned serious. "Now Clyde Clawson is the one doing the lion's share of land grabbing. He's bought nearly ten-thousand acres of heirs property for next to nothing these past few years. What's going to be left after he's done?"

"Nothing," said Matt emphatically. "He's going to keep on grabbing until there's nothing left. We've got to do something about this, Hannah. We can't let any more people lose their homes. I want to help, but honestly, I don't know where to start."

Hannah slumped back, sipping her beer. She folded her legs crisscross and buried her head in her hands.

"It's too much for just the two of us to handle," she murmured dejectedly.

For a moment, they both sat lost in thought, Matt stroking Hank's warm back and trying not to stare too openly at Hannah's long bare legs.

"Well," he said finally, "we can start by exposing this sick scheme of his."

"Which one?" asked Hannah, "The one to grow 'people nuggets' or the one to make 'chicken' ones out of toxic waste?"

"Both," said Matt with gusto, "they're equally revolting."

"And illegal, too," said Hannah, visibly brightening. "Using toxic waste to grow chicken meat? Check! And cultivating...whatever... for rich weirdos to buy? Double check, I say."

"Well," drawled Matt, "I don't know about his plan to grow chicken meat in a lab from his waste . . . he can probably get away with that. The government will make CCM—cell-cultured meat—legal very soon. But the way he's going about it...using waste from his slaughterhouses to make a slurry to feed the cell cultures? That probably isn't legal at all. As for the 'other thing' he wants to sell to his Circle of Tantalus friends, no way in hell is that legal. Using a person's genetic material without their permission is a crime, although it's been done before. You've heard the story of Henrietta Lacks, right?"

Hannah tilted her head and nodded tentatively. "I think so . . . wasn't she that black woman who donated her cells to a university back in the fifties? I can't really remember the whole story."

"You got it," Matt said "She actually *unknowingly* donated her cells to Johns Hopkins University in 1951. Scientists still use her cells—"HeLa cells," they call them. They're unique because they literally never die. You can find HeLa cells in every major biological research facility around the world. I read, or actually, listened, to an audiobook about her while I was working on the boat: *The Immortal Life of Henrietta Lacks.* Pharmaceutical companies have made millions from selling her cells, while her family never even got one dime. Not to mention the fact that Ms. Lacks hadn't even consented to any of it."

Matt paused and held up his hand. "Wait—I think I've got it, Hannah! That's how we can hang Clawson. For theft of property—genetic material being the property stolen. This business with the barges, that's not right either. I don't care how high his bribes and payoffs go...they don't go all the way up and at some point the law has to catch up with him. We just have to get the truth out there. If all of this becomes public knowledge, he'll have nowhere to hide."

Hannah nodded in agreement, tapping her knees excitedly. "You know, one of my college friends is a reporter for WCHRS news in Charleston. We could send her my files, maybe even get some photos or videos from the barges and see if she could run the story."

"That sounds great," Matt enthused. "I was just thinking...I've got a friend, Bruce, back in Austin, who's a computer geek and used to be a major hacker. I think I need to call him and see if he's willing to hack into the Circle of Tantalus website. If he could uncover anything about the identity of these people, that would give us even more leverage."

Hannah clapped her hands, her eyes shining despite the darkening sky.

"Yes! Yes! That's a great idea, Matt." She let out a tremendous sigh and reached for his hand, pulling him toward her.

"You were right. The two of us alone can't bring down Clawson. We're going to need a team and it sounds like we've got the makings of one already!"

Hank suddenly found himself on the floor of the cockpit and Matt found himself beside Hannah on the bench, her slim arms around his neck, and his mouth on hers. They jumped apart suddenly as a knocking sounded on the boat's hull. Leaning over the lifelines, they saw one of Tiny's cousins pulled alongside in his fishing skiff.

"Hey y'all, didn't mean to scare you. I'm just heading back home. Nana B was hoping you'd come to dinner, but figured you were having fun visiting." He passed a paper plate, wrapped in foil, up toward Matt.

"Shrimp and grits, buttered cornbread and sweet potato pie from Nana B. She says "Breakfast 'll be on at 'day clean'" - that means daybreak, don't be late!

Matt and Hannah thanked him profusely and waved as he pushed off and paddled slowly back toward shore.

Hustling down below deck, Matt grabbed a couple of forks, and for the next few minutes they ate in silence, savoring Nana's excellent cooking and the peaceful sounds of the evening.

Hannah was the first to break the silence.

"You know, if I wasn't so worried about what Nana B thought about me, I just might stay and keep you company tonight. But...I don't want her to think I'm being a 'loose girl'—Nana's words—so I probably should get back to shore."

Matt was searching his brain for something clever to say when he glanced over to see the kayak that she'd borrowed, which apparently had drifted back to shore, being pulled up out of the water by a kid down at the dock.

"I guess that settles that," said Matt, nervous and excited all at once.

Hannah grinned, her teeth white against the backdrop of the darkening sky.

"And I guess I need a *real* sailor to show me how to tie a knot next time!" she said in a campy voice, fluttering her lashes and flapping her hands in faux helplessness.

That night, for the first time in over two years, Matt fell asleep cradling a warm body that wasn't Hank's, against his own. Or at least besides Hank's, for the little dog had scooted his butt against Matt's head and made himself comfortable on the pillow. Matt breathed in the rich coconut scent of Hannah's springy curls and felt the heat of her smooth skin press against his palms. The curves of her body fit against his in a way that felt both familiar and totally new. Tiny's words came to him then, and he knew that he'd reached a turning point. Maybe he didn't need to run so far from home to find happiness. Maybe it was closer than he'd thought.

Drifting across the water from the house up on the hill, they could hear the gentle sound of the old woman singing what sounded like an ancient love song. Obviously, Nana B didn't mind what Hannah got up to, as long as it was with that nice boy from Texas.

CHAPTER 19

The clang of the breakfast bell came far too early for Matt and Hannah. They crawled out of the V-berth wearing twin sleepy smiles, dressed hastily, and carried Hank up to the deck to do his business. While Hannah found the bag of kibble and fixed the little dog's breakfast, Matt hauled out the dinghy, which he'd rolled up and stored on deck for the voyage. He attached its little Yamaha outboard, and the trio climbed in, preparing to make the short ride over to the dock.

The morning was sunny and warm, without a cloud to mar the pristine blue sky. Matt cut the engine as they neared the shore and let the dinghy drift up to the pilings. As they pulled alongside, Hannah grabbed the bowline and stood up to tie the line to the metal deck cleat.

Matt rose beside her and nudged her playfully with his shoulder as he peered over her at her handiwork.

"You look pretty handy with that knot there. Do you only tie non-holding knots when you're hoping to get stranded?"

Hannah giggled and mock-slapped Matt's shoulder.

"No!" she protested, "But I was in a hurry to come aboard, so maybe I wasn't at my knot-tying best!'

Matt laughed, scooping Hank up onto the dock, then extended a hand to Hannah as the pair climbed out of the dinghy. The dog ran ahead toward the house and the promise of a second breakfast. Hannah seemed nervous as they approached the house, as if expecting a little side-eye judgment from Nana B, but none came. The old woman welcomed them with a smile that spread right up to her eyes. She laughed and said,

"I'm going to feed you, then I'm going to put you two to work. Eat up, because you'll be earning every bite."

Nana B was true to her word, and they soon found themselves climbing a ladder up to the roof, their bellies full and ready for their assigned project. The same strong cold front that had rattled *Lonesome Dove*'s perch in the boatyard had blown hard through the island, ripping several shingles off the roof and resulting in a leak directly above Nana B's bed. One of Tiny's cousins was just getting started making shingles in the old-fashioned way. He sliced pieces of cypress wood from a short log using a long ax-like tool he told them was called a *froe*, which he drove into the wood with a large wooden mallet. As Matt and Hannah located the damage and cleared away debris, Clive passed the freshly cut shingles up to the pair, who wiggled the edge of each piece underneath the remaining old shingles before finally nailing them into place.

The view from the rooftop was spectacular. To one side was deep, lush forest, and to the other was the family's

neatly tended fall garden, where plantings of onions, col-
lards and cabbage stretched out in neat rows, watched over
by a gangly homemade scarecrow. To the east, Matt could
see the neat little half-moon-shaped bay where *Lonesome
Dove* was anchored, mast set to swaying slowly side to side
by the small waves. As picturesque as this image was,
though, it was hard to ignore the "fowl odor" wafting their
way. Just outside the harbor, in the bay, six large barges,
filled to the brim with what surely was putrid chicken-farm
waste, leaked their particulate matter into the air and likely
into the surrounding water as well.

While waiting for Clive to make more shingles, they
took a quick break. Hannah lay back on the roof's gentle
incline, stretched her arms overhead, and rested her head on
her palms, gazing up at the sky. Matt wrapped one of her
curls around his finger and smiled down at her. Then,
catching a strong whiff of Clawson by-product, he wrinkled his nose.

"It's time. We need to get this...thing, going. I'm going
to give my friend Bruce a call while we're on break. We
should have a good signal up here." Hannah nodded and
turned her head, frowning slightly as she watched Matt
reach for his phone and pull up his contacts.

His old college friend was one of the earliest "old
school" hackers, and had known his way around a computer long before Austin had earned its reputation as
"Silicon Hills." Over the years, Bruce had caused his share
of mischief on the web, gotten himself arrested once or
twice for breaking into government networks, then finally
went legit, starting what was now one of the world's largest

antivirus software companies. Matt thought fondly of Bruce's complete and unrelenting nerdiness and of the depth and loyalty of his friendship, especially during Matt's most trying times. Whenever Bruce got excited or hyper-focused, he adopted an Austin Powers/Doctor Evil voice. As Matt waited for his friend to answer his call, he reminded himself that Bruce's voice thing was just one of his quirks and to try not to let it distract him.

Bruce was obviously excited to hear from his friend, and Matt heard a little Austin Powers before he could break in with, "Bruce, old buddy. I've got a favor to ask you."

Matt did his best to convey an abbreviated version of the Hopkins/Mitch/Clawson/Circle of Tantalus tales and how they all intersected. Bruce listened patiently, and then to Matt's shock, replied with, "Man, they've been on my radar for a while now. Are we talking utilizing my...special skills?"

"Well, yes," Matt responded, momentarily confused.

"Hang on...um, I want to switch this conversation over to that secure app I told you about, okay? You have it on your phone, right? Hang up and I'll call you right back."

Matt ended the call, and seconds later Bruce called back using what he had explained was an end-to-end encrypted app, which would allow them to talk with no possibility of a government audience listening in on the call.

"Okay, where were we...I've tried to hack into the Circle of Tantalus before, but no such luck. They use biometric authentication, and I just can't seem to get past it. Right after they enter their password, members have to put their eye up to a retinal scanner. I can hack the password by..." Bruce rattled off a bunch of steps that Matt didn't understand. "But I can't see a way past the biometric authentication part."

Matt sighed heavily. "Whatever you can do, man, I'd sure appreciate it. We need to bring this bastard down. If anyone can help us, you're the guy."

Bruce chuckled appreciatively. "Danger's my middle name, baby. It's all going, or going to go, perfectly to plan. Give me a few hours. I'll get back to you tonight."

They said their goodbyes and ended the call. Hannah was grinning. Bruce's voice was loud, and she'd caught a lot of his end of the conversation.

"Austin Powers?" She wiggled her eyebrows and winked at Matt. "*Oh groovy, baby.*"

For the next hour, they worked quickly to finish the patch job on the roof. Down below in the yard, they could see Hank meandering around. He'd befriended a much bigger old hound dog of Nana B's called Potcake. They were about the same age, mismatched in size, but with similar gray muzzles and foggy, gray old dog eyes. The pair were almost inseparable now and each of them followed the other like shadows as they explored the island, never wandering too far from their humans, but obviously just far enough to taste adventure.

After enjoying a delicious lunch of homemade, farm-raised, pulled-pork sandwiches that thankfully were not followed up by another project, Matt and Hannah excused themselves and headed back down to the dinghy, trailed by Hank and the old hound dog.

"You ready to do this?" Matt asked as he untied the dinghy. Hannah pulled out her cell phone, brandishing it in one hand and giving him an enthusiastic thumbs-up with the other.

The two old dogs were trying to get in the dinghy as well, so Hannah lowered them both carefully into the craft, where they made themselves comfortable on a pair of old life vests Matt kept for old-doggy ease. He fired up the engine, and they made their way slowly through the barely lapping waves toward the waste barges. As they approached, he cut back on the throttle and let the dinghy slow, not wanting to draw too much attention to their reconnaissance mission.

The putrid smell was overwhelming, and after judging the wind direction, Matt came alongside, upwind of most of the stench. Matt had smelled death itself before, in places like Fallujah and Baghdad, and the odor was only slightly different from the foul vapors that now caused them to choke and cough, even on the windward side of the barge. It was the smell of corruption and greed—of evil and suffering. The two old dogs even seemed to hate the stench as well, both of them lying down in the dinghy and pushing at their noses with their front paws.

A small stream of reddish-colored sludge leaked into the water from the side of one barge. Hannah aimed her phone in the leak's direction and began filming. Matt cut the engine, and they drifted along between the barges, Hannah's camera tracking as they came alongside a barge without a tarp to conceal its grisly cargo. Seagulls flew back-

and-forth overhead, slimy bits of chicken-plant waste clenched in their beaks.

"That's enough right there to get Clawson shut down," Hannah whispered as she stopped the recording, but kept a tight grip on her phone, pressing it against her chest.

Matt started the engine again, and they made their way slowly toward Salt Pond Island, once apparently as lush and beautiful as Jasmine, but now barren of all but Clawson's unique brand of functional and crude architecture. Now renamed "Clawson Island," it was home to a huge chicken-processing plant and dozens of long industrial buildings where thousands of chickens had to live out their brief lives in cruel, cramped conditions.

The island's harbor bustled with activity, workboats coming and going, with all the clamor and chaos of an enterprise dedicated to making money as quickly and efficiently as possible. As they approached, a tugboat was pulling away from the dock with another barge in tow, piled high with a steaming load of smelly chicken guts and feathers from the processing plant. It was enough to make Matt once again swear off ever eating another chicken product.

As they pulled up alongside the dock, a security guard eyed them warily and motioned for them to move on. Matt held up a fishing pole in one hand as he drifted by, and the guard nodded, turning away and returning to whatever he was doing on his cell phone. Cutting the engine, they coasted up against the mangroves about a hundred yards past the main dock. They were alongside the shore near one of the large, long metal buildings, which housed thousands of chickens crammed into tiny metal cages. Matt knew these poor birds never even saw the sun during their short miserable lives, instead forced to live in a cycle of artificial light and darkness, which would make one day seem like four to the poor things. This artificial acceleration of time, along with their hormone-laced feed, caused the birds to grow much faster—and bigger—than nature had ever intended.

Tinny music drifted over the water from inside the chicken barn.

Matt frowned. "Is that *'La Macarena'*? What the hell?" he asked in a low voice.

Hannah leaned over and nodded, whispering. "That's Mitch's pride and joy." Her tone was bitter. "They play music just before the automatic feeders dispense chicken feed into their cages. It's like with Pavlov's dogs. They hear the music, and it makes them salivate. It gets their digestion system going before they eat, just so the feeders can speed up the process of cramming in more food and speeding up the chickens' growth. Mitch's research found that out of all the sounds and songs he sampled, the poultry responded best to the rhythm of 'La Macarena.'" She added, "Mitch said that the Colonel really hated the song, calling it 'filthy foreign music,' but tolerated hearing it because it was like 'the sound of money being made.'"

Matt imagined hundreds of chickens bobbing their little heads to the silly old song, and it seemed funny—but only for a nanosecond. "I thought growing human tissue for cult members was weird, but playing 'La Macarena' for chickens?" He shook his head as if in disbelief.

Hannah set her phone back to video and aimed her lens at a stand of bulrushes which barely concealed a rusted pipe disgorging a nasty orange slurry into the bay. All along the shore, dark green moss grew in thick mats, a telltale sign that sewage was being regularly discharged into the water.

She turned off the camera as Matt started up the engine and cut a wide arc in the water, heading back to Jasmine Island. They didn't speak until Clawson Island was well behind them. Then Hannah announced she was calling her reporter friend.

"I'm giving Traci everything we've got. She can blow this thing wide open." Hannah's eyes glinted with triumph as she found her friend's contact and pressed to connect the call. After a moment, she gave Matt a thumbs-up. "Hey Traci! I know it's been forever, but I've got a helluva story for you down in the Sea Islands—Clawson Island, to be more specific. My battery is running low, so I'm going to send you some video and call you right back."

Hannah ended the call, and fingers flying over the screen, selected several of the video clips and shared them to Traci's email. Before Hannah had a chance to call her friend back, her cell rang, a riff from an old Rick James song: *she's a very freaky girl...* Matt rolled his eyes and shook his head as Hannah connected the call, hitting the speaker function so they could both hear Traci's side of the conversation. She sounded out of breath.

"I'm coming down the day after tomorrow. I gotta see this shit for myself. Clawson is having a ribbon-cutting ceremony at the plant on Tuesday. I saw the press release the other day. No one wanted to cover it—it's an awful

company—but I want in, now. My news director can get you a press pass. In the meantime, I'm going to see what else I can uncover."

When Hannah ended the call, Matt pointed to the motor. "Do you mind steering for a sec? I want to check if Bruce has left me any messages."

They carefully slid around each other and Matt absent-mindedly scratched the old hound dog's ears while opening up the secure app and checking for a message. There was only one: *Call me, dude, I think I know a way to crack it.* Hands shaking with excitement, Matt called his friend via the encrypted app.

"What have you got, old buddy?" he practically shouted as soon as his friend answered. He wasn't sure if it would be Austin Powers or Dr. Evil who answered, but it was just plain old Bruce, and for that, he was thankful.

"I can get you a retinal scanner by FedEx overnight. It's a little viewfinder-looking device you can put over the eye-piece of anything—from a camera to a telescope—really, anything that you could get that guy Clawson to look through. All it takes is a quarter second, then I've got his biometric ID. I've already got his password...got that in about five minutes with a new AI rainbow table program I'm messing around with..."

Matt did not know what a "rainbow table program" was, but thanked Bruce profusely and told him he'd send him the address of the little general store over on the mainland, where most of the locals got their parcels. He didn't have a clue yet how he'd get the Colonel to look through a telescope, or a camera, but he was sure as hell ready to give it his best shot.

With Hannah taking over the steering, Matt was free to pet the dogs and tell her all about his phone call. He shrugged helplessly as he told her about the retinal scanner, and was surprised when laughed, her eyes sparkling.

"Oh my God, it's perfect!" she shrieked. "Traci can set the video camera on a tripod, all set up to take flattering images of the factory and call the Colonel over for his 'approval' on the shot. That's how you'll get his...biometrics, or whatever it is Bruce is after."

Matt sat bolt upright, leaning over to high-five Hannah's free hand. This was it—it was really going to happen. They were going to bring down the Circle of Tantalus, and with it, Clawson and his whole damn evil empire.

CHAPTER 20

An easterly breeze was picking up, throwing choppy little waves into the harbor. Hank dozed on a pile of old towels, feet twitching sleepily as his dream counterpart set off on another adventure. Setting aside a water-stained paperback, Matt rose and made his way to the bow, where he checked his anchor line still held fast. Hannah was back at the boat-house, holed up in the loft, trying to finish up a paper *without distractions* as she had put it, before they headed over to the mainland to meet her friend Traci.

Matt missed the burble of Hannah's easy laughter and her radiant energy, among other things, and had been trying to enjoy his temporary solitude with little success. A chorus of whining boat engines provided a ready distraction. A line of boats stretched into the distance, motoring past him into the harbor. Each had several people, ranging from toddlers to elderly folk aboard, and appeared to be loaded down with food, judging from the mouthwatering scents he savored as they passed nearby. He waved as each craft drifted by, keeping an eye out for Tiny's skiff, but didn't see his friend among them. Dozens of families were headed to Jasmine for a reunion, some boating in from as far away as Georgia, others having trailered their boats up to Moss Landing to make the crossing.

Heading back toward the cockpit, Matt heard the chime of his cellphone and lunged for it before the call could cut out. It was an incoming call via the secure app. With trembling fingers, Matt swiped to connect. "Bruce, man...what's up?"

His friend's voice was shaky with excitement. "Matt, I'm in...I'm into their network. This is huge! This is some seriously fucked-up shit, baby!"

"Oh my god, you're in? The Circle of Tantalus?" Matt could hardly believe what he was hearing.

"No man, not the Circle . . . the whole frickin' chicken plant. I've hacked into their mainframe. I'm in here now, looking at the whole damn network, baby!"

Matt could hear furious clicking on a keyboard, then Bruce was back.

"Boom! I just made their overpriced vending machines give out free drinks. I can control the whole frickin' thing from right here in Austin...right down to when the chickens eat. I could even open the chicken cages if I wanted...Oh, but wait...Holy crap, this shit is crazy..."

Matt hesitated, letting the silence yawn, knowing that when Bruce was laser- focused, he was a furious speed reader. He wanted to know exactly what it was Bruce had discovered.

Bruce let out a sound that echoed, strangely like a screech. Matt could picture him grabbing fistfuls of his own hair—a thing he did when he was overstimulated—as if trying to give his brilliant mind even more room to stretch.

"So…" he continued. "This Mitch guy you told me about—your girl's ex—he's helping Clawson grow samples of human 'meat' in a secret lab in the plant's basement! His notes…that's what I'm looking at right now. They reference the live cultures of human cells from at least five different people. Each of the cell cultures they're growing has a code name, like "Rocket Man" or "Songbird," and from these notes I think they're from actual…living people."

Matt was on his feet now, heart pounding.

"No…" he whispered. Bruce's voice filled his ear, but it was almost too much for him to process. His friend continued.

"Okay, okay…I'm looking at another file now. This one's about, um…waste management for the processing plant. They're working on extending a secret pipeline off shore, where they can dump the worst of their slaughterhouse waste without having to pay any disposal or environmental fees."

Matt thought about the time he and Tiny had stopped to fish and had been warned away from the spot by the "gas pipeline company" security guards.

"Oh man…and, what waste he doesn't dump out there, even if it's full of detergents and all kinds of crap, is what he's going to use to grow his cultures of lab-grown chicken-nugget meat. Ohh…that could gag a maggot…"

Austin Powers, or rather Fat Bastard this time, was back. Bruce was going to be hard to rein in. Matt broke in gently and explained Hannah's plan to use the retinal scanner over the video camera viewfinder to capture Clawson's biometric ID. They'd picked up the package Bruce had FedEx'd the day before and stowed the tiny device carefully out of harm's way up in the V-berth.

"Oh yeah, baby—that's the ticket!" exclaimed Bruce. "Once you've got the scanner in place, connect to the app I'm sending you. It's Bluetooth enabled." As soon as the Colonel looks through that viewfinder, we'll be able to get inside the Circle of Tantalus."

This was it. They were so close Matt could almost taste sweet justice.

"We're on it, Bruce. Man, you're fucking amazing. Thank you, buddy!"

"You got it. Later, man."

Matt checked his watch. It was nearly ten and time to take the dinghy over to the dock to pick up Hannah and head on over to the mainland at Moss Landing, where the little general store was located. From here, they'd join her friend Traci in her TV van before driving on over to Clawson Island, recently connected to the mainland by a long, narrow bridge. Thinking of Mel Fisher's optimistic mantra *"today's the day"*, Matt wondered if this might be theirs when they finally unearthed the treasure trove of data that could take down Colonel Clawson.

After waking his sleeping dog and getting him to potty on his poop-deck pad, Matt set Hank up in the V-berth. He did not know what they'd be getting into, but he figured if Clawson island was a dangerous place for chickens, it probably wasn't a haven for old, half-blind dogs either. Leaving the hatch open to allow the fresh air to fill the cabin, he grabbed the package Bruce had sent, then went topside, untied the dinghy's lines, and cranked up the motor. He could see Hannah over on the dock, her tangle of curls lifted by the wind. Neatly pressed chinos and a close-fitting polo shirt replaced her usual baggy cargo shorts. He'd tried as well to look less like a threadbare sailor and more like a young professional. With press passes, they could at least pass for members of the camera crew.

Once Matt had told Hannah the latest news from Bruce, they were mostly silent as they motored back to the mainland. There was so much to think about—so much to process—that it was hard to pull out a single thread of conversation and follow it before getting trapped in the tangles of the wcb they were about to rip open. Matt kept a hand on Hannah's slim thigh as he steered, feeling the heat of her skin against his palm. As they approached the shore, Matt could see a woman waving at them from beside a big TV van with satellite dishes festooning the roof and *WCHRS Eyewitness News* emblazoned across the side. He slowed the engine, then cut it as they pulled alongside the dock. Hannah was the first to climb out of the dinghy, securing the bowline first before running down the dock to her old friend. Matt finished tying the lines, then followed her.

Traci's greeting was warm, and her dry handshake was firm. Her close-fitting navy pantsuit said she was all business, and her matte makeup and seemingly poreless skin said she was too professional for things like perspiration. She winked at them.

"Well, y'all...you ready to go fry a chicken king?"

They climbed into the van, Hannah up in the front beside Traci, and Matt in the back. Hannah was chattering to her friend, filling her in on all the things they'd learned about Clawson. Matt opened the bubble-wrapped envelope his friend had sent him, pulled out the device, and powered on the little fake viewfinder. It was about as big around as a half dollar and featured a cushioned eyepiece that resembled the ones on most professional video cameras. Matt clicked on the small switch, just as Bruce had instructed, then carefully paired the little device with the app he'd installed on his phone.

As the three of them made their way toward the bridge to Clawson Island, Matt leaned over the seat and joined the conversation, catching Traci up on the information Bruce had gleaned from his network breach.

Traci sighed. "Unfortunately, I can't risk using that information directly from your friend, but if he can get everything together, and dump it on WikiLeaks or a similar site, that would be outstanding. And just one thing, guys...we never had this conversation. Okay?

They both agreed.

The narrow bridge to Clawson Island was crowded with cars heading toward the looming plant, which had foul-smelling smoke and steam billowing from multiple stacks on its roof. Traci's pretty nose wrinkled. By now Matt had gotten slightly nose-blind to the stench, but even he was shocked by the odor's growing intensity.

Clawson could have afforded a much wider bridge, but the nearly single-lane design was clearly intentional. Since most of the chicken feed and processed meat came and went by barge, the traffic on the road was mostly workers, and they were surely at the bottom of his priority list. In addition, the skinny bridge helped control the flow of the occasional visitors. Hannah's networking had yielded a rich supply of information on the place. According to a cousin of hers who worked at the plant, if any of Clawson's cronies received word that a state or federal inspector was coming, they would start a "code Fed" alert. A loud siren would sound inside the plant. This would alert workers to hastily reinstall the federally mandated safety guards and protective shields on meat grinders and other dangerous equipment, as well as turn off any valves that were discharging toxic waste into the bay. The entire process could be completed in fewer than thirty minutes, while a fake "road crew" held up the inspectors as they pretended to patch potholes on the long bridge. Weekly drills kept the machinery of duplicity running smoothly. Matt was certain they had enacted this protocol the day Tiny's wife had suffered her fatal injury, stalling the first responders, which could have saved her life with a more timely arrival.

As they neared the main area of the plant, it looked like a carnival was underway in the shadow of the ugly industrial buildings. Behind a sign reading "Pony Rides," a sour-faced old woman with leathery skin smoked a cigarette while leading a young boy around on an ancient swayback mare. The boy was grinning from ear to ear, but the rest of the carnival crew bore the distinct distant look of people who'd rather be doing just about anything else.

Clawson's people were clearly attempting to curry favor with any locals they weren't actively trying to intimidate and were offering free chicken nugget dinners to everyone who showed up. The Colonel was notorious for bragging about the vast crowds he drew to his events and used free food as an enticement to folks who were hungry and desperate or lacking in taste buds and ethics.

Parking was tight, as most of the spots were taken up by employees and those seduced by the prospect of the carnival. They squeezed into a spot in the dusty gravel lot. Traci passed out laminated press passes and grabbed a smaller handheld video camera. While Hannah and Matt walked awkwardly behind her, trying to look like they were part of her team, the reporter took some footage of the tawdry event. In a temporary pen at the end of the parking lot, a "chicken derby" was underway. Several dozen poor birds, who'd probably never even seen sunlight before, wore paper numbers glued to their backs, and were corralled in a small temporary pen next to a larger one about the size of a basketball court. A machine next to the pen dispensed tickets corresponding to the numbers on the pitiful fowl as a stone-faced man stood by droning out "one ticket per person" and "next" over and over. The sign attached promised that the birds would be released to "race" to the opposite side of the enclosure. Whoever's ticket matched the "winning" bird's would be the lucky recipient of a year's supply of Clawson Chicken Tenders.

Near the chicken derby corral was a section of the parking lot where orange traffic cones had created an obstacle course. Here, a beefy security guard showed what was apparently the newest addition to the plant's security force: a futuristic-looking robot dog like the ones some big city

SWAT teams were now using. The guard put the robot through its paces with the usual dog tricks: fetch, roll over and play dead, then got to the part of the demonstration which clearly brought him the most pleasure. His piggy little eyes crinkled with delight and he shone with perspiration as he tapped a command into a handheld controller. The robotic dog strode jerkily toward a crude dummy, which stood a few feet away. Its speaker issued an ominous warning in a tinny voice:

"Stop. You are trespassing on private property. Leave at once. This security robot has been authorized to use force." Seconds later, it issued the same rapid command, followed by, "Use of nonlethal force has been authorized in...five, four, three, two, one..."

The robot dog extended a front arm menacingly toward the noncompliant party. The appendage held a powerful stun gun, which emitted a wide, sizzling spark—almost touching the dummy—before the guard issued a command for it to stand down. A few members of the crowd oohed and aahed while the robot crabbed faithfully back to the guard's side. Some folks, probably employees or their family members, looked decidedly uncomfortable. A couple gasped aloud, but the guard seemed oblivious to their discomfort, obviously thrilled with this new extension of his power.

"This concludes the demonstration. Please disperse...er, move on to the next exhibit and...um...thank you for your cooperation," the guard said awkwardly, as if unwilling to revert to customer-service mode. The point of the demonstration was patently obvious: *Welcome to the carnival, y'all, eat Clawson Chicken, and stay the hell off our property unless we say different.*

At the opposite end of the parking lot was Clawson's "Cluck Truck," his own take on the Oscar Meyer "Weinermobile." The Cluck Truck was a gaudy, jacked-up monster truck with enormous tires and a huge, animatronic fiberglass chicken head attached to the roof. The driver, a short, unsmiling young man in a sleeveless T-shirt and baggy jeans, gunned the engine periodically, releasing columns of black diesel exhaust from the twin stacks behind the cab. It was, no doubt, his dream job. Whenever the young man tugged on a hydraulic lever that extended from the dash, the huge tail feathers, located where the truck's tailgate would ordinarily have been, would sweep up and down, sort of like the handheld fans old ladies once used in country churches in the days before air conditioning. Four large speakers—in the shape of fast-food chicken-nugget containers, each facing in a different direction—sat in the back, blaring out a jingle extolling the deliciousness of Clawson Chicken Nuggets. With some more lever- pulling and button-pushing, the chicken's head swiveled and its beak jerkily opened and closed.

Presiding over this ignorant spectacle of animal cruelty—real and mechanical—was Colonel Clawson himself, dressed in his trademark Southern colonel uniform, complete with a jangling chestful of fake medals. He chomped on a fat cigar and tugged roughly at the leash of an unhappy-looking little female Corgi he called "Nugget"—a company mascot. Supposedly the Colonel despised the dog, and Nugget spent most of her time locked up in a cage, only to be released if there was the chance of a cute photo op. Clawson always did what he could to offset the negative publicity wrought by the animal rights activists, whom he made it his personal mission to persecute. The sight of poor Nugget being dragged along on her leash reminded Matt of the little dog in *The Grinch Who Stole Christmas,* who was also an unwilling victim in his owner's cruel machinations.

While the chicken derby was getting underway, Traci set up her staging area for the flattering shot of the chicken plant's facade with which she planned to lure the Colonel to the camera. The entrance to the office area of the plant was a grotesque version of the Tara plantation in *Gone with the Wind* that featured several large faux-marble columns and a pair of oversized U.S. and South Carolina flags. These fluttered next to a slightly larger and taller Clawson Chicken flag which bore a strong resemblance to the Confederate battle flag. In place of stars along the "bars," it featured small chicken silhouettes and drumsticks, along with the company name emblazoned across the bottom. The gaudy-looking banner was Clawson's idea and simultaneously offended both those who abhorred the sight of the original flag and those who saw it as part of their Southern heritage.

Matt and Hannah helped set up the tripod, mounting the heavy news camera and rolling out a smart-looking red carpet on which Traci hoped to convince the Colonel to stand. Traci then set about working her reporter magic, capturing the moment when a young boy from Edisto Island won a year's worth of chicken tenders as lucky chicken number 53 beat its competitors to the other side of the enclosure. Matt kept his head down and face averted. It was unlikely that Clawson would recognize him from his day in court—he'd barely looked up from his phone—but Matt was taking no chances. It was a good thing that Traci was a woman, because that was the only gender for which the Colonel seemed to have an eye out. Clawson seemed especially pleased that a real TV reporter, and a female one at that, was presenting a favorable picture of his operation, and waddled over to where she was shooting, clearly hoping for some press of his own. When Traci sweetly asked if she could record him saying a few words about the day's events over on the red carpet, his chest puffed out and he swaggered into place.

Matt had already slipped Bruce's fake viewfinder over the video camera's eyepiece, so now all they needed was for Clawson to put his eye to it for his hacker friend to gain access to the Circle of Tantalus website.

"Right this way, Sir...or do you prefer Colonel?" Traci inquired courteously.

"Colonel's just fine, Honey Pie," the old man drawled, his eyes lasciviously roaming her figure, as he fairly drooled around his cigar.

Traci was no bimbo, and she didn't lose a beat as she directed the Colonel into place and stepped neatly out of reach of his grabby hands. She'd helped break some big stories in her career, including exposing voter suppression efforts and penning hard-hitting environmental pieces which landed a couple of Charleston city councilmen in jail. The councilmen had taken part in a scheme that pocketed federal funds targeted to pay for replacing dangerous lead pipes in the city water system, producing fake work orders showing that the job had been done when it hadn't. Colonel Clawson did not know who he was up against.

Traci was back behind the camera. "How does this look, Colonel? Do you like the shot that we've got of the plant?"

"Sure, Honey Pie, I'm sure it's just fine," slurred the Colonel, looking glassy eyed as he stared openly at the pretty reporter.

"Are you sure? If you would just pop over here and have a peek through our camera lens, I can make sure everything looks perfect for your first interview with WCHRS."

"Aw, all right, Honey Pie. Shoot, if it'll make ya happy, I'll take a look," he said reluctantly and shuffled over. As Clawson bent down and peered through the small viewfinder, Matt felt his phone buzz from a notification. They'd done it! The little device had just scanned the Colonel's retina. Bruce would now have the Clawson's biometric ID.

The old man, holding his poor dog Nugget in a choke hold under his arm, rambled on a bit more than Traci had expected, talking about the merits of free enterprise, progress, and ability of the local people to "gain dignity through hard work" at his plant. When he'd finally wrapped up his speech, Traci thanked him courteously and asked him a few more questions, this time in a more investigative reporter kind of way, while Matt and Hannah began taking down the camera setup.

As soon as they were all back in the van, Matt received a call from Bruce over the secure app. "Smashing job! I'm inside the Circle of Tantalus! Yeah, baby!" Bruce said rapidly in his dorky Austin Powers voice. "Gimme a few, and I'll let you know what I dig up." Matt thanked his friend effusively and disconnected the call.

Hannah and Traci talked nonstop on their way back to Moss Landing. The reporter was thrilled with the scoop and was eager to bounce ideas around with her old friend. They made the trip back in good time, and Traci dropped them off at the general store before heading back to Charleston. She seemed high on the prospect of the story that would shortly be breaking. Today's footage would be nothing more than ironic backstory to the sordid tale that was about to unfold.

At the small local market, Matt bought a box of liver treats for Hank and a couple of cold sodas, and they soon got underway in the little dinghy. Matt took it easy this time, the little outboard putting along as they made their way out past the moss-covered trees along the sides of the inlet, then out into the bay. For a few long minutes, they just sat quietly, sipping their drinks and contemplating the shitstorm to come. The proverbial chicken poop was about to hit the ventilator, but neither of them had a clue that the countdown had already begun. They'd barely hit the bay when Matt's phone chimed. The secure app—again. Matt cut the engine and let the dinghy drift as he answered the call. He didn't want to risk losing the signal as they got farther out.

"Buddy, tell me. What have you found?"

"It's freaking huge! Matt—what the actual fuck! It's..."

"Slow down, buddy. Take a breath. What?" Matt could hear his friend drawing in ragged breaths before Bruce continued. He tapped the speaker icon so Hannah could hear as well.

"Well, for one thing, I can tell you who Clawson's co-conspirators are. I can see every message in his private inbox, and I'm pretty sure that I know who at least three of the people are who're in the market for his cell-cultured human flesh. One of them is James Brazos, owner of that big online shopping company. Apparently, he just wants to own a bit of Jaron Tusk, you know, the genius gazillionaire that's competing with him to make rockets and go to Mars."

Hannah gasped, and Matt grabbed her hand and squeezed. Her eyes widened, and she shook her head in shock. Bruce kept talking.

"Another is—and you're gonna love this one—is that cute singer-chick, Baylor Sweet, she wants to . . . you're gonna love this one, consume a tiny bit of the country singer Polly Darton herself to get some of her 'singing powers.' Smashing, baby! The Colonel is growing a culture of freaking Polly Darton cells! I don't even know how the hell he got *her* stem cells, but...I've been able to grab their IP addresses and trace where they transferred money from their banks to buy the Bitcoin that they used to pay the Colonel. They're rich, but these Circle jerks are not very smart and most of them didn't even use a VPN when they logged in. I guess they figured with the whole biometric ID thing, that's all they had to worry about. I'm gonna dump everything that I find on the Circle of Tantalus site, as well as from the chicken plant's mainframe, on WikiLeaks. After I do, you never talked to me, okay?"

"You got it," said Matt, and Hannah echoed his words in a whisper.

Hannah's eyes locked with Matt's, and she grabbed him in a tight embrace. The dinghy rocked as they held on to each other. Tears sprang to Matt's eyes as Hannah's arms tightened around him and he rested his chin on the top of her head. He smiled and then drew in a long, deep breath of the salt air, taking in his fill of delight at being young and alive and here in an old dinghy, in the middle of a bay, about to see justice finally served.

CHAPTER 21

The following morning, Matt woke with a cottony mouth and a pounding head. Tiny had finally made it back to Jasmine Island in time for the family reunion, and after another of Nana B's glorious feasts, the pair had headed back to *Lonesome Dove* where they'd shared a bottle of Tiny's "fishing rum" and Matt had caught his friend up to speed on the past few days. Tiny was understandably shocked to hear of the goings-on, and a little sad that Hannah, not wanting to remind him of Marie's tragic death, had carried the burden of her tale alone for so long.

After they'd polished off the rum, and discussed all the ways they could imagine karma being visited upon the evil Clawson, the pair had wrapped up their drinking session with a couple of lukewarm beers from Matt's cooler before Tiny awkwardly set out for shore on one of the kid's small kayaks.

Crawling out of the V-berth seemed to take an inordinate amount of effort, but the prospect of caffeine and its magical medicinal effects fueled the endeavor. Hank was

awake now as well, stretching his plump body forward and
lifting his stubby-tailed butt in the air. Matt quickly
scooped up the old dog and carried him topside, depositing
him carefully on a fresh pee pad to do his business while he
dropped back below to make the coffee.

He'd just lit the stove and was measuring out the aro-
matic coffee grounds when Hank began a chorus of sharp
little barks. Matt squinted and rubbed his eyes as he took a
couple of steps up the companionway ladder to see what his
old dog was fussing about. He blinked into the sunlight,
craned his neck, then widened his eyes. Scrambling all the
way up into the cockpit, he leaned out over the lifelines to
get a better view. In the distance, he could hear what
sounded like sirens and alarm bells ringing from over by the
far side of the bay toward Clawson Island. A plume of dark
smoke rose skyward from one of the cooling towers.

A burst of adrenaline cut through the surfeit of Añejo
rum, propelling Matt back into the cabin, where he
switched on the VHF with trembling fingers. Cranking up
the volume, he listened impatiently as the captains of various fishing vessels chimed in with their own queries and
speculations about the alarms and the smoke. No one
seemed to know anything besides the obvious: something
bad was going down on Clawson Island. Matt spun
around, looking for his cell phone, then dove for it when he
saw it lying abandoned in the rumpled sheets. He cursed
when he realized the battery was dead. Locating the charg-
ing cable, he shoved in the connector and held down the
power button, waiting for the phone to juice up. After
what seemed like an eternity, the phone powered up and he

swiped past the home screen. Matt was about to open up the local news when he saw a red notification beside the secure messaging app's logo. He clicked. The first message read:

Hey old buddy—there's some crazy shit going down near you. Check it out.

There was a screenshot image at the end of the message from the website of an independent news agency. The featured stories were titled, *"Hackers Take Control of Clawson Plant and Free the Chickens'* and *"Billionaire Chicken King Clyde Clawson: Leader of an Elite Cannibal Cult?"*

Matt opened the second message. It read,

Drop your phone in the saltwater after you read this. I'm wiping your Apple account along with mine—This is not a joke!

Matt's head was spinning. What the hell was going on? He ignored Bruce's directive. Sure, he'd ditch the phone shortly, but didn't want to miss any news from Jasmine Island. He opened his messages and was reading the first of many from Hannah (*The plant is burning—we're on our way to help evacuate...*) when he heard her yelling his name. He grabbed his phone, noticed the stove burner was still on, shut off the gas, then jumped up into the cockpit.

"Hey man, let's go!" yelled Tiny. The skiff bobbed in the water by *Lonesome Dove*'s hull, his friend at the wheel and Hannah beside him, obviously worried, but still smiling radiantly.

"Gimme a sec," Matt called back, scooping up Hank and taking him down into the cabin and his safe little cubby in the V-berth. On impulse, he grabbed the tiny bag of "mojo" given to him by Nana B. While Matt wasn't especially superstitious, he thought that from the looks of the situation, they could use all the luck they could get.

He scrambled back up the ladder and over the side, dropping into the skiff. Matt's feet had barely touched the deck when Tiny cranked the engine and the craft took off with a loud roar, careening over the waves as fast as she could go. Clutching the back of the seat with one hand, Matt still gripped his phone in the other. With a sigh, he turned and launched the phone into the boat's foamy wake.

"What did you do that for?" Hannah called over the boat's engine. Her pretty brow was furrowed with confusion.

"Saving Bruce's ass—and mine," he yelled back.

The wind had picked up, and the column of smoke Matt had seen earlier was now blowing almost horizontally over the bay. As the skiff bounced over the white-capped waves, Matt heard something sliding and bumping on the floorboards. He caught sight of a gleaming piece of metal and realized it was the froe that Clive had been using to cut shingles back on the island. Hannah trapped the sliding tool with one booted foot and called back to Matt over her shoulder, pointing to the tool with her index finger. "Tiny thought it might come in handy!" Matt didn't have a clue what they were heading toward, but he figured an old-school hand tool couldn't hurt their chances any more than the mojo.

The bone-jarring ride seemed to take forever. Around them, the water churned with the wakes of other boats, all headed into the haphazard rescue mission. Across the bay they could see dozens more "rooster tails"—spray thrown up from powerful outboard engines—as they barreled in from every direction toward one point: the docks at Clawson Island.

Every captain among them would know they'd probably beat the emergency vehicles to the factory, and all engines were cranked up as fast as they'd go. As the main dock came into view, Matt took a deep breath. The air was thick with the acrid smell of billowing gray smoke, and everywhere people were running and shouting, panicked and terrified. Flames licked the upper windows of one building, and from another came the sound of a minor explosion. Matt hadn't seen this degree of chaos since the war in Iraq, and for a fraction of a second, he was right back there again. Then, Hannah grabbed his hand and held on tight, her smooth fingers gripping his as Tiny skillfully maneuvered the big skiff up toward the plant's main dock. Matt let go of Hannah's hand and jumped up onto the wide planks, grabbing the lines that Tiny tossed him and throwing them around the rusty bollards to secure it alongside.

As they ran up the long, neatly manicured lawn that flowed down from the wide office steps to the water, the robotic patrol dog they had seen at the carnival appeared out of thin air. Sunlight glinted off the shiny chrome body as the machine bounded slowly toward them, pausing periodically to leap and paw into the air as if chasing imaginary butterflies. Matt felt his stomach clench as it neared, but instead of tasing them, the robot, its cold electronic "eyes" gazing straight ahead, galloped right past them, making a beeline toward the dock where it sprang easily into the air and launched itself into the waves. For a moment, Matt turned and stared as the robot emitted a puff of white smoke and a shower of sparks, then slowly sank into the waves, one mechanical paw appearing to reach skyward like a messenger from the future delivering a final warning.

Then, he heard something—*a cry for help*—and he was off, sprinting past Tiny and Hannah toward the sound.

Flames curled around the roof of the multistory office complex and shot skyward from a ventilator shaft. The jagged remnants of a broken window on the top floor framed the face of a terrified woman, screaming desperately for help, heedless of the blood streaming from fingers ripped by splintered wood and shards of glass. A fall or jump would cause serious injury—or worse—from that height. Catching sight of a recently abandoned John Deere tractor parked off to the side, mowing deck attached and engine still idling, Matt sprang into action.

"Just hang on!" he shouted to the woman, waving both hands to draw her attention. Recalling a lesson in "improvised egress techniques" from his ranger training, Matt quickly jumped aboard the tractor, pulled a lever to raise its front-end loader bucket, and steered it toward the trio of flagpoles just outside the entrance. Motioning for the woman to back away from the window, he drove the little tractor headlong into the tallest pole from which Clawson's grotesque banner still flapped. The heavy aluminum pole snapped at its base, and like a tree falling, keeled over and landed squarely up against the upper part of the fourth-floor window. The woman reappeared at the window.

"You're gonna have to climb out and grab the pole. We've got ya," he called. Matt nodded at Tiny, who moved into position, ready to catch the woman if she fell. Clearly terrified, the woman leaned out, grabbed the metal flagpole with blood-slick hands, then clambered awkwardly out of the window frame. For a moment, her legs kicked at open air, then she wrapped first one foot, then the other, around the post, and slid swiftly down. Just before she landed hard on the gravel, Tiny caught her in his enormous arms and set her gently on the ground. Hannah squeezed her shoulder and pointed to where a line of workers were running toward an empty barge. A tugboat was heading toward the docks, obviously ready to pull the barge and its passengers to safety. The woman turned in a slow circle, clearly disoriented and in shock. Tiny put his arm around her shoulder, and when she crumpled, scooped her up and took off at a run toward the dock.

"I'll stay here and make sure we're clear," Matt called to Hannah, showing the line of buildings beyond the offices. "You go with Tiny." His throat tightened as he scanned his surroundings and tried to listen for sounds of life. Other than the hiss and roar of the blaze pouring from the open window, all was quiet. Orange flames now danced over the roof of the office complex, and he knew there wasn't long to act.

"No," Hannah yelled, grabbing his hand. "I'm going with you." There wasn't time to argue. She squeezed his fingers and jerked her head in the factory's direction. "The plant! We need to check the plant."

They ran together past the complex with its gaudy co-
lonial facade and toward the ugly metal outbuildings of the
plant. Entering through the open doors, Matt sensed motion and gave a start—then he almost laughed out loud.
Humans had abandoned the plant, but a half-dozen squat
little utility robots wandered aimlessly between the long
rows of meat-processing equipment. Two repeatedly
crossed paths, banging into each other like little metal sumo
wrestlers. Matt and Hannah hurried past a long, shallow
vat growing cell-cultured "lab meat," into which a number
of electrodes had been placed to help "texturize the product." Randomly, parts of the expansive vat would twitch,
as if part of some creepy high school science experiment involving an unfortunate frog. Matt wondered if a nerve
response meant pain for the lab "animal-matter." Was
Clawson's proprietary lab meat process nothing more than
animal cruelty on a larger scale, just with no anthropomor-
phizing features to stimulate an empathic response?

Nearby, a sausage machine, obviously another hacking
victim, propelled tubular meat links across the room and
through a broken window where they formed a waist-high
pile. A flock of seagulls, never ones to pass up a free meal,
were grabbing beakfuls of sausage and flying off with their
unexpected bounty.

Straining to be heard over the cacophony of all the malfunctioning equipment, Matt yelled: "Let's get out of here,
before these machines turn on us!"

Hannah nodded and took off at a run toward the entrance, Matt on her heels.

Then she stopped and turned, grabbing Matt's arm.

"Wait...Matt—what about all the poor chickens?"

"Awww shit," he sighed. "The chickens. Let's go!"

They ran around the plant toward the five squat buildings where the Colonel had bragged he kept more than a quarter million birds. The sheer number was staggering to contemplate, but on rounding the corner, the sea of fluttering white bodies, seemingly unable to do more than flap helplessly about, was so thick that Matt and Hannah had to slow and literally wade through them. Apparently, the hackers had opened the electronically controlled latches on the doors and cages. Four pairs of doors yawned wide, revealing a few straggling fowl blinking into the harsh bright light of day. Unaccustomed to sunlight or fresh air—and freedom—the stunned birds were waddling about with no instinct for self-preservation. The doors of the farthest barn were stuck fast. Flames from the blaze at the front of the property swept along the rooftops, pushed along by the wind. Gray smoke turned to black, and the billows swelled, stinging their eyes and peppering their skin with ash.

The couple beat their hands against the locked doors and tugged with all their strength, trying to find a weak spot, but the heavy panels wouldn't budge. Matt's heart sank. He turned toward Hannah, hands raised in surrender. Then, he saw Tiny rounding the corner, heavy iron froe gripped in one hand.

Tiny's chest was heaving as he approached them, quickly taking in the situation, and circling the yard once, before he saw what he needed. With his free hand, Tiny stooped and wrapped his fingers around a large, heavy rock. Then, he motioned for his friends to step back and steeled himself for the task. Carefully, he placed the sharp blade of the shingle-making tool on one of the chain's heavy links. Then, he raised the rock overhead and with one swift move, brought it crashing down. The chain cleaved in two, like it was a shingle sliced from a log. Then together, the three of them pulled the two heavy chicken barn doors open to reveal the cacophonous, chaotic scene inside. Released from their cages, thousands of birds tumbled over each other, a rolling pile of feathers bound to suffocate or crush the half of them.

Matt looked at Tiny in dismay. The big man shrugged his shoulders and pushed into the barn, wedging himself among the birds and pushing them outside by the handful.

"Wait, guys—I've got a plan! Follow me!" Hannah cried and then took off at a run toward the ugly, jacked-up monster "Cluck Truck" which was parked by the barns. Not having a clue what she was up to, but fully trusting her instincts, Matt raced alongside. The monster truck's step rail was almost to Hannah's shoulders.

"Give me a boost," she called to Matt, who cupped her raised foot and hoisted her up into the cab. The key was still in the ignition, and Hannah cranked it hard, bringing the diesel engine to life and causing a gust of thick black smoke to pour from the oversized exhaust pipes poking up behind the chicken-head-shaped cab. Matt ran around the front of the truck and, with difficulty, swung into the passenger seat. Reaching into the pocket of her cargo shorts, Hannah grabbed something and pressed it into his hand. He realized it was her cell phone and gave her a quizzical look.

"Go to Spotify," she directed. "Find 'La Macarena.' Hurry!"

After a moment of clumsy fumbling, the catchy song jangled from the phone.

"Okay, now pair it . . . argh—not like that."

Hannah grabbed the phone from Matt and started tapping. Soon, "La Macarena" was blaring from the Cluck Truck's massive speakers. Their seats rumbled with the thumping bass of a song that Matt figured had probably been played, and danced awkwardly to, at more than a billion weddings by now.

"Look!" yelled Hannah, pointing. Matt leaned over her shoulder, catching a whiff of her coconut scent. The bobbing, weaving flock of chickens heading their way looked like a giant, undulating white wave flowing toward the sound of what was essentially their dinner bell.

Hannah carefully put the monster truck in gear and began driving slowly away from the barns, crawling past the plant and the offices, away from the malfunctioning machines and the fire, and toward the bridge leading to the mainland. Matt turned in his seat, watching the spectacle unfold. It was quite a sight to behold: a quarter of a million chickens, all bobbing their heads to "La Macarena," scurrying along behind the two pied pipers in the jacked-up monster truck, shepherded by a huge, muscular Gullah man, waving his arms and funneling the last few stragglers into line.

As they finally eased out onto the bridge, Clawson's gaudy, white mansion came into view. A large helicopter was rising slowly skyward from a helipad on the emerald-green lawn. The sleek-looking chopper banked briefly to one side as it flew over the smoking plant, then headed out toward the open sea—away from the mainland. It had to be the Colonel.

"There he goes, the evil bastard," exclaimed Matt. "That's why nobody called the fire department. He was too busy destroying evidence and getting ready to haul ass."

Just as they reached the end of the bridge, and the last of the chickens had made its way safely across, a long line of law enforcement vehicles came streaming past, lights flashing and sirens blazing. A lone, ancient-looking fire truck belonging to the local volunteer fire department attempted to navigate its way through a crowd of onlookers gathered at the end of the bridge. Judging from the apocalyptic cloud of smoke billowing on the horizon, there was little that the old fire engine could do if it ever made it through.

Bringing up the rear of the procession were a handful of marked FBI vehicles and Traci in the WCHRS Eyewitness News van. From high in the driver's side of the Cluck Truck, Hannah waved down at her friend, gave two long pulls on the air horn's cord, and received an enthusiastic wave and a thumbs-up in response.

Matt gazed in open admiration as Hannah's long, well-toned leg pressed down on the clutch pedal as she grabbed the second gear. All he could utter at the moment was, "How do you know how to drive a...before he quickly corrected course and wrapped up with, "Damn, you sure look a whole lot better driving this thing than that skinny redneck!"

With a quick sideways glance and a smile, she replied, "Yeah, you bet your ass I do!"

Far behind, in the Cluck Truck's wake, people were scooping up the bewildered- looking chickens and carrying them off to the safety of boats and cars lining the mainland side of the causeway. Matt was confident the birds would soon be adopted by locals and become free-ranging chickens living their best lives...or at least better lives than Clawson chickens.

A sudden long, mournful—eerily human—wail pierced the jangle of "La Macarena." Matt frowned and glanced over his shoulder. Then he spun all the way around, got up on one knee and leaned over the back of the seat.

"Oh, my God!" he shouted, catching sight of a tiny metal cage filled with a honey-colored Corgi. It was Nugget, the Colonel's sometime mascot.

"Who? What is it?" Hannah cried, trying to keep her eyes on the road.

Matt hung all the way over the seat, released the latch, and grabbed the warm, trembling body in both hands. He carefully lifted Nugget up and over, settling her in his lap. She shook violently, but managed a tentative lick as Matt offered her his palm to sniff. Hannah let out a long sigh and held her free hand to her heart for a moment before settling her fingers in Nugget's wavy fur.

"Matt..." said Hannah hesitantly, "when you heard her make...that sound...Did you think it sounded like, I dunno...a person? Like maybe, a famous singer?" she added, only partly joking.

Matt nodded. "Yeah, that's what I was thinking. You don't think Nugget's been eating...scraps of Polly Darton cell culture, do you?"

Hannah grimaced. "With that sick, cheap bastard as her owner? I wouldn't rule out anything."

Matt reached for Hannah's hand and threaded his fingers through hers. He squeezed and she squeezed back, a small smile dimpling the corner of her mouth. With his free hand, he gently stroked Nugget's knobby spine. Her trembling eased and her breathing slowed. Long-lashed, colored eyelids drifted closed, and she gave a soft sigh that Matt swore sounded like that of a very...well-satisfied...woman. *Maybe they could call her Polly*, he thought. The honey-colored Corgi dozed, and Matt and Hannah held hands all the way back to the general store at Moss Landing.

That night, Nana B cooked her biggest feast yet to celebrate the end of Clawson's long campaign of abuse against pretty much everyone outside of the now infamous "Circle." Platters of tender roast pork, crispy fried fish, savory shrimp and oyster perloo, and steaming bowls of peas and rice, okra, and collard greens covered the scarred surface of the long wood table. Later on, out in the courtyard, old and young sang and danced around a big crackling fire.

Matt felt grateful that despite all the division that was still going on in the country, at least here, in the magical place that was Jasmine Island, these warm and generous people had simply welcomed him, without reservation or hesitation, to join in their celebration as if he were truly part of their family. On this calm evening, as tiny embers from the fire seemed to drift up and transform themselves into yellow stars, he and his new friends celebrated the defeat of their common foe, as well as the joy of life itself—lived simply and to its fullest.

On a creaky old porch swing, Matt and Hannah swayed slowly and held hands. Their bellies were full of food, their minds with stories, and their hearts with something that felt complex, but which was really pretty simple. At the end of the long porch, Nana's old hound dog gnawed sleepily on a meaty pork bone and eyed her next paramour—a big shaggy mutt who had been hanging around the boatyard and whom Tiny had brought to the island to stay. At their feet, mindful of the movement of the swing, Hank and his new lady love, rechristened "Polly," spooned together, the bigger honey-colored body curved around the old spotted one.

The sparkle of lightning bugs winked on and off in the cool night air. High above them, thousands of stars shone brightly. As was his ritual every night since his journey had begun, Matt located the constellation Orion the Hunter and traced a downward path from the three stars in Orion's belt to Sirius, the Dog Star—the one he thought of as Julie's star. He took a deep breath, gazed hard at the shining point of light, and willed a message up to the cosmos—to wherever his sweet girl's spirit had flown—putting in it all the love, memories, and pleas for guidance and understanding that churned around inside him like pebbles caught in a tumbling wave. For a fraction of a second, so quickly he almost missed it, her star pulsed with light, shining more brightly than all the others. His heart filled with love: for Julie, for his new friends, for Hank and Polly, for his old boat, and the whole big-old wide planet he called home. And also...for Hannah.

Tiny was right. He would never forget Julie. Whenever he looked up at the night sky, especially on clear, velvety nights like tonight, he would always seek her star. But in his own hand, he held a chance at a new life. He'd already reached out. Now, all he needed to do was keep holding on.

Hannah's dark eyes caught and held the starlight as she turned toward him. Her voice was soft, barely a whisper. "Well, what's next for you? Will I see you again now that everything's...over?"

Matt took a deep breath, then plunged. "I don't know that *everything* is over. I think maybe some things are just getting started. Maybe you want to keep working on your writing . . . on the road or the water?"

Hannah frowned, confused.

Clearing his throat, Matt tried again. "What I meant was, can you come sailing with me? Or do you *want* to come sailing with me...and Hank, and I guess Polly as well?"

He knew he was babbling. He felt like an idiot, but that feeling vanished when Hannah's warm lips pressed against his own and her strong arms tightened around his neck. She pulled back just enough to whisper,

"I'd go anywhere with you, Matt."

At that moment, Nana B's old hound dog let out a long howl, talking to a crowd of crying coyotes far across the water on the mainland. Polly abruptly awoke from her slumber, raised her head and joined in, sounding just like her country-singer namesake hitting a high note in her very best song. Hank sleepily joined in the chorus, tilting his little head back and giving his finest old-dog yodel.

Matt looked at Hannah and laughed. "Sounds like we've got the makings of quite the band here."

Hannah, imitating the canines, tilted her head back and bayed at the moon overhead. She smiled widely and her cheeks dimpled. "Well, in that case, Captain, maybe we should head back to the boat and practice making some music together."

They rose in unison, hands still linked, and together they walked down the path toward the vast blue ocean to begin their journey.

EPILOGUE

One year later

The story of the Colonel's flight from Clawson Island has been transformed from top news story to fodder for urban myth. Reliable sources all agree that Clawson fled "his" island by private helicopter to Cuba, then boarded a private jet in Havana bound for somewhere in the Pacific. Authorities believe he has a secret compound somewhere far up in the remote jungle highlands of New Guinea where he'd spent those formative years of his youth. Rumors are that the twisted old man has now amassed a veritable army of bloodthirsty mercenaries to protect him, and demands that all in his employ now call him "General Clawson." Unfortunately for the seekers of truth and justice, the country of New Guinea does not have an extradition treaty with the U.S.

While the authorities have still not pinpointed the exact location of "General" Clyde Clawson's lair, they could take at least a part of him into custody. On Clawson's helipad, federal agents reported finding a bloody severed hand, along with several hundred-dollar bills glued to its sticky fingers.

Video footage got from the mansion's security cameras showed the cause of the amputation. Just as the rotation of the chopper's blades was gathering speed, a briefcase the fleeing Clawson was clutching suddenly sprang open. As bills flew out and scattered, the Colonel, never one to let a buck slip through his stubby little fingers, snatched at the vortex of bills being swirled skyward. His grasping fingers reached just a little too high in their pursuit of the airborne loot, and the chopper's rotor caught him...well, red-handed.

Sightings of the Colonel/General—for months the top-trending social media topic—have dwindled to only a handful, no pun intended.

There are now plump white chickens all over Jasmine and her neighboring Sea Islands, being schooled in the ways of country chickens by their free-ranging cousins.

The plant and the chicken barns are now nothing more than mountains of rubble and ash. A couple of months ago, the EPA sent out a team to investigate Clawson's environmental crimes and to direct the cleanup of the toxic stew caused by the fire. A big demolition company out of Charleston is now hiring local men to help clean up the remains of the chicken plant. They're paying good wages to the crew, with the promise of additional work to do in the coming months. After a brief legal battle, the ownership of the land has reverted to its original Gullah owners, and soon ground will be broken for the construction of a new school and community center.

Long gone are the patrol boats full of armed henchmen, along with Clawson's sleazy lawyers, and their land-grabbing schemes to steal heirs property from its rightful owners.

A well-known animal welfare group took some credit for the hack that set the destruction of the plant in motion, but vehemently denied setting any of the fires. A recent investigation has revealed that it was Clawson employees—including Hannah's ex-boyfriend, Mitch—who started the fires as they attempted to destroy incriminating documents about the human flesh project. When a paper shredder failed to keep pace with their efforts, someone had the bright idea of using a metal office wastebasket as an incinerator. Arson investigators have now determined that lighter fluid set ablaze inside the flimsy trashcan was the source of the inferno that destroyed the plant.

Freed from fear of the Colonel's wrath and enticed by the prospect of five minutes of fame, workers from the plant have spilled its secrets. From their stories, the world has learned of Mitch's fate. From the experimental flesh lab beneath the chicken plant, scraps of whatever—or whomever—they were growing, sometimes became an impromptu meal for the alligators living in the swamp that bordered the backside of the plant. For whatever reason, these gators developed a fierce attraction to the scent of humans. If they caught a whiff of that distinctive aroma, they would swarm in, jaws snapping wildly, in anticipation of a feeding frenzy. According to eyewitness accounts, Hannah's ex was last seen dumping trays of "evidence" into the water for the gators to dispose of. One of the largest—a wily fourteen-footer who could move at a speed belying his bulk—had grabbed Mitch's right leg, toppled him into the fetid water, and dragged his bounty down into the depths of the swamp.

Although Clawson's henchmen destroyed much of the physical evidence of his deranged schemes, the white-hat hackers successfully released enough incriminating evidence for the feds to bring indictments against Clawson and many members of the now-infamous Circle of Tantalus.

The smell from the burned chicken plant has finally faded, and after tugboats removed the last remaining barges of fowl waste, Jasmine Island once again smells more like its floral namesake.

At the reunion that took place the night before the fire, Tiny had met a smart, beautiful, and very outspoken real estate lawyer named Elisa, who is now working with local families to protect heirs property. A few months ago, Tiny quit his job at the boatyard and moved back to the island with his new bride. Now, the only boat he works on is his own Carolina Skiff. With the help of his cousin Clive, Tiny is building a camp for inner-city youth. It will be a place where mainland kids can connect to their roots, learn skills in self-sufficiency, and escape the pitfalls of urban living—at least for the summer. Each of the small cabins will have its own name. The first one they constructed already has the name "Marie" neatly engraved on a wooden placard beside its front door. Tiny has made a small fortune selling the exclusive rights to his story, which will help get the program started. Over the entrance to the camp, he will place the froe that played a minor role in toppling the Clawson empire.

With the support of Tiny's industrious new bride, Nana B recently became the author of a cookbook: *Farm to Table with Nana B.* They're selling like hotcakes on Amazon. One buyer, MattnHannah7789, has purchased and donated one thousand copies to urban community gardeners and volunteers around the country.

Shortly after breaking the Clawson story, Traci tracked down the source of the original leak. After one top-secret interview with the reclusive but beguiling hacker, the reporter was smitten by his wry humor and classic good looks. Last month, she transferred to a TV network affiliate in Austin. When "off the air," she occasionally dons a frilly babydoll and furry mules and transforms herself into the fembot of Bruce's wildest fantasies.

Hank is still a happy, healthy super-senior dog with a much younger girlfriend who now has a custom life jacket very much like his own. She serenades him most nights, but sadly, he cannot hear her hit the high notes. Hank very much enjoys snuggling with Polly during the more stressful episodes of blue-water sailing. She's so tickled to have a proper home—not a metal cage—that she's in a constant and even contagious state of bliss! Hank will be much happier when he has some powdery sand between his toes and the horizon quits tilting.

Lonesome Dove has now spent a leisurely, if eventful, year sailing the crystal waters of the Caribbean. With Hannah's help, Matt recently finished writing an account of his adventures. With the advance he received, he's helping fund the camp for urban youth on Jasmine Island. Hannah is working on a children's book about Hank's journey from shelter dog to first mate, all the while keeping up their travel blog— "The Not-So-Lonesome-Dove" —which has become wildly popular. They are keen followers of the "coconut telegraph" which keeps them apprised of Clawson sightings. The latest locates the corrupt one-handed bandit in the remote highlands of Papua, New Guinea, the place where his demented desires had been kindled so long ago.

Matt isn't sure if he'll follow Clawson's trail or chart a new path. One night, when the moon is full, and the sea is calm, they lay the big sailing chart across the dinette table, tenderly smoothing out the folds. Matt carefully sets the nautical protractor over the lines and curves and names of faraway places and tentatively traces two paths. Then Hannah sets her hand over his and gives it a gentle push. Matt's destiny is no longer tied to the Colonel's. He's free to find his own way—their way. And so they do.

ABOUT THE AUTHOR

Like his protagonist, Hollan once pulled up anchor in Corpus Christi Bay, and set off in search of adventure and a new beginning. For three years, he sailed his patched-up 1967 Pearson Vanguard around the Caribbean and to parts of Central and South America. These days, he does his exploring in a well-used pickup truck with a rooftop tent, exploring the less-traveled backroads of the U.S. and Canada with his wife and two spoiled rescue dogs.

Visit the author online at Cluckedthenovel.com.

NOTE FROM TROY HOLLAN

Word-of-mouth is crucial for any author to succeed. If you enjoyed *Clucked*, please leave a rcview online—anywhere you are able. Even if it's just a sentence or two. It would make all the difference and would be very much appreciated.

Thanks!
Troy Hollan

We hope you enjoyed reading this title from:

BLACK ROSE
writing™

Subscribe to our mailing list – *The Rosevine* – and receive **FREE** books, daily deals, and stay current with news about upcoming releases and our hottest authors.
Scan the QR code below to sign up.

Already a subscriber? Please accept a sincere thank you for being a fan of Black Rose Writing authors.

View other Black Rose Writing titles at www.blackrosewriting.com/books and use promo code
PRINT to receive a **20% discount** when purchasing.

Milton Keynes UK
Ingram Content Group UK Ltd.
UKHW010812081123
432193UK00001B/22